"How'd you ~~get through my~~ door ~~~~?" he asked.

"I'm not completely without resources," she murmured as she moved toward him. "I brought a bottle of wine. Would you like a drink?"

"No, thanks. I'm already drunk on the sight of you."

"I didn't come here for flattery," she said. "I told you that I get all the empty praise I can stand from other men."

"Then what do you want from me, princess—?"

His breath gave out when she reached up to unfasten the top button of his shirt. Then the second and third buttons came undone—along with his willpower. His heart thudded against his chest so hard he thought the blow might have broken a rib.

"I've decided I want the same thing from you that you said you wanted from me," she whispered. "I want to be naked with you, Coop. Do you have any objections?"

* * *

Cooper's Woman
Harlequin® Historical #897—May 2008

Praise for Carol Finch

"Carol Finch is known for her lightning-fast,
roller-coaster-ride adventure romances that
are brimming over with a large cast of characters
and dozens of perilous escapades."
—*Romantic Times BOOKreviews*

McCavett's Bride
"For wild adventures, humor and Western atmosphere,
Finch can't be beat. She fires off her quick-paced novels
with the crack of a rifle and creates the atmosphere of
the Wild West through laugh-out-loud dialogue and
escapades that keep you smiling."
—*Romantic Times BOOKreviews*

The Ranger's Woman
"Finch delivers her signature humor, along with
a big dose of colorful Texas history,
in a love and laughter romp."
—*Romantic Times BOOKreviews*

Lone Wolf's Woman
"As always, Finch provides frying-pan-into-the-fire
action that keeps the pages flying, then spices up her
story with not one, but two romances, sensuality and
strong emotions."
—*Romantic Times BOOKreviews*

CAROL FINCH
COOPER'S Woman

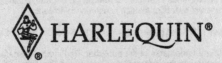

HARLEQUIN®

TORONTO • NEW YORK • LONDON
AMSTERDAM • PARIS • SYDNEY • HAMBURG
STOCKHOLM • ATHENS • TOKYO • MILAN • MADRID
PRAGUE • WARSAW • BUDAPEST • AUCKLAND

ISBN-13: 978-0-373-29497-8
ISBN-10:   0-373-29497-2

COOPER'S WOMAN

www.eHarlequin.com

Printed in U.S.A.

This book is dedicated to my husband, Ed, and our children
Christie, Jill, Kurt, Jon and Shawnna. And to our grandchildren,
Kennedy, Blake, Brooklynn and Livia with much love.

Chapter One

~~~~~~~~

Santa Fe, New Mexico Territory, 1880s

Alexa Quinn stood tensely in the doorway of the ballroom. Although the last half-dozen guests were milling about, her attention and her thoughts fixated on her father and Elliot Webster. The pair stood beside the fireplace, each with a drink in hand. Elliot had dogged Alexa's steps most of the evening and she sincerely hoped he hadn't pulled her father aside to ask for her hand in marriage. Dissatisfied as she was with her life, it would be infinitely more boring if she married Elliot. Even his dashing good looks, wealth and outward charm couldn't overshadow the fact that Alexa didn't like him.

She had learned to trust her instincts, as they pertained to zealous suitors, and they hadn't failed her yet.

"You've done it again, my dear," Benjamin Porter praised as he approached. "No one hosts a better party in Santa Fe. I'm sure your father is exceptionally proud of your skills."

Alexa dragged her anxious gaze away from her father and Elliot Webster to nod graciously to the short, pasty-faced math whiz who was one of her father's closest advisors. "Thank you, Ben. I appreciate that."

The truth was that Alexa didn't give a whit if she could organize a political or social function for her father and see that it ran smoothly. Harold Quinn might have fulfilled his ambitions as the territorial governor's appointed director of finance, who also served in several other capacities, and was considered the governor's most trusted counselor. She even understood that her father was preoccupied with his administrative duties to serve the greater good. Still, it was hard on her pride to know that her father saw right past her more often than not. Furthermore, he hadn't realized her potential. That cut her to the core.

Her ambition extended beyond social director for his political gatherings. Her soul was screaming for the opportunity to find her true calling. She definitely couldn't find it if her father consented to a match with Elliot Webster.

After Ben Porter strode out the door, Ambrose Shelton approached. "Your party was passable," he remarked as he straightened the cuff of his black jacket.

You sourpuss, thought Alexa. The puffy-jowled, round bellied gent never failed to find more fault than praise with his acquaintances. According to her father, Ambrose Shelton had a brilliant political mind. His perspectives and guidance were invaluable.

Alexa was in no position to argue with her father's opinion, but she thought Ambrose had the social skills of a cranky grizzly. Keeping her observation of the dour, middle-aged, slightly balding man to herself, she said wryly, "There's a chill in the air tonight, Ambrose. Don't catch cold and lose your voice."

Ambrose snapped up his double chin. His ferretlike gray eyes bore into her. He puffed up to such extremes that she thought he might pop like an over-inflated balloon.

She flashed him a teasing grin, knowing she had gone too far with her father's valued associate. Mentally scrambling she added, "I don't know how Papa would manage if he couldn't hear your wise advice."

A tense moment passed. Then Alexa noticed a small crack in his stern veneer. She thought Ambrose might have smiled slightly, but it was difficult to tell because she'd never seen the man smile. Ever.

"I'm not sure your father deserves you, young lady," Ambrose said finally. "But then, we aren't allowed to pick family, are we? We're just stuck with what we get."

"So true of our families and our family's friends—" Alexa slammed her mouth shut so quickly that she nearly clipped off the tip of her tongue.

Usually she managed to control her thoughts before they flew from her lips. Indeed, she had years of practice at concealing her true feelings. She blamed her lack of discretion on her apprehension over her father's continuing conversation with Elliot Webster. Either that or she had stifled her true nature for so long that it was about to burst loose.

Then the most peculiar thing happened. Ambrose Shelton, the persnickety, faultfinding advisor to Harold Quinn, snickered. Even Benjamin Porter halted on his way down the front steps, pivoted and did a double-take.

"Your poor father," Ambrose said with a slow shake of his wiry red head. "He's stuck with you and with me. Well, good night then." He pursed his lips and added, "Perhaps you should put your snippy tongue to bed early."

What an odd man, she thought as Ambrose waddled off on his tree-stump legs. Benjamin Porter scuttled alongside him, chattering nonstop, same as he did while he labored over accounts that pertained to territorial finances and budgets.

After John Marlow and William Trent, two other members

of her father's advisory committee, said their farewells and ambled off, Alexa turned her full attention to her father. She grimaced apprehensively when her father and Elliot shook hands, and then finally parted company. Alexa stared warily at the tall, swaggering gentleman, who was decked out in the finest evening wear that money could buy. Elliot paused to bow over her hand and kiss her knuckles.

She controlled the shiver of dislike and reminded herself that she had years of experience masking her hidden feelings. However, she was more than a little worried about the outburst that had tumbled off her tongue so carelessly with Ambrose. It was a sure sign that her discontent with her present lifestyle was about to erupt.

"Ah, my lovely Alexa," Elliot purred. "I shall miss your enchanting company."

"You're leaving town?" She tried very hard to keep the hopeful note from flooding her voice.

"Eventually, my dear, yes. I have a mercantile business and a ranch to run in Questa Springs. However, I shall be here until the end of the week. I hope to have the pleasure of your company again before I depart."

Not if I can avoid it, she thought, but she said, "I'll look forward to it. However, I must tell you that I have a busy schedule. Obligations to Papa take precedence."

Elliot's hazel eyes crinkled at the corners and a lock of thin blond hair tumbled over his forehead as he glanced sideways. "Of course. I understand that your father is a busy man. Invaluable to the citizens of this territory."

"Extremely invaluable," she confirmed.

She all but collapsed in relief when Elliot released her hand then lurched around to swagger through the door. "He is going to make some woman an annoying husband," she said under her breath. "I pray to God that it won't be me."

"What do you think of Elliot Webster?" her father asked as he came to stand behind her.

Alexa spoke plainly, just in case her father had ideas about marrying her off to that cocky gent. "I don't think much of him. Pretentious. Calculating. Premeditated charm so sticky sweet that it gives me an instant toothache and—"

"By all means, don't hold back, dear," Harold chuckled. "Ah, where is that tact and diplomacy that I've tried so hard to drill into your pretty head?"

She spun to face her father directly. This was a crucial moment and her future might be at stake. This was no time for diplomacy. "You asked for my opinion and I gave it to you. I don't like Elliot Webster and I can't imagine that I ever will."

She stared through the open door, watching a man in a military uniform, whose slight, lean physique seemed familiar to her, approach Elliot. The two shadowy figures spoke briefly before Elliot bounded into the carriage to return to his hotel.

"Webster expressed an interest in you, Lexi."

"It is not returned," she reiterated. "We are two entirely different people. At least I like to think I'm not that aloof and annoying."

Harold's brown eyes narrowed pensively. "He claims that he's taken an instant liking to you and that he would like to begin a courtship that leads to marriage."

Just as I thought, she mused uneasily. "I'm sure his supposed interest in me has everything to do with the prospect of becoming *your* son-in-law, not *my* devoted husband."

And there was the crux of her problem with men. Alexa could never be certain if men liked her for what she was inside or because her father was powerful and influential in the territorial government. She had learned early on that she was viewed as a tool to gain favors from Harold Quinn. She had never forgotten that humiliating lesson five years earlier. Back then, she had been naive and idealistic. Now she understood that love was an illusion and that men saw her as a pawn.

Turning, Harold motioned to Maria Gomez, the housekeeper. "Please bring Lexi and me some coffee. We'll be in the parlor."

The Mexican housekeeper strode off as Harold guided Alexa to the tuft chair. "Actually, I'm glad you have no romantic interest in Webster. I don't know what he's up to or where he is getting privileged information, but it disturbs me that he knows things the rest of the public doesn't," he murmured.

Alexa perked up. Her father seldom took her into his confidence when it came to his business. He was usually too distracted and too busy to notice her in any capacity besides his hostess.

She savored this rare moment and vowed to do whatever was necessary to ease his concerns. She loved her father dearly, even if he had little time to spare her.

"What is it, Papa? You know I will help in any way I can."

Harold plunked down on the sofa, then expelled a frustrated sigh. "Thank you, honey. But I'll muddle through. No need to bother you with my concerns."

Bother me! Include me in your life! Notice me! Please stop overlooking me! "What has Elliot Webster done to draw your concern?" she prodded. "And it best not be entangled with a scheme to marry me. I don't want him."

Her decisive tone drew Harold's attention. He blinked, as if just realizing he had raised a daughter teeming with spirit and fierce independence. "When did this happen?" he mused aloud.

"About twelve years ago when Mama took Bethany and headed back East," she replied, then wished she'd kept her trap shut. The comment caused her father to wince and shift self-consciously on the couch.

"That fiasco wasn't fair to you, Lexi. I loved your mother, but I swear I will never understand why she left you behind."

Alexa clasped her father's hand, giving it a fond squeeze. "If I had been given a choice I still would have remained here with you," she insisted. "Now tell me what Elliot Webster has done to upset you."

Harold blew out his breath and set aside the troubled past. "In addition to his expressed interest in you, he asked about the government contracts to sell livestock to the forts and Indian reservations in the territory. The fact that I'm not satisfied with our last contract with him and have considered finding new suppliers is not common knowledge. I mentioned it at our last meeting. I fear that one of my trusted confidants has been compromised. I'd like to strangle whoever betrayed our policy of keeping such information quiet."

"I'm not surprised to hear that Elliot has found a mole and that he might be paying for information," said Alexa. "I don't trust that man because I get the feeling he always has an ulterior motive."

She also had a hunch about who might be willing to relay private information for a fistful of money. Ambrose Shelton headed up her short list of suspects. She predicted Ambrose believed himself far more capable of holding a powerful position in the territorial government than her father. Undermining Harold Quinn's work on various government boards and committees might allow Ambrose Shelton to move up the political ladder. It was speculation, of course, but Alexa would eagerly volunteer to investigate.

"Elliot Webster will be leaving Santa Fe at the end of the week," Harold continued. "Until he heads south to Questa Springs I will have someone shadow him."

"Good idea. The sooner you find the snitch the better," Alexa agreed.

"I also intend to hire an investigator to monitor Elliot's activities when he returns to Questa Springs," Harold confided.

"I can't entrust this inquisition to any of my associates, in case one of them is involved. That means I must enlist the help of an outside agent."

Her father was frowning so intently that Alexa swore he was going to give himself more wrinkles. She could understand his dilemma. Everywhere Harold Quinn went the press followed. He lived under a microscope... Which made the solution to his problem so simple that *she* could resolve it over their evening coffee.

Excitement bubbled through Alexa while she waited for Maria Gomez to set the silver tray on the coffee table. After the servant retreated, Alexa turned to face her father directly.

"This situation can be resolved easily," she declared while she watched her father sip his coffee.

Harold sniffed in contradiction. "I hardly think that is possible, my dear. I'm not sure who I can trust."

"Thank you so much for the insult."

Harold blinked owlishly then waved her off with a flick of his wrist. "Present company excluded, of course. But this is over your head, Lexi. Besides, I'd shoot myself before I placed you in possible danger."

There he goes again, ignoring my potential.

"Who better to undertake the task of discreetly hiring an investigator to monitor Elliot's activities?" Alexa argued. "Even *you* refuse to consider the prospect of sending a woman to do a man's job."

"But I—"

Alexa cut him off with a slashing gesture of her arm. She was bound and determined to present her case without interruption. "Perhaps I could consult the sheriff or city marshal in Elliot's hometown to hire an investigator. Provided that Elliot doesn't have the local lawman in his hip pocket." If

Elliot was in the habit of paying for information that was always a possibility. "Now that Elliot has expressed an interest in me, I have the perfect excuse to visit the area. I can pretend an interest in him, too."

"No. Absolutely not," Harold objected strenuously.

Alexa's mind was brimming with possibilities. This was her chance to prove to her father that she had talents and abilities that extended far beyond the skill of drawing up a guest list, organizing seating arrangements and hiring entertainment for social and political gatherings. If she pinpointed the information leak, he might perceive her as what she was—a young woman aching to find a meaningful purpose in her life and accept new challenges.

"It's perfect," she enthused. "Kate Hampton, my dearest friend from finishing school, lives near Questa Springs. I can schedule a visit and make myself available for Elliot's supposed courtship. I can oversee the hiring of an investigator and make certain the man does his job properly. In no time at all we will know who is leaking information to Elliot."

"*No.*"

His brown eyes flashed and his thick brows swooped down in a sharp V. However, Alexa was not to be deterred by her father's evil eye and uncompromising frown.

"I have spent years guarding my tongue and refraining from speaking my mind," Alexa declared. "Even the pompous asses you deal with on a weekly basis have no idea what I think of them."

Harold's brows shot up so quickly that they nearly rocketed off his forehead. "My God, who *are* you? And what have you done with my daughter?"

Alexa sat up a little straighter on the couch. She batted her blue eyes and smiled sweetly. "Why, Papa, whatever do you mean? I am the same devoted daughter who knows her place and happily remains within the narrow confines men have established for women."

She was very much afraid her father's eyes were about to pop from their sockets. She had altered her persona so quickly that he couldn't keep up. Well, too bad. It was high time Harold Quinn accepted that she had a mind of her own and ached to use it. It was also time that he realized she didn't intend to live in his shadow, performing mundane social duties when her heart cried out for the chance to pursue a worthwhile cause.

Harold slumped against the sofa and sighed audibly. "I can't let you do this. I promised myself the day your mother left with Bethany that I would care for, and protect you better than she ever did. I also swore to see you well schooled and properly married. You don't have to work a day in your life or struggle to attain envied social status. Furthermore, I will not purposely plant you in harm's way and allow you to deal with investigators of questionable background and few scruples. Bounty hunters and detectives tend to bend the law to suit their purposes."

"Papa, I regret to inform you that the life you envision for me is in direct contrast to the one I crave for myself." She stared intently at him as she took both of his hands in hers. "I *want* to do this for you. I *need* to do this for you. Who better to guard your back than the one who loves you most? The one who will be loyal and true-blue to the end."

Harold grimaced. "It better not come to that. I couldn't live with myself."

"Please, Papa. Let me prove to you that I am *your* daughter, not Mama's. When the going got tough, she packed up and left. I'm still here and I'm strong and capable. I can hire an agent to contact an investigator, who will monitor Elliot's activities, if that will relieve your concerns."

She *could* hire an agent if she were inclined, which she wasn't. But she wasn't about to tell her father that. She intended to be actively involved to prove her worth.

"Pretending an interest in Elliot will explain my extended visit to Kate Hampton's family ranch," she insisted.

Harold stared at her for so long that she squirmed impatiently. She knew he was struggling to equate his previous expectations of her with the woman who was bearing down on him. When he started to pull his hands away, Alexa clamped on to his fingers and refused to let go.

"I'll be just fine," she reassured him. "I can take care of myself. I certainly managed while I was away at school in Albuquerque. Why can't you see that I'm grown up and champing at the bit to accept this challenge? You accept every challenge that comes your way. And I am the proverbial chip off the block that Mother left behind because I acted too much like you."

Finally Harold grinned and nodded his head. "I'm glad I don't have to debate you at board meetings. You'd plow over me."

Alexa beamed at the rare compliment. Indeed, she lived for moments like this one.

He shook his finger in her face. "But you must promise me that you'll hire a go-between to meet with the detective. Most of them are glorified gunslingers, paladins and guns-for-hire. Not the sort of scoundrels a lady should associate with. I don't want you endangered in any way so I'll send Miguel Santos along as your chaperone and bodyguard."

Alexa didn't want her childhood friend and playmate—not to mention her walking conscience—following her around. But she had won the major battle so she conceded this skirmish. "Agreed. After all, Miguel is exceptionally handy with a knife and a fair shot. Not that I can't handle my own dagger and pistol."

One dark brow elevated in wry amusement. "Finishing school must have expanded its curriculum."

"I hounded Miguel until he taught me to use weapons," she confided. "Every woman should know how to protect herself. A free-spirited woman doesn't have the time or inclination to wait around for a man to rescue her."

"This is worse than I thought," Harold murmured with a bewildered shake of his head. "I have neglected you since I was appointed to this political position that consumes so much of my time and energy."

That was true, but this conversation went a long way in opening her father's eyes to the strong-willed twenty-two-year-old woman she had become. He wasn't overlooking her or misjudging her now. Apparently he was seeing her for what she was and it scared him a little. Alexa, however, was eager to embrace the unknown and the unfamiliar. Her soul craved excitement and adventure.

"I will resolve this problem with Elliot Webster," she vowed determinedly. "You will know which one of your business associates is passing information. I will expose him for the unscrupulous scoundrel he obviously is."

Harold looked her over long and hard, as if reevaluating the young woman he thought he knew and understood. "All right, Lexi. But you will only be acting in an advisory capacity. From a safe distance. Let the investigator handle this case. If you come to harm I will never forgive myself. *Be careful.*"

She smiled brightly, knowing she did not intend to hover on the sidelines during this investigation. She figured that what her father didn't know wouldn't worry him. "Elliot Webster won't suspect my ulterior reason for being in town and that will become his downfall."

"I hope you're right about Webster underestimating you."

Alexa hoped she was, too. Her pride and self-esteem were

riding on her ability to complete this assignment. She wanted her father to recognize her worth. She wanted him to be proud and confident in her abilities. If she fell flat on her face, it would be hell to crawl home, ashamed and unsuccessful.

If things went sour, she'd have to take an extended vacation in Europe to nurse her bruised pride.

No more of those negative thoughts, she chastised herself as she mounted the stairs to retire for the night. By damned, this was her golden opportunity and she was going to do her father proud.

She hoped...

Wyatt Cooper swung down from his horse then scanned the scenic canyon north of Questa Springs. There were some spectacular landscapes in the rugged Sacramento Mountain Range that rose up between the Rio Grande and Pecos Rivers. In the distance, he heard the murmur of rapids tumbling down the spring-fed river that meandered toward town. The vibrant colors of sunset splashed across the horizon. The setting was so awe-inspiring that he had to remind himself that he was here on business not pleasure.

Cautious by nature and by habit, he tucked himself beside a pine tree and fished out the card he carried in his vest pocket. For the umpteenth time in a week, he asked himself why he had decided to take this particular assignment. Then he studied the carefully printed card that read like an invitation to a formal social function and he remembered what had piqued his curiosity.

Whoever had contacted him anonymously at his headquarters in Albuquerque had been sending him specific instructions for this secretive rendezvous. Each elaborately written message was as impressively worded as the previous ones.

He figured he'd have to wait until dark to meet his mysterious client. It's what he would've done. Sure enough, the sun dipped behind the looming precipices before a stout, round-bellied man emerged from the bushes. His hat sat low on his forehead. A gray beard and mustache concealed his facial features. Scant light reflected off his wire-rimmed spectacles. He didn't approach, just lurked by a tree, as if prepared to bolt and run at the first sign of trouble.

"Are you Wyatt Cooper?" The hushed, gravelly voice carried an Eastern accent.

"Yes, but I prefer to be called Coop," he insisted.

"Very well then, Coop, let's proceed with our business. I have been hired by my client to contract you to keep surveillance on a man named Elliot Webster."

Coop nodded his dark head in recognition of the name. Webster owned and operated a mercantile shop in Questa Springs, in addition to a cattle ranch two miles northeast of town. Coop had heard that Webster had gained the reputation of a price gouger and a ruthless competitor who tried to monopolize the dry goods business in the area.

"You want me to document underhanded business dealings?" Coop presumed.

"Yes," the agent replied. "In addition, my employer wants to know who comes and goes from the store and the ranch. We want to know who contacts Webster personally and professionally."

Coop arched a thick black brow. "Do you work for a branch of the territorial government?"

"*I* work for my *employer*, who will pay *you* handsomely to keep track of Webster's associates, on and off his ranch," the agent said evasively. "I require names and a detailed list of Webster's activities so I can obtain a clear understanding of his leisure pursuits and business practices."

The man tossed a stack of banded bank notes into the air. They landed at Coop's feet, causing his horse to shift uneasily.

"Easy, Bandit," Coop murmured to his black gelding.

Without taking his eyes off the short, stocky man who clung to the shadows, Coop scooped up the money. He blinked in surprise when he counted five hundred dollars. "I was only going to ask my going rate of two hundred fifty dollars a month."

"Most detectives only charge one-fifty," the man pointed out in his arrogant tone and thick Eastern accent.

Coop grinned. "Yeah, but you get what you pay for."

"Then I expect quick results. I doubled your going rate since I want you to play a certain role while in Questa Springs. Because of your widespread reputation, your arrival in town might draw unwanted curiosity and suspicion. Although you are well-known in this territory, I want you to keep a low profile."

Coop barked a laugh. "How do you intend for me to accomplish that? Cooper Investigations is a thriving business. And, at six feet two inches tall and one hundred ninety-five pounds, I'm hardly invisible and I don't blend into a crowd."

"That's why I came up with a plan."

"It better be a damn good one," Coop smirked as he tucked the money in the pocket of his buckskin vest. "Let's hear it…"

Chapter Two

From behind the spectacles, fake mustache and beard, Alexa Quinn appraised the powerfully built gunfighter who loomed in the shadows. She was pleased that her disguise—and the padding that made her appear overweight and barrel-bellied—protected her identity. The less Coop knew about her the better.

Despite her attempt to focus on the business at hand, her gaze kept wandering over Coop in appreciation. His coal-black hair, vivid green eyes and swarthy complexion had captured her attention when he first reached the rendezvous site. She kept recalling how impressive he looked against the pastel hues of sunset.

Wyatt Cooper looked to be in his early thirties and he possessed a striking physique. He radiated self-assurance, strength and keen intelligence. Of course, she had checked him out thoroughly before contacting him and discovered that he was considered the premier detective in the Southwest. Reportedly he was hell on outlaws and deadly accurate with the two ivory handled six-shooters strapped around his lean hips. He also carried a Winchester rifle in the sling of his saddle and he was reportedly accurate with it as well.

According to the information she had gathered on Coop, he had worked as a bounty hunter and a deputy U.S. Marshal who rode for Isaac Parker—the well-known "Hanging Judge" who presided over lawless Indian Territory. Coop's five-year stint had earned him a reputation as law and order's last resort against the most violent criminals plaguing society. All reports indicated that he was one of the quickest men on the trigger in the West.

No one knew where he was born and raised. It was almost as if he hadn't come into existence until the age of eighteen. That fact aroused her concern, but despite her best efforts, she couldn't find anyone who knew about his mysterious childhood.

He had moved to New Mexico Territory two years ago and opened his own investigation agency. It was said that the Pinkerton Detective Agency had tried unsuccessfully to hire him, but he refused. Whether it was because of his unethical methods of capturing criminals or his preference to be his own boss, she didn't know. But the man was in constant demand, corrupt or not.

"Well? What's this grand plan of yours?" Coop questioned impatiently. "It's been a long ride and I'm ready to settle in for the night."

His rich baritone voice filtered into her thoughts and Alexa forced herself to concentrate on the business arrangements at hand. *Not* on her unexpected and unwanted fascination with the ruggedly handsome gunfighter.

"The story is that you have come to Questa Springs to recuperate from an injured leg after your recent shootout with a band of outlaws," she announced.

"How many cutthroats did it take to wing me?" he asked, mildly amused.

"Four, but you prevailed and won the day, of course."

"Interesting tale, but I prefer straightforward and simple."

"I don't," she insisted. "I have made arrangements for you to be the substitute bartender at Valmont Saloon during your recuperation." She tossed a battered cane to him. Even in the gathering darkness, his lightning quick reflexes enabled him to catch it in midair.

He stared at her long and hard then glanced distastefully at the cane. "You are kidding."

"I have no sense of humor, Mr. Cooper," she said somberly.

"I'm beginning to realize that," Coop muttered as he stared at the cane he was to use as a prop.

Alexa suppressed a smile. She had formed an instant liking to this brawny gunslinger. She attributed part of her attraction to his appealing physique and his deep voice. Another part of her fascination stemmed from the fact that this man didn't treat her as if she were a socialite who was kin to a government dignitary and heir to a fortune. Of course, Coop had no idea that she was a female and he wasn't trying to put on airs the way her wanna-be suitors usually did. This was a novel experience for Alexa and she was enjoying it thoroughly.

"As bartender and bouncer at Valmont Saloon you can monitor Webster's activities," she insisted. "I don't know if the local law enforcement officer is in Webster's pocket. That is for you to find out."

Coop slid the cane into the leather sling that held his Winchester rifle. Absently he patted his horse. "You've made all the advance arrangements, I see."

"Of course. That is my job."

"You're very thorough, Mr...." His voice trailed off, waiting for her to fill in the blank.

"*Chester,*" she replied without missing a beat. "My client requests that you rendezvous with me at the end of next week to report your information. Same time. Same place."

"You want a written report, I suppose," Coop remarked.

"Naturally. My employer and I expect it."

"Fine, I'll take a room at one of the hotels—"

"I made those arrangements, too," she cut in. "You have a room facing Main Street, directly across from Webster Mercantile and Dry Goods. Room number four at Walker Hotel and Restaurant."

"Your employer obviously hired you because of your organizational skills. Very impressive, Mr. Chester," he praised.

"Thank you. I believe in being thorough."

"Anything else before I go?" Coop asked.

"Yes, make sure you don't drink your salary at Valmont Saloon. I want you to remain alert and observant at all times. I'm paying you according to *your* impressive reputation. Do not disappoint me."

"Don't worry, Chester," he said and snorted. "This isn't my first investigation. I'll even tell you how many times a day Webster relieves himself and behind which tree, if you want to know."

Alexa tried not to react to the comment. She decided there were some disadvantages to disguising herself as a middle-age, overweight man.

"Thank you, Coop, but my only interest is acquiring a list of Webster's associates and his social activities," she replied, careful to give nothing away. The less Coop knew the better.

Alexa's attention remained on Coop while he swung effortlessly onto the muscular black gelding that sported four white stockings and white circles around both eyes. The horse was as striking and unique as his rider. Her gaze and thoughts remained fixed on the impressive masculine silhouette until it blended into the night.

She had a good feeling about Wyatt Cooper. With this legendary ex-lawman on the case, she could conduct her own discreet inquiries from a different angle. Of course, she would have to portray the role of a fluff-headed socialite to quell all suspicions about her real reason for being in Questa Springs. However, if it provided her with valuable information and helped her father, she'd do it.

"I do not like this, Lexi. Your father won't, either."

Alexa nearly leaped out of her padded disguise when Miguel Santos's quiet voice drifted from the darkness. She clutched her palpitating chest and drew in a calming breath.

"How did you find me?" she demanded as her walking conscience approached.

"I have the nose of a bloodhound where you are concerned." Miguel gestured in the direction Coop had disappeared. "This man, he is dangerous, *querida*. I can feel it. No matter how you try to sugarcoat it, he is a gun-for-hire and his kind walk a fine line between good and evil."

"This man is superbly skilled and experienced and that's all that matters," she countered as she lumbered awkwardly toward the horse she had tethered in the trees. "And if you breathe one word about my taking an active part in this investigation to Papa I won't speak to you for the rest of my life."

"What will it matter?" Miguel scoffed as she shed her disguise then crammed it into the carpetbag tied behind the saddle. "If you persist in remaining in harm's way, you'll be dead."

"*Pfftt!*" she erupted in contradiction. "You worry too much. You always have. I'll be fine."

"*Si*, you and Mr. Chester. He will be back here next week?" Miguel gave Alexa a boost onto her horse and she thanked him kindly.

"You will indeed see Mr. Chester on occasion. He can go places that I cannot."

"Then you should be prepared for more off-color comments from your detective," Miguel said as he mounted his horse. "Since Coop doesn't know you're a woman he will speak to you man-to-man."

"I have no problem with that," Alexa assured him as she reined toward Hampton Ranch where she was staying with her school chum, Kate, and her family. "At least he won't be putting on airs. I've had plenty of that already."

While Miguel categorically listed everything that might go wrong with her charade and her self-appointed investigation, Alexa turned her thoughts back to Wyatt Cooper. She knew she had chosen well. The gunfighter would help her ferret out information that she could take back to her father, who would undoubtedly be impressed with her abilities. Meanwhile, she had to make herself available to Elliot Webster's courtship and pretend she enjoyed his company.

Alexa sincerely hoped her acting ability was up to snuff. Pretending to like Elliot would require considerable effort.

Scowling, Coop limped along on his cane, silently cursing that toady little Yank named Mr. Chester, who had dreamed up this stupid ruse. Coop never should have agreed to it. Yet, he had tied splints to his right knee to ensure that he didn't forget to walk stiff legged. Mr. Chester apparently thought that a lame gunfighter-turned-bartender wasn't as intimidating as a shootist with two good legs under him. Fact was, Coop had trained himself to be a crack shot, whether he was at full gallop on a horse, rolling across the ground to dodge bullets or squaring off for a showdown in the street.

Despite the attention he received as he hobbled down the boardwalk, he focused on familiarizing himself with the town. Questa Springs boasted a population of two thousand. One-fourth was the Mexican community that had settled the area decades earlier. Another quarter consisted of ranchers whose livestock grazed the nearby mountain slopes and grassy valleys. Another fourth of the population consisted of railroad workers who were building spurs to serve the copper and silver mines in the mountains to the west. The Johnnies-come-lately were drifters, gamblers and shysters who preyed on cowboys and miners.

Besides the bubbling springs in the town square, the community had ten saloons, four hotels, five restaurants, seven gaming halls, brothels and a lumberyard. There was also a bakery, two boutiques, a bank, livery stable, newspaper office and telegraph office. Coop had made note of the two dry goods stores—Webster's and one that challenged its high-priced competitor.

When two women made a big production of crossing the street to avoid encountering him, Coop rolled his eyes and sighed. He'd told Mr. Chester that he was too well-known in the area not to be recognized. Obviously, word spread quickly that he was in town. The God-fearing and Cooper-fearing citizens walked on the opposite side of the street to prevent breathing the same air as a man with blood on his hands. They didn't know the half of it.

Before Coop reached Valmont Saloon, the town marshal exited from his office—to lay down the law, no doubt. Coop blinked in surprise when he recognized the man who had a tarnished silver badge pinned on his vest.

"Well, I'll be damned," Gil Henson said as he ambled forward. "Long time no see."

Coop surveyed the rangy, six-foot-tall man whose reddish-blond hair protruded from the rim of his Stetson. The amber-eyed, ex-bounty hunter that Coop had worked with two years earlier had added several pounds since their last meeting.

"Didn't know you were here, Gil," Coop said as he draped his cane over the crook of his elbow so he could shake hands.

Gil gestured toward the cane. "What happened to you?"

"I found myself in a shootout against lopsided odds and took a bullet in the knee. I don't remember much about it because it happened so fast." He didn't remember *anything* about it because Mr. Chester had made it up. Coop inclined his raven head toward the saloon. "I thought I'd do some bartending in this mountain haven while recuperating."

"You came to the right place to convalesce. The scenery is magnificent. You might have to break up the occasional fight between drunken cowboys and crooked gamblers, but it shouldn't be too strenuous," Gil replied. "With your reputation, no one with any brains will try to cause trouble on your watch…."

His voice trailed off and his attention drifted over Coop's shoulder. Bemused by Gil's sudden distraction, Coop half turned to see a vision of mesmerizing beauty alight from a carriage. The blue-eyed blonde, dressed in the finest silk and lace that money could buy, twirled her frilly parasol—and sent his mind into a whirl.

Coop had seen some attractive women in his day, but this shapely specimen was a feast for the male appetite. Springy blond curls surrounded her heart-shaped lips and face. Her skin was the color of cream. Her blue gown accentuated her shapely figure and matched the vivid color of her thick-lashed eyes.

"I tell you for sure, Coop, that's the prettiest woman I've ever seen," Gil breathed appreciatively. "Every time she arrives in town activity grinds to a halt." He motioned toward the other gawking men on the boardwalk.

Coop's attention swung back to the young woman who looked to be a decade younger than he was—and a hundred years less experienced in dealing with the hard knocks of life. Lovely though she was, she represented the hoity-toity aristocrats who hired him to do their dirty work and resolve their unpleasant problems. His wealthy clients didn't consider a man with his background their social equal. In their opinion, he was merely a second-class servant who was handy with a gun and whose tracking skills kept him dogging the steps of wanted outlaws.

When Elliot Webster strode from his mercantile shop to bow over the woman's hand, Coop frowned. "Who's the woman that Webster is slobbering over?"

"That is Alexa Quinn. Her father, Harold, is the territorial governor's right hand man and his most valued advisor. As you can plainly see, Elliot Webster is at the head of the line when it comes to offering to escort Alexa around Questa Springs. I suspect Webster is interested in marrying *her* and her *money*."

"Not a bad combination," Coop murmured.

And then it dawned on him who his real client probably was. No doubt, Mr. Chester worked for Harold Quinn, who wanted his potential son-in-law checked out thoroughly. Coop speculated that his true purpose was to find out how many harlots Webster kept at his beck and call and how much corruption was involved in his mercantile and ranch dealings. Harold Quinn wanted all the dirt he could dig up on Webster, just in case Alexa decided to marry him.

It made perfect sense now. The discreet and elegantly written notifications arriving at his office. A secret meeting in the upper canyon with Mr. Chester. It was understandable that the financial director of the whole damn territory would want to ensure his future son-in-law was not a crook who might become an embarrassment to the politician.

His thoughts wandered off when the enchanting female tittered and cooed at whatever Webster had said to her. No doubt, she was a spoiled, pampered tenderfoot whose world consisted of soirees, fine dining and expensive accommodations. She was everything he wasn't and had no desire to be.

For that reason, he disliked what she represented, even while her outward beauty continued to dazzle him.

"Probably as shallow as a tub of bathwater," he said under his breath.

Gil tossed him a quizzical glance. "Pardon?"

"Nothing. Where's the royal princess staying?"

"At Hampton Ranch. I heard that Alexa Quinn and Kate Hampton were best friends at boarding school in Albuquerque."

Coop was sure he would have remembered this beguiling beauty if he'd seen her before. But then, they didn't travel in the same circles and Albuquerque was a damn sight larger than Questa Springs.

He was sorry to say that his thoughts scattered again when the voluptuous blonde pivoted away from Webster and swanned across the street. A short, wiry man of Mexican descent, who looked to be in his late twenties, followed ten paces behind her.

The bodyguard or chaperone, no doubt. Bodyguard, Coop decided when he noted the nasty looking, foot-long dagger strapped to the man's thigh. Apparently Harold Quinn didn't allow his dainty daughter to traipse around the rugged Sacramento Mountains without a competent protector watching her.

As Alexa approached, all dimpled smiles and radiant beauty, Coop forced himself not to change expression. He willfully battled down his unwanted physical attraction. In addition, he reminded himself that there were too many Alexa Quinns flitting around high society and he didn't like any of them.

"Good morning, Marshal," she greeted Gil then nodded politely to Coop. "And good day to you, sir." She glanced directly at his battered cane. "I'm sorry to see you are nursing an injury. I hope it isn't too serious."

"Nothing I can't live with," he replied as she swept past.

The alluring scent of her perfume infiltrated his nostrils.

Coop took a step backward to prevent the fragrance from clogging his brain and smothering his good sense. Distracted though he was, something familiar niggled him. Maybe he *had* seen her before in Albuquerque. Maybe he had heard her voice somewhere. No, that was impossible, he told himself. He would have remembered everything about this woman.

With her expensive hat sitting at a jaunty angle on her head, twirling her parasol on her shoulder like a carousel, she sashayed into one of the boutiques. No doubt, her greatest interest in life was shopping. Here was the crowning example of the idle rich. She might be every man's fantasy, but he doubted she had a brain in her pretty blond head.

"Damn Webster's luck," Gil grumbled enviously. "Can you imagine the possibility of marrying a woman like that and bedding down with her every night?"

"Nope," Coop replied. "Wipe your mouth, Gil. You're drooling."

Gil shook himself from his erotic thoughts. "Well, I won't keep you from your part-time job. Maybe we can have dinner and a drink tonight when we're both off duty."

"Sounds good." Coop cast one last glance at the boutique to note the bodyguard waiting outside with feet askew and arms crossed over his chest. As one servant of the affluent to another, Coop nodded and the Mexican nodded back.

There is one job I'd refuse to take, Coop thought as he headed for the saloon. He wouldn't want to be Alexa Quinn's lackey. He sincerely hoped the bodyguard was well paid for his trouble.

As for a potential match between Harold Quinn's daughter and Elliot Webster, they probably deserved each other, he decided. Nevertheless, Mr. Chester had paid Coop considerable money to monitor Webster's activities. Coop would do his job to the best of his ability. The last thing he needed was the high and mighty Harold Quinn spreading word that he was an incompetent investigator.

Alexa expelled a sigh of relief while she sorted through the day dresses in the boutique. She had underestimated her reaction to Wyatt Cooper. In broad daylight and at close range he was even more arresting than he'd been while he loomed in the gathering shadows of sunset. His piercing green eyes, wavy raven hair and muscular physique combined to make an impressive package of masculinity. She had noticed how other women on the street had taken a wide berth around him, but there was no mistaking the speculative glances he received from them. He might be considered a hard-edged, dangerous gunfighter, the angel of doom to outlaws, but he was still a tempting specimen.

Completely off-limits, she reminded herself sensibly. There could be no association between them whatsoever. Webster might become suspicious and she shouldn't have spoken to Coop on the street, but she hadn't been able to resist. From now on, she would avoid encounters with him.

A curious frown knitted her brow when she glanced out the window to see Elliot Webster striding into Valmont Saloon. She'd like to be a fly on the wall and hear what Coop and Webster had to say to each other, if anything. But she quelled her curiosity and reminded herself that tomorrow she'd have a chance to familiarize herself with Webster's home. He had invited her to supper, as she'd hoped he would. As for tonight, Kate would be joining her in town to dine at one of the local restaurants.

Alexa sighed impatiently. She was anxious to hear what the townsfolk had to say about Webster. The more she could learn about him the better she would understand him. With that in mind, she turned a smile on the female proprietor of the boutique and made a few casual inquiries.

Coop had been on the job less than five minutes when Elliot Webster sauntered inside, looking arrogant and defensive at once. Out of pure orneriness, Coop plunked down the nameplate that said, Wyatt Cooper, Bartender and Bouncer on Duty. Provided by the efficient Mr. Chester, no doubt.

"Need a drink, friend?" Coop asked cordially.

Webster nodded his blond head and requested a shot of the best whiskey in the house—no surprise there. After he downed it in one gulp, he stared straight at Coop and said, "There's an unspoken rule in society that states that men with your reputation don't associate with women like my soon-to-be fiancée, Alexa Quinn. No offense intended, of course. I'm just reminding you of that fact."

Better men than Elliot Webster had tried—and failed—to put Coop in his place. He had no respect for the rich, for they seemed to think they were entitled to privileges that he wasn't.

"And you are?" Coop asked, as if he didn't know.

He drew himself up to full stature and tilted his chin to an aloof angle. "Elliot Webster. I own and operate the town's most profitable dry goods store."

And you gouge miners, ranchers and cowboys to feather your nest, every chance you get, Coop thought.

"I also own a ranch outside of town and sell livestock to the forts and Indian reservations," he boasted proudly.

Coop suspected this man was cheating the soldiers and Indian tribes to increase his profit. The bastard.

"Just for the record," Coop said, "I didn't strike up a conversation with your soon-to-be-fiancée. She spoke to me first."

"Obviously she had no idea who she was talking to."

"Obviously." Coop forced a smile and envisioned himself planting his fist in Webster's jaw. The man was an ass.

To his surprise, Webster leaned close to request another drink then said, "I wonder if I might hire you to check my neighbors' ranching practices. A few of my cattle have gone missing lately."

Coop suspected it was probably the other way around.

Three jobs at once? he mused. That might be an interesting twist. Mr. Chester wouldn't like it, but he could work for the man he'd come to investigate. "You mean at night when I'm off duty at the saloon? This is gravy money. I'm not giving it up."

"Yes, at night. That's when the rustling takes place," Webster replied sarcastically.

"Could be some of your own hired men," Coop speculated as he refilled Webster's shot glass.

"Doubt it. They are well paid to be loyal. You will be, too."

This was too perfect to pass up, thought Coop. If he were on Webster's payroll, he'd have an excuse to come and go from the ranch without inviting suspicion.

Coop shrugged. "Sure. Why not? As long as I don't have to get into a foot race with rustlers. My leg won't hold up."

Webster grinned as he straightened away from the bar. "Just shoot them from horseback. I hear you're good at that. And not to worry, the city marshal won't arrest you."

When Webster strutted off, Coop frowned warily. He was going to be disappointed if Gil Henson was on the take and had been paid to look the other way when Webster dealt severely with his competitors at Hampton, Barrett and Figgins Dry Goods Store.

Coop discarded his pensive thoughts when one of the calico queens sashayed over to introduce herself. Now this was the kind of female Coop was familiar with. This uncomplicated woman offered and expected no more than a moment's pleasure for a price. Women like Alexa Quinn were like porcelain dolls in shop windows. Untouchable. Unattainable. Too delicate to associate with a rough-edged man like him.

So why was he giving Alexa Quinn a second thought? Damned if he knew. Coop smiled rakishly and devoted his full attention to the buxom brunette named Polly Sanders.

Chapter Three

 ⟡⟡⟡

Later that evening Miguel Santos stared accusingly at Alexa. "You poisoned me!"

"Don't be ridiculous," she replied as she tucked the quilt under his quivering chin while he lay sprawled on the bed. "Why would I do such a thing?"

"So you can tramp about without me there to tell you that it's too risky. I—" He moaned miserably and battled to prevent himself from losing his supper.

Alexa patted her friend's shoulder consolingly, then surveyed the hotel room she had rented when he became ill a half hour earlier. Hurriedly she walked over to fetch a washcloth then dipped it in water so she could wipe Miguel's clammy face. He looked as peaked as a dark-skinned man could get. Furthermore, his expression was as sour as his upset stomach.

"I did not poison you, Miggy," she insisted, using the nickname he had acquired as a child.

While she blotted his face, someone tapped lightly on the door. "Who is it?" Alexa called out.

"Kate." She swept into the room without waiting permission and hovered over Miguel. Her thick-lashed brown eyes were filled with concern. "You poor man. Is there anything I can get for you to make you more comfortable?"

"No, *señorita,* but thank you for your kind offer. I will live…I hope."

Kate glanced at the gold-plated watch pinned to her belt. "We need to ride to the ranch before dark, Lexi. There is always the risk of bandits and rustlers in the area. Papa lost five head of cattle last week."

"Go with her, Lexi," Miguel beseeched. "I'll be fine."

"I'm staying with Miguel," Alexa told her friend. "You have your chaperone for your protection. Miguel and I will ride out to the ranch tomorrow when he's back on his feet."

"Are you sure about this?" Kate questioned hesitantly as she backed toward the door.

"Absolutely. I want to be close by so I can check on Miguel."

"I'm concerned about you," Kate said. "First you strike up a conversation on the street with that hired gun that everybody is whispering about and now you plan to stay in town when Miguel can't defend you."

"I believe those types prefer to be called detectives or investigators." Alexa tossed Miguel a silencing glance so he wouldn't chime in and tell Kate that he was worried about her reckless encounter with Coop. "Furthermore, I spoke to the town marshal on the street at the same time and it would have been rude not to speak to Mr. Cooper when he was standing right there."

"There are certain rules we're supposed to observe when it comes to our social class," Kate reminded her dourly. "Never mind that I dislike that one person can't be kind to another without inviting rumor and gossip. My father harps on the subject constantly and I heard Elliot Webster muttering when you paused to greet the marshal and the gunslinger."

Alexa gnashed her teeth. Elliot's snobbery was another of

his annoying flaws. The man was lousy with them. Too bad that Kate's father was also prejudiced.

Kate checked her timepiece again then glanced back at Miguel. "Well, I should be going. Papa is so overprotective that if I'm not home before dark he'll send out a search party."

"As well he should," Miguel murmured weakly. "If I could, I would see you home safely."

"You are so sweet, Miguel." Kate surged forward to brush her hand over his forehead. "You have always been wonderful to me. Alexa is so lucky to have you."

"Which is why I intend to stay at the hotel until he's feeling better," Alexa remarked.

She glanced speculatively at Kate then down at Miguel.

"I don't trust you here," Miguel said after Kate left.

Alexa tried to look properly affronted. "That doesn't speak highly of your abilities as a tutor. You taught me to take care of myself. Are you saying that you failed and I'm helpless?"

"I'm saying that you're too daring for your own good...." His voice trailed off momentarily and he grabbed his belly when another cramp clenched his abdomen. "Go to your own room and stay in it," he wheezed. "I don't want you to see me so miserable."

Alexa pressed a kiss to his forehead. "I'll be back to check on you."

"Don't do anything stupid in the meantime," he demanded sickly.

Deciding that she would have the local physician check on Miguel, she hurried off. Although she wasn't responsible for what was ailing Miguel—as he accused—she did intend to take advantage of the situation. She wanted to know what Elliot did after he closed up shop for the evening. Did he frequent saloons? Hurry back to his ranch? Alexa intended to observe his after-hours routine.

Alexa paid a visit to the doctor then tramped off to position herself in the alley beside Webster's mercantile shop. She only had to wait a quarter of an hour before Elliot locked the door and strode down the street. Enjoying her new career as a detective, Alexa darted down the alley, following at an inconspicuous distance.

Coop had been off duty at the saloon for over an hour and had dined with Gil at one of the restaurants. He was on his way to the livery stable to fetch Bandit when he spotted Webster—and the fancy-dressed female lurking in the alley. Coop was both surprised and amused at Alexa Quinn's daring. She was amazingly swift of foot and effective at lurking in the shadows so Webster wouldn't realize he was being followed.

Although Coop hadn't given the socialite credit for processing much thought in that pretty blond head of hers, she wasn't as naive as she let on. Coop veered into the alley to follow the woman who was trailing her soon-to-be-fiancé—or so Webster claimed. When Webster scurried across the street toward the dimly lit brothel on the edge of town, Alexa hiked up her cumbersome skirts and darted toward the side window of the brick building that housed Lily's Pleasure Resort.

"See anything interesting?" Coop whispered as he stepped up beside Alexa.

She yelped in surprise and clutched her chest. "You scared ten years off my life. What the blazes are you doing here?"

"I could ask you the same question," he pointed out.

He grinned at the pinched expression on her shadowed face. Her clipped tone of voice and her unconventional antics offered him insight into this woman's complex personality. She didn't seem to fit the expected mold. Which was too bad because he really didn't want to like this wealthy heiress.

"Sorry, Mr. Cooper. I didn't mean to snap at you."

"No problem. But I'm dying to know why a proper lady is playing Peeping Tom at a bordello window. You might get far more of an education than you bargained for...unless you like to watch."

"You are an ass," she sputtered as she brushed past him.

He wasn't sure if her elbow accidentally jabbed him in the belly or if she had done it on purpose. He suspected the latter.

"I only followed Elliot to confirm what I expected to be true," she said as he fell into a limping stride behind her. "Like all of my other suitors, who were supposedly smitten with me, Elliot is undoubtedly after my social connections and my money. He will never be faithful. But whether he likes me at all has nothing to do with anything. I only wanted to be sure we were both playing by the same rules."

Coop clucked his tongue. "So cynical for one so young. I didn't expect that."

When Alexa stopped short Coop did, too. The light from the street lamp illuminated her enchanting face and high-lighted her soft, kissable mouth. Lust sucker-punched him so hard that he staggered back a step.

Damn! Coop didn't recall other women making such a fierce and immediate impact on him. And hell, he could list a score of reasons why he should keep his distance from Alexa. Yet, he couldn't stop himself from gazing down into those incredible blue eyes and craving a taste of those honeyed lips.

"And what of you, sir? What do you see when you look at me? Dollar signs? Invitations to high society's soirees?"

A slow smile worked its way across his mouth. "All I want is to see you naked with me," he told her frankly.

That should scare the dickens out of her and send her scuttling off, frightened and embarrassed, he predicted. Which would guarantee that she would never allow herself to be alone in the dark with him again. Then he wouldn't be tempted and tormented with the want of this forbidden female.

To his stunned amazement, she met his rakish grin and didn't recoil in shock and indignation. "You would hang the money and the prestige?"

"From the tallest tree in the territory," he assured her. "No reason you shouldn't give good ole Webster the same lack of fidelity he's practicing right now."

She chuckled when he waggled his eyebrows suggestively. "You are an unabashed scoundrel, Mr. Cooper."

"Coop," he corrected. "An *honest* scoundrel."

She studied him pensively. "You consider appeasing your lust more important than wealth and status?"

"Tonight I do," he teased playfully.

Then the most astonishing thing happened. Alexa Quinn, who was rather tall for a woman—perhaps five feet eight inches, give or take—pushed up on tiptoe and pressed those dewy, heart-shaped lips against his. Coop stood frozen to the spot. His eyes flew wide-open and he stared incredulously at her while he accepted the quick taste of her kiss. Her shapely body brushed against his masculine contours and white-hot sensations bombarded him from every direction at once. He'd never been lightning struck but he was pretty sure this was what it felt like.

She dropped back on her heels and gave him that killer smile that cut dimples in her cheeks. "Good thing my chaperone is under the weather this evening," she murmured. "I would have missed out on this grand adventure."

"What's wrong with him?" Coop questioned, his voice wobbly, despite his attempt to appear unaffected.

"He claims I poisoned him."

She pivoted to amble down the street.

"Did you?" he called after her.

She glanced over her shoulder. There was a flicker of mischief in her gaze. "Poison Miguel? My childhood friend and companion? Really, Mr. Cooper—"

"Just Coop," he reminded her. He studied her thoughtfully, fascinated by the contradictions that he saw in this breathtakingly beautiful woman.

"Well then, good night, Coop."

"You didn't answer my question," he reminded her.

She tossed him another impish smile as she passed beneath the second street lamp. Then she was gone and he was left to wonder if Alexa had doctored her bodyguard's food or drink so she could dart off in the night to do as she pleased.

Right there and then, Coop made a mental note not to eat or drink anything that passed this siren's hands…just in case.

Two hours after Alexa's encounter with Coop she checked on Miguel and was relieved to find him sleeping comfortably. The bottle sitting on the nightstand indicated the physician had paid a visit and prescribed medication to soothe Miguel's stomach.

When Alexa returned to her own room, she doffed her gown. She smiled impishly, remembering her conversation with the ruggedly attractive detective. Matching wits with Coop had been more fun than she'd had with a man in years. Her longtime friendship with Miguel being the exception. He was like the brother she never had.

Coop had teased her and tried to shock her rather than bowing and scraping, attempting to win her favor. She had teased him right back, especially when he quizzed her about poisoning Miguel. Which of course she hadn't. Miguel was sensitive to certain foods but he refused to consider the possibility because the reactions weren't long-lived or serious. She'd known when he'd ordered the main dish smothered with a sauce containing pecans and almonds at dinner that he'd be down for the count.

She'd never been able to convince him that something as simple as eating walnuts caused his stomach ailments. Therefore, his temporary illness was self-inflicted. He couldn't exactly call that *her* fault, now could he? She had mentioned the possibility years ago, but he refused to believe it and she had stopped bringing it to his attention.

Her smile faded as she brushed her fingertips over her lips, remembering the impulsive kiss she had bestowed on Coop. She knew she had no business making the slightest contact with Coop, for fear of complicating this case. Not only had she struck up a conversation with him on the street that morning, but she had also kissed him that night. Perhaps she'd been caught up in the exciting intrigue of following Elliot and talking her way out of the situation with Coop. Maybe that had led to her impulsive embrace.

Although her father forbade her from taking an active role in the investigation, she had discovered that she *thrived* on the challenge and adventure. She had also experienced the most delicious tingles of desire when she brushed against Coop's masculine body and tasted his sensuous lips. That kiss in the dark was guaranteed to incite erotic dreams tonight—

"Stop that," she ordered herself sensibly.

Her startling reaction to Coop was one-sided, she knew. No doubt, he'd been with his share of women. One brief kiss wouldn't turn his world upside down and she was determined not to let it upend hers, either.

"You have another objective to accomplish while Miggy is out of commission tonight," she reminded herself.

She was on a crusade to help her father and to prove to him that she was worthy of his respect and his pride.

Alexa dug into her carpetbag to retrieve the second disguise she carried with her. Not Mr. Chester, but rather the elusive cloaked rider who blended with the darkness. She fastened herself into the trim black breeches, black shirt, boots and cap. Then she donned the cape that concealed her size and shape and gender. She had rented a mount from the livery on her way back to the hotel and tethered the steed in the alley. It was ready and waiting for the midnight jaunt.

She planned to be at the brothel when Elliot exited so she could follow him to his ranch, which was located two miles northeast of town. She was curious about other activities on his agenda before he bedded down for the night.

Five minutes later Alexa crept down the back steps of the hotel to retrieve her waiting horse. She followed the alley to avoid notice. When she reached the four brothels in the red light district, she veered toward a nearby grove of bushes to hide. Elliot had entered the most respectable-looking brothel of the four. *If* you could call any house of ill repute respectable. The other three were hastily constructed clapboard buildings into which dusty cowboys, miners and railroad workers came and went.

She waited ten minutes before Elliot appeared. He weaved a bit unsteadily as he hiked off to the mercantile shop to fetch his horse. Impatiently she waited for Elliot to mount up, light his cigar then trot away from town. She perked up immediately when he veered off the path leading to his ranch house and headed due east. Five minutes later, he dismounted to relieve himself then entered a shack nestled against the hillside.

She assumed it was on his land. Perhaps a line shack or abandoned bunkhouse, she speculated.

Another horse was tied to a scrub bush near the shack. Alexa was anxious to know who was waiting for Elliot. This could be the mysterious informant or his agent. If she could crack this case wide-open in less than a week all by herself, her father would be impressed and she would be assured that she was capable of handling an investigation alone. Nothing would please her more.

Her thoughts skittered off when her horse whinnied at the two mounts near the shack. She cursed her horse silently then hurried to take cover in a nearby stand of cottonwood trees. If she wanted conclusive evidence then she had to slither on her belly to eavesdrop at the window.

Securing her horse, Alexa dropped onto hands and knees and moved forward until she ran out of the cover of bushes. Then she sprawled in the grass to slither toward the window.

Coop scowled as he stared at the unidentified rider who dismounted in the trees. He appeared to be keeping surveillance, same as Coop was, on the shack that Webster had entered a moment earlier.

"Damn that Mr. Chester," he muttered under his breath.

Coop stationed himself at a point near a cedar tree so he'd have a clear view of the door of the shack and the caped crusader who slithered on his belly like a snake. It was glaringly apparent that the Yank, Mr. Chester, didn't trust Coop to do the job he'd been paid to do. Chester had obviously hired a second detective to tail Webster. Either that or someone else had hired an investigator to monitor Webster's activities for other reasons.

Earlier, he had seen Webster leave Lily's Pleasure Resort and he had decided this would be the perfect time to hammer out the details of his employment and insist on advance payment. That was when he first spotted the unidentified rider, who dressed in black and wore a cape that flapped in the breeze like bat wings.

It was turning out to be an interesting evening, thought Coop. First he had watched Alexa spy on her wanna-be fiancé.

Now someone else was hot on Webster's heels. Hell, there might be so many people trailing Webster that it caused a traffic jam.

Coop jerked to attention when the door creaked on its rusty hinges and two shadowed silhouettes appeared on the rickety stoop.

"I'll be in touch in a few days," came a quiet voice Coop didn't recognize.

He watched Webster fish into his pocket then place what Coop presumed to be several coins in the man's hand. "You tell our mutual friend that the last tidbits of information aren't enough to satisfy me. I'm paying for better tips than this."

"I'll relay the message," the other man murmured so quietly that Coop barely made out his comment.

Webster lurched around and staggered clumsily toward his horse. He belched loudly then scooped up the reins. Coop smirked, wishing Alexa were here to see this jackass at another of his defining moments. She might as well know what she was getting if she decided to marry Webster.

When Webster clomped off on his horse, his associate closed the door to the shack then strode hurriedly toward his mount. Coop couldn't trail the short, lean figure of a man who galloped north because Webster had halted near Coop's hiding place to take a swig of whiskey from the bottle in his pocket. When Webster was finally out of earshot the cohort was long gone.

Coop turned his attention back to the caped rider. "Well, I'll be damned." Coop looked every which way but he saw no sign of the man in black. "Where'd he go?"

Exasperated, Coop reined back to town. Contacting the drunken Webster could wait until the following evening, he decided. Besides, he was anxious to return to his hotel room, remove the cumbersome splints and enjoy a warm, relaxing bath. Plus, he wanted to wash away the alluring scent of Alexa that clung to him and to his shirt after she had kissed him. He needed no reminders of that intriguing female if he hoped to put aside all thoughts of her and get a good night's rest.

Alexa eased open the door to check on Miguel one last time before bedding down for the night. Obviously he was feeling better for he propped himself up on an elbow and glared at her.

"Come in and close the door," he demanded sharply. "Where have you been? I dragged myself from my deathbed an hour ago to check your room."

Alexa pursed her lips as she stared at her friend whose black hair was sticking out in all directions. "I thought you learned long ago that I don't always do as you order."

"Don't remind me," he grumbled. "I've spent half my life fretting over you and your daredevil streak." His gaze narrowed. "Now where were you?"

She sank down beside him. "I had investigative work to do."

Miguel sighed audibly. "Your father will have my head for this."

"Not to worry. I'll give him mine instead," she volunteered.

"Not funny, *querida*. You keep up these death-defying stunts and you won't be alive to give anybody anything. Now tell me specifically what you were up to."

"I followed Elliot to a brothel where he drank heavily, etcetera, etcetera." Although Miguel sputtered in annoyance, she hurried on. "Unfortunately Coop was also tailing Elliot at the time and I ran into him."

She had to pause momentarily because Miguel spewed Spanish curses. Not that it mattered because Alexa spoke fluent Spanish.

"How did you explain spying on Elliot to Coop?" Miguel finally got around to asking after he depleted his supply of succinct oaths.

She shrugged nonchalantly. "I told him that I wanted to know the real Elliot Webster…in case I decided to marry him."

Alexa didn't confide Coop's intimate remark about getting naked together or the kiss she initiated during a momentary lapse of sanity. Miguel would pitch a fit and she figured he'd had a rough night already. No sense aggravating his condition.

Furthermore, the encounter with Coop was much too private and personal. She wasn't prepared to share it with anyone.

"What time did all this take place?" Miguel interrogated. "It was eleven o'clock when I visited your room." He gestured toward the bottle on the nightstand. "I took my second dose as the doctor ordered and then I went to look for you."

Alexa fidgeted uneasily. "Um…it was earlier this evening. I returned to my room to don a disguise about ten o'clock."

Miguel erupted in another stream of Spanish curses. "And you did what?" he said through clenched teeth.

When he reared up in bed, Alexa pressed the heel of her hand to his rigid shoulder and pushed him down. She smiled reassuringly, but her friend continued to glare stonily at her. "Calm down, Miggy. Your sour expression will sour your stomach all over again."

"Too late," he growled.

"I wanted to know where Elliot went after he left the brothel. My persistence paid off. I followed him to a shack that sits on the edge of his property…I think. He met a man but I couldn't get a clear look at him in the dark."

Alexa was annoyed that she had slithered all the way to the window, only to have the men step outside before she could spy on them. She had been in the wrong place to get a description of Elliot's associate or to identify his voice. At least she knew Elliot was conducting secret meetings. She didn't know if the encounter provided him with information from the territorial capital or if it involved some of Elliot's other shady dealings.

"I don't like any of this," Miguel complained before he gulped down another dose of the pasty liquid medicine. "I especially don't like you spiriting off in the night. I wish you could have come up with a safer scheme to gain Harold's notice and impress him with your skills and intelligence."

Alexa withdrew slightly, causing Miguel to snicker.

"Don't you think I know what motivates you to stick your neck out so far with this case? Not that I mind accompanying you to Questa Springs. I've always liked your friend Kate."

"More than I suspected...until today," Alexa remarked.

It was Miguel's turn to squirm self-consciously. "Yes, well, I am a realist at least. In her parents' eyes, I am the hired help. Your chaperone and bodyguard. I'm certainly not considered marriage material for Kate."

"She would be lucky to have you," Alexa insisted loyally. "Plus, she seems genuinely fond of you. Had I realized this earlier I would have arranged to get you two together more often."

"Which would have made admiring her from afar all the worse," said Miguel. He waved his hand dismissively. "That is beside the point. You need your rest and so do I. *Please* go to your room...and stay there."

She offered him a playful salute. "Yes, sir."

"Promise me, no more midnight rides alone," he demanded. "If you are compelled to snoop around, at least let me go with you next time."

She arched an amused brow as she rose to her feet. "Without complaints or lectures?"

"No. You'll have to endure those, but at least you won't be alone and I can offer protection."

"I love you, Miggy," she murmured on her way out the door.

"Me, too... But you drive me crazy."

"I heard that," she said from the other side of the door.

Chapter Four

⟨⟨⟨⟨⟩⟩⟩⟩

From his posted lookout at his hotel room window the next morning, Coop surveyed the street. A strange sensation filtered through him when he spotted Alexa, who was dressed in a stylish mint-green satin gown. She and her bodyguard were ambling toward Donovan's Café, which was directly across the street. Coop was tempted to strap on his splint, grab his cane and limp over to eat breakfast, just to get another close look at her.

"You're an idiot," he told himself as he wheeled away from the window—and the tantalizing scenery beyond. He'd had enough trouble falling asleep because erotic visions of Alexa danced in his head all night. No need to torture himself this morning, he decided. He'd grab a bite at one of the other four cafés before going on duty at the saloon.

With his leg bound up, Coop crammed his hat on his head and hobbled off. For the most part, the patrons in Sawyer's Café pretended he wasn't there. The waitress approached tentatively, but she relaxed when he didn't grab his six-shooter and fill her full of holes. He considered himself one of the good guys, but anyone touted as quick on the draw was subjected to suspicion, conjecture and approached with caution. Yet, this mountain town was no different to him from other places, he reminded himself. He never stayed in one place long enough to make friends. He made a few casual acquaintances, completed his assignment then moved on to the next job.

"Morning, Coop. Mind if I join you?"

Coop smiled and nodded at Gil Henson, who parked himself in the adjacent chair so he, too, would have a clear view of the door and windows. It was a common practice for gunfighters to sit with their backs to the wall…just in case. Wild Bill Hickok had failed to follow that practice only once, Coop reminded himself grimly. The oversight had cost Hickok his life in a saloon in Deadwood, South Dakota.

Coop wasn't taking any chances.

He inclined his head toward the patrons who were pretending he wasn't there. "I'm making people nervous. Are you sure you want to be seen with me, Gil?"

"Sure. Why not? I'm considered a necessary evil in Questa Springs," Gil said, then asked the waitress to bring him his usual breakfast of biscuits, gravy and coffee.

That explained Gil's widening girth, Coop mused as the waitress placed the steamy plates on the table. As for Coop, he preferred steak whenever he could get it. Morning, noon and night.

He wondered about Alexa's tastes in food and then chastised himself for allowing her to cross his mind…again.

"How good of a friend are you to Elliot Webster?" Coop asked conversationally. "Good enough to be invited to his wedding, if there is one?"

Gil chewed, swallowed then smirked. "Doubt it. Webster only deigns to speak to me when he wants something. Six months ago, he wanted me to arrest Hampton, Barrett and Figgins, his business competitors, for undercutting his high prices at his mercantile store.

"Another time he demanded that I arrest Andrew Barrett, who is not only his business competitor but also one of his ranching neighbors," Gil continued. "Webster claims his live-stock has gone missing on several occasions and that either Barrett or Percy Hampton, who shares his fences, is respon-sible. Or maybe both. According to Webster there is a con-spiracy at work to bankrupt him."

Coop wondered if Webster wanted to marry Alexa, in case his finances hit rock bottom. "In my spare time, Webster wants me to check neighboring herds to see if they carry his brand," Coop said confidentially.

Amber-colored eyes riveted on him. "Are you signing on Webster's payroll?"

"Are you already on it?" Coop questioned the question.

A wry smile pursed Gil's lips. "You think I can be bought, is that it? Thanks for the vote of confidence."

Coop cut his steak then tossed Gil a sideways glance. "Just checking, old friend. It's always important to know who has your back and who doesn't…when bullets start flying."

"I'm not on Webster's payroll, but it's not for his lack of trying," Gil confided. "You need to know that Webster has several hired gunmen on his staff, guarding his cattle and horse herds and his home. I wouldn't turn my back on any of those bastards, I'm tellin' ya for sure."

Coop studied Gil intently. He believed him. But he'd be mad as hell if Gil turned out to be a liar. For now, he gave Gil the benefit of the doubt.

"I was going to meet with Webster last night, but he hotfooted it to Lily's Pleasure Resort before I could catch up with him on my gimpy leg." He grinned wryly. "Does Webster have a favorite among the soiled doves at the brothel?"

Gil grinned back. "Why do you want to know? You planning to beat his time for spite?"

Coop shrugged nonchalantly. "Sure, why not? I doubt Webster settles for anything less than the best. Just look who he's courting for a potential bride."

Despite what Coop said, in his effort to dig for information, he had developed a forbidden fascination for the spirited blonde whom Webster wanted to marry. The thought of Alexa wedding Webster annoyed the hell out of him, although he told himself that it really wasn't any of his business.

"Webster obviously has a strong appetite because I know he and Lily Brantley have standing appointments three times a week," Gil reported. "Maybe more."

"As in *Lily's,* the owner? Webster and the madam?"

Gil nodded his reddish-blond head. "She also has two sisters who run brothels in the territory. Must be a family tradition passed from one generation to the next."

Coop vowed to pass along the information about Webster and his intimate companion to Alexa. He figured a prospective wife ought to know where her would-be husband went for lusty passion. After all, Alexa claimed she didn't want to enter into a marriage blindly, *if* she decided on Webster.

"Marshal Henson?"

Coop glanced at the young man who called out to Gil from the door of the café.

"Harlan Fredericks is on the rampage again. You better come quickly."

"Damn that old fool," Gil grumbled as he tossed aside his napkin then bolted to his feet. He cast a longing glance at his half-eaten breakfast then sighed defeatedly.

Coop tossed money on the table for their unfinished meals and clambered to his feet, silently cursing the inconvenience of his splinted leg. "I'll come along to back you up," he offered. "Who's Fredericks?"

Gil led the way onto the street. "About once a month the

old bastard starts drinking heavily and convinces himself that his wife is cuckolding him. He takes after her and causes a public commotion."

"Is she cheating on him?" Coop asked curiously.

Gil barked a laugh as he veered toward the residential area behind the bank. "Doubt it."

A moment later Coop knew why Mrs. Fredericks, who looked to be in her early fifties, wasn't cheating on the older man, who looked to be in his early sixties. Fredericks was scampering around his front lawn in his long handles, swishing a tree branch threateningly, as if brandishing a sword.

He was chasing after a homely woman, whose gray eyes were a mite too close together to be attractive. Her salt-and-pepper gray hair was piled atop her head, exposing her oversize ears. Her hips were as wide as an ax handle and her shoulders were exceptionally broad. She was six feet tall if she were an inch and she dwarfed Mr. Fredericks, who was rail-thin and stood about five foot nine inches tall in his stocking feet.

"Harlan!" Gil bugled loudly. "Put down that stick and leave your missus alone! I will never understand why she is loyal and true-blue to an idiot like you. You're the one who needs a good thrashing for running around in your underdrawers. Go put on your breeches!"

"Stay outta my business, Marshal," Harlan shouted without breaking stride. "What's between a man and his wife is private."

He swung his stick, missing his wife by a few inches. She yelped and quickened her pace.

"This isn't private because you're attracting public attention." Gil gestured toward the gathering crowd that watched Harlan perform his monthly ritual.

Coop's gaze settled on Alexa who stood on the street corner with her bodyguard. She watched Harlan chase his wife in circles and her annoyed expression indicated she was offended by his behavior. Coop inwardly groaned when Alexa marched across the street to plant herself directly between husband and wife.

"Here now!" she spouted off. "That is no way to treat a lady!"

"Lady? Hell!" Harlan raised his stick menacingly. "Get outta my way, lass, or *you'll* get what *she's* got coming. A man has a right to expect fidelity!"

Alexa, curse her courageous hide, simply crossed her arms over her breasts, lifted her chin belligerently and stood her ground. "Mrs. Fredericks?" she called to the woman behind her.

"Yah, ma'am?" the older woman said, panting for breath.

"Have you been faithful to your husband?"

"Yah, but the old fool doesn't believe me." Her voice carried a distinct Swedish accent.

Alexa focused intently on Harlan. "There you have it, sir. Your wife has not betrayed you. I plan to hire her so she won't have to put up with your nonsense all the livelong day."

"Hire her?" Harlan hooted. "Then who's gonna feed me if she ain't here to do it?"

"I'll take the job," Mrs. Fredericks said enthusiastically.

"You don't even know what the job is," Harlan snapped at her.

"Doesn't matter. It has to be better than getting chased down the street when you're having one of your mean streaks."

When Harlan raised his stick again, looking as if he intended to whack Alexa for interfering—before he went on his way to thrash his wife—Coop lunged forward. He used his cane to deflect the blow aimed at Alexa. To his surprise, she didn't need his assistance. She agilely darted sideways and the tree branch collided with the upraised cane.

In the blink of an eye, her bodyguard pounced on Harlan.

Before Harlan could react, the nasty-looking dagger that Miguel Santos kept strapped to his thigh was pricking the older man's throat. Harlan squealed like a stuck pig and his eyes popped when he noted the size of the knife.

"Alexa, my dear!" Webster cried. "You shouldn't witness such distasteful goings-on! Why, the old codger isn't even dressed!"

Coop muttered under his breath when Webster showed up to fuss over his intended bride. The hypocrite scurried over to latch on to her elbow then shepherd her back to Main Street. He fussed and fawned over Alexa as if she were the light and love of his life. Coop doubted the two-faced bastard had whispered Alexa's name while lying naked in Lily Brantley's arms the previous night. Clearly Webster's devotion was pretentious and calculated.

When Alexa glanced over her shoulder at Coop, he felt marginally better. Her smile indicated that she wasn't falling for Webster's theatrics and that she saw through him, too.

"C'mon, Harlan," Gil said, grabbing the man by the scruff of his neck. "You can cool down in jail."

The Mexican bodyguard tucked away his dagger and stared somberly at Coop while Gil frog-marched his prisoner to jail. "Thank you for your assistance, *señor.* My employer often acts before she thinks, when it comes to her desire of righting wrongs."

"Obviously." Coop extended his hand. "And you are—?"

"—Not sure we can be friends, *gringo.* Not if you can't offer Alexa the respect she deserves," he said pointedly.

"I see you are direct. Good. I appreciate that." Coop smiled dryly. "I hear you were ill last night."

The comment earned him a scowl. "*Si.* I am Miguel Santos." He clasped Coop's outstretched hand. "Harold Quinn pays me handsomely to keep Lexi out of trouble." A grin spread across his lips. "I am not overpaid, believe me. I earn every cent of my salary."

Coop chuckled. "I don't doubt it. By the way, I'm Wyatt Cooper."

"I know who you are." Miguel's expression sobered. "And you know you are overstepping your bounds. Men like you and I are not allowed to mix and mingle with the Alexa Quinns of the world. It is true that we are off the beaten path here. But if we were in Santa Fe you would have no association whatsoever with Lexi."

"Only in the capacity to serve her and people like her? Yes, I know," Coop replied. "Are you one of her many besotted admirers?"

Miguel laughed, unoffended by the direct question. His midnight-black eyes sparkled in the sunlight as he shook his dark head. "No, *señor.* I know her too well."

Coop stared speculatively after Miguel as he walked briskly toward Alexa, who was being propelled toward Webster's mercantile shop. With each passing hour, Coop discovered there was indeed more to Alexa Quinn than superficial beauty. Even her bodyguard acknowledged that she was difficult to handle. Maybe even temperamental when she didn't get her way. Coop couldn't say for sure. But thus far, he had caught glimpses of her courage, curiosity, quick intelligence and daring. Those weren't the characteristics he usually attributed to the idle rich who asked him to resolve their problems for a price.

Tossing aside his fruitless thoughts, Coop limped toward Valmont Saloon. He was already a few minutes late because of the Fredericks altercation. As he hobbled along, Mrs. Fredericks buzzed past him in pursuit of Alexa. Coop predicted that Alexa had made a devoted friend of Mrs. Fredericks, by boldly standing up to Harlan the way she had.

Coop frowned curiously, wondering how much pressure Alexa was under to select a suitable match from her elevated social class. Even if she saw Elliot Webster for what he really was, would she accept his marriage proposal and agree to a loveless match, in order to assume her expected role among the muckamucks?

"Mind your own damn business," Coop grumbled at himself. "You're here to do the job you're paid to do."

He wasn't being paid to understand why Alexa permitted Webster's courtship. Coop was on a fact-finding mission and he had to answer to Mr. Chester at the end of the week. Thus far, all he had was that Webster saw Lily Brantley exclusively when he visited the brothel and that Webster drank heavily on occasion. That and Webster held secretive meetings at a line shack late at night, Coop tacked on.

He doubted those tidbits would be enough to satisfy Mr. Chester, who had obviously hired a second detective to ensure quick results. The thought soured Coop's mood. He was going to confront the Yank about the issue of professional competency and trust the first chance he got.

"I cannot thank you enough," Selma Mae Fredericks gushed in her thick Swedish accent. "You are a lifesaver, Miz Quinn. Truly you are."

Alexa patted the older woman's hand. Selma Mae alternately bowed and curtsied until Alexa clamped a hand on her shoulder to stop her. "You're entirely welcome. I was glad to be of assistance."

Although Alexa had offered to employ the woman, she had no idea what to do with her. At least the woman wouldn't constantly be subjected to Harlan's misguided tantrums. "Are you a seamstress?" she asked while Miguel stood in the corner of the hotel room, rolling his eyes in exasperation.

"Yah, I am a fine seamstress," Selma Mae declared. "After my first husband died, I worked for the gentry in the old country to pay my way to America. I cooked, cleaned and mended." She pulled a face. "Then I married that dimwit Harlan Fredericks. His first wife ran off with an actor in a theater troop. He expects me to do the same. I keep telling him that I've had two husbands and that is plenty. But he refuses to believe me."

Alexa wondered if Harlan, like Elliot Webster, frequented brothels but expected his wife to remain faithful. She knew Elliot would never be faithful. She wondered if the same might be true of Coop. Perhaps infidelity was indigenous of the male species in general.

Coop's views on fidelity are completely irrelevant, she admonished herself. Her association with Coop shouldn't exist at all. If it did, it had to be strictly business. She hadn't come to Questa Springs in search of romance. Indeed, she wasn't even sure she believed in it. The constant squabbling between her parents during her childhood convinced her that romance didn't exist. Besides, she had come here to prove her skills and intelligence to her father by exposing Elliot for the shyster he was. She wanted to remain focused on her mission.

"I can wash and press your garments, too," Selma Mae insisted, breaking into Alexa's wandering thoughts. "And your bodyguard's as well."

"That would be nice," Alexa said. "I have an evening engagement with Elliot Webster at his ranch and I want to look my best."

Selma Mae's weathered face puckered. Clearly she disliked Elliot.

"Have you had unpleasant dealings with Mr. Webster?" Alexa questioned.

"Yah. When we first arrived in town, Harlan was a prospector. Elliot Webster refused to grubstake Harlan and me without demanding outrageous interest. Things got better when Harlan signed on with the railroad crew and began to receive a steady income. It took a few months to get our feet under us, and Mr. Webster took advantage of our situation the entire time."

Selma Mae shook her head. "The man is not good enough for you, missy. If not for Webster seeing to it that his competitors can't acquire all the necessary items to sell to miners, ranchers and prospectors, most of us wouldn't have traded with him at all the past few years."

Alexa frowned, wondering if the mysterious man Elliot had met at the line shack might be connected to this facet of corruption. Time would tell, she decided. If Elliot was cheating the townspeople for his personal gain, she vowed to stop him. Her strong sense of fair play refused to let him get away with murder. Figuratively or literally. Maybe both.

Time would tell about that, too.

Later that evening Alexa sat across the table from Elliot, who was decked out in his finery, trying to impress her with his comments, his expensive attire and his elaborate residence. It wasn't working. He must have had his house servants working overtime because the expensive, two-story stone and timber ranch house was free of dust. In addition, the woodwork, furniture and floors had been polished until they shined. The fact that Elliot had most likely acquired his costly furniture, imported rugs, tapestries and china at his customers' expense didn't escape her attention.

Elliot raised his wine goblet in toast. "To us, my dearest Alexa. You are such charming company and so lovely to look at that you take my breath away."

"You are too kind," she purred and batted her eyelashes for effect. "Your home is quite impressive, Elliot. A spectacular mansion in the mountains."

"I'm glad you approve." He took a drink of his wine and then smiled charismatically. "Perhaps one day you might be interested in living here with me."

Not a chance in hell! "Why, Elliot, are you suggesting what I think you are suggesting?" Alexa murmured coyly.

"I'm in need of a wife," Elliot remarked before he gulped down more wine. "At thirty-five I'm ready to start my family."

My, the man was a lush, Alexa noted as he filled his glass again. Another reason for her to dislike him. Her mother had the same problem.

"And my father thinks it's high time that I took a husband," she replied. "But I don't wish to be too hasty. After all, it is a commitment meant to last a lifetime."

Elliot reached across the table to clasp her hand in his. "Perhaps tonight can be a celebration of sorts. Would you consider me as a prospective—?"

"There he is. Never mind, Oscar. I found him."

Alexa tried very hard not to react to the unexpected sound of Coop's voice rolling into the room. To her surprise, he emerged from the shadows and limped into the middle of the dining room. Oscar Denton, the armed guard she'd met at the front door, looked quite annoyed as he lumbered along at Coop's heels. She noticed that Elliot made a point to cling overly long to her hand so that Coop was aware of the possessive touch.

"What are you doing here?" Elliot demanded of Coop.

"Didn't know you had company." Coop glanced at Alexa and touched the brim of his hat in greeting. "Ma'am, pardon the interruption. I'll come back later."

"Sorry, boss," Oscar Denton mumbled as he grabbed Coop's arm. "He just sort of breezed in here like he had no manners."

Alexa hid her frown of concern and curiosity behind the wine goblet as she took a sip. What the blazes was Coop doing here? He was supposed to monitor Elliot's activities from a distance, not barge in as if he owned the place.

Her attention shifted to the burly cowboy who was one of Elliot's hired gunmen. Oscar was two inches shorter than Coop and slightly heavier. He was armed with two six-shooters strapped to his hips, a dagger like Miguel's on his thigh and a bandoleer filled with ammunition draped diagonally across his thick chest.

She watched Elliot surge to his feet then cast her an apologetic glance. "Please excuse me for a moment, my dear. I might as well speak to the man since he's here." He stared pointedly at Coop. "If for no other reason than to remind him of his manners." He gestured for Coop to lead the way through the dining-room door.

When the three men exited, Alexa breathed a sigh of relief. Pretending to be enamored with Elliot was taxing. She was grateful for a moment of reprieve. She helped herself to another sip of wine and tried to puzzle out Coop's unannounced appearance.

Disturbing though it was, it provided a much-needed break in her conversation with Elliot. Listening to him, ad nauseam, while he chided her for speaking to Coop on the street the previous day and then for thrusting herself into the melee with the Fredericks this morning had become tiresome. She had apologized for her rashness, only because it was what he expected of her. Alexa didn't want to tip off Elliot that she wasn't exactly what she seemed.

Elliot had forgiven her for her impulsiveness but pleaded with her to be careful, because he had become exceedingly fond of her. Ha! He was fond of her father's political connections and her social status. Otherwise, he wouldn't have rushed to the brothel to seek satisfaction with a harlot.

Alexa helped herself to more wine, wishing she could tiptoe

to the door to eavesdrop on Elliot's conversation with Coop. But she figured she'd be caught and have some explaining to do.

Wine and *waiting,* she mused impatiently. She was stuck here, drinking, until Elliot returned.

"What the devil is the matter with you?" Elliot snapped at Coop. "The next time you barge in my home unannounced I'll have you shot—"

He shut his trap when Coop jerked his arm from Oscar Denton's grasp and gave both men quelling stares. Coop let it be known—here and now—that, although he could be friendly and agreeable if the mood suited him, he was not a man intimidated by verbal threats.

"Send your lackey on his way or I'll do it for you," Coop demanded harshly. "My business is with you, Webster. By the way, don't push me. Next time I might not be in a forgiving mood."

When Webster dismissed Oscar Denton with a flick of his wrist, the henchman scowled at Coop. They traded disrespectful glares before the guard lumbered outside to stand watch on the front steps.

Webster motioned for Coop to follow him to the far side of the elaborately furnished parlor. Out of Alexa's hearing range, no doubt. Coop was exceptionally pleased with his timing. From the looks of the intimate dinner, Webster planned to ask for Alexa's hand. Coop couldn't think of one reason why he should feel jealous and possessive, but he was, damn it. He didn't want that intriguing woman to marry this scoundrel.

Furthermore, where was Miguel Santos, the bodyguard? Had Alexa poisoned him a second night in a row so she could come alone to Webster's ranch?

"What do you want?" Elliot demanded irritably. "As you can plainly see, I'm entertaining an important guest this evening."

Coop stuck out his hand, palm up. "Advance pay is my policy," he announced. "One week's advance to be specific."

Elliot grumbled under his breath but he reached into the pocket of his trousers to retrieve several large bank notes. "Next time I'll meet you at the line shack on the south edge of my property. At midnight. I don't want you coming and going from my house. It looks suspicious."

Coop shook his head. No way in hell was he going to arrive at the line shack and find himself bushwhacked by Elliot's henchman or the unidentified colleague. "We'll meet here or your store or not at all. If you're going to be contrary I'll notify the marshal that you're paying me to find fault with your neighbors' ranching practices."

Elliot puffed up like an offended toad. "I will deny it!"

Coop shrugged lackadaisically then stretched the truth. "Doesn't make a damn to me because some of your neighbors want to hire *me* to check on *your* ranching practices. I'm a gun for hire and a job's a job, Webster. I go to the highest bidder."

Elliot snapped to attention and his gaze narrowed sharply. "*Who* wants to hire you away from me? Hampton? Barrett?"

"Client confidentiality," said Coop, his hand still outstretched. "So which is it? You or them?"

Muttering, Elliot slapped the money into Coop's waiting hand. "You work for me. Now get out of here and do what I'm paying you to do. Find out if my neighbors are guilty of rustling my cattle."

In other words, unjustly accuse them of wrongdoing, Coop translated. "Sure, you're the boss."

"You're damn right I am," Elliot contended aloofly. "And don't you forget it."

Coop watched Elliot stride quickly across the room to rejoin Alexa. He'd give anything to have the chance to tell her about Webster's intimate connection to Lily Brantley. Alexa needed to take that into consideration before she accepted or rejected the forthcoming marriage proposal. Although Coop knew he wasn't the right man for Alexa Quinn, he knew for damn certain that Webster wasn't, either.

When Coop hobbled outside, leaning heavily on his cane, Oscar Denton was there to confront him with a sneer and a loaded Colt .45. Coop twirled his cane, knocking the pistol from Denton's hand. It clattered down the steps and Denton cursed foully.

"Watch where you point that thing," Coop ordered. "You might shoot someone accidentally."

"When it comes to you, there won't be anything accidental about it," Denton sneered as he doubled over to scoop up his weapon. "Next time you go barging in on the boss I'll drag your dead carcass out by your boot heels—"

Denton's voice dried up when he realized Coop had drawn a six-shooter and had buried it in his soft underbelly. Coop had used the art of intimidation against outlaws dozens of times. He didn't like the looks of this whisker-faced, tobacco-chewing hooligan whose sketch could likely be found on a Wanted poster.

"One quick shot and I'll have *your* job," Coop threatened. "Doesn't make a damn bit of difference to me, as long as I get paid."

Coop retrieved both of Denton's pistols and his dagger. He tossed them into the bushes as he limped toward his horse. "I don't think we're going to be best friends," he said before he reined away from the burly henchman.

He heard Denton cursing a blue streak while he groped in the shrubs to locate his weapons. Coop had the distinctive feeling that he had made an enemy of Oscar Denton. But then, Coop had many enemies among the outlaw population of the world.

One more didn't make that much difference.

Chapter Five

⤜⤛⤜⤛⤜⤛

Alexa had endured as much of Elliot's tiresome company as she could stand that evening, while taking their meal in the dining room then adjourning to the parlor to sip wine. She was relieved when Oscar Denton lumbered inside around ten o'clock.

"Pardon, boss, but this message arrived for you. I thought you might want to see it immediately."

"Goodness, look at the time." Alexa rose to her feet. "I should be going. Thank you, Elliot, for a most delightful evening." She was quite pleased with herself because she hadn't gagged on the words.

Alexa exited the room before Elliot called her back. She had even managed to avoid further discussion of a possible betrothal. She had chattered nonstop, hoping to bore Elliot into a coma. She had nearly succeeded. Then Oscar showed up to provide her with an excuse to leave.

Once outside the house, Alexa inhaled a restorative breath of evening air. She scurried toward the rented carriage that waited on the circle driveway. She grinned, recalling that she had outsmarted Miguel this evening by sending him into town with Kate to retrieve the carpetbag she had purposely left behind at the hotel.

Alexa hadn't wanted Miguel hovering around, in case she had the chance to do a little snooping—which she intended to do now. She was eager to find out who had sent the missive to Elliot. Miguel, of course, would have nagged her relentlessly to let Coop do the investigating.

Unfortunately, his arrival this evening disturbed her and left her wondering whose side he was really on.

Alexa drove the carriage down the beaten path then veered into a grove of pine trees to avoid detection. She had a clear view of the office window and noticed a lantern had flared to life. She could see Oscar's and Elliot's silhouettes in the window. A moment later Oscar exited.

The guard dragon returned to his post on the front porch. Good. If he wasn't circling the house at regular intervals, she could tiptoe up to the window to see what was going on in Elliot's office.

Suspicion continued to hound Alexa. She wondered if Coop would show up for another consultation with Elliot. What was he up to? Was he planning to double-cross Mr. Chester?

She'd shoot him herself if she discovered he was professionally unreliable and corrupt. She'd shoot him *twice* to compensate for the disconcerting realization that she couldn't trust her instincts as well as she thought she could. Then she'd blast him a third time for disappointing her personally.

Maybe her father and Miguel were right. Maybe ex-bounty hunters and so-called detectives couldn't be trusted completely. Her instincts might have failed her in this instance because of her fierce physical attraction to Coop.

She pricked her ears when she heard the clatter of hooves, indicating a late-night visitor had arrived. She squinted, trying to determine if it was Coop or the unidentified man from the line shack who approached the ranch house.

Alexa cursed under her breath when she stumbled over the hem of her gown. Halting near the garden gate, she shed her petticoats, and then tossed them over the white picket fence. Hurriedly she fashioned her dress into breeches so she could scurry through the shrubs without being snagged.

In the near distance, she could hear muffled voices. With her curiosity on high alert, she quickened her pace to reach the corner of the house. Removing her slippers to ensure better footing, she scaled the jagged stones to reach the elevated office window. The feat wasn't too difficult, but clinging to the side of the house like a spider on the wall, to maintain her balance, took considerable strength and effort. Although she broke several fingernails, she managed to sink in her hands like cat claws. She stretched out a leg—practically doing the splits—to find purchase on another protruding stone.

Frissons of excitement coursed through her as she inched sideways so she could peer into the office. She had found her true calling, she realized. This was the kind of thrill and challenge that had been missing from her life. Gathering information, piecing it together and solving puzzles filled her with a sense of purpose.

This new job made her *happy*. However, if Coop was the late-night caller, who arrived to meet secretly with Elliot, she was going to be mad as hell.

She tossed aside the disparaging thought when she heard Elliot's voice drift through the office. It wasn't the cooing, sticky-sweet tone he employed when he was with her, but rather a soft, seductive voice that alerted her that it probably wasn't Coop who had arrived on the scene.

Alexa leaned sideways as far as she dared, and then craned her neck to peer into the window. Elliot stepped into view. He had removed his dark jacket and silk cravat. His crisp white linen shirt hung open, revealing a light furring of blond hair on his chest.

The sight did nothing to stimulate Alexa. However, the auburn-haired woman, dressed in a red satin gown that displayed her ample bosom to its best advantage, seemed to appreciate the sight of his bare skin. She smiled provocatively as she sashayed up to Elliot.

Alexa watched the woman trail her fingertips down the middle of Elliot's chest then skim her hand over the placket of his trousers. That appeared to be all the incentive Elliot needed, for he hooked his arm around the woman's waist and hauled her roughly against him. They commenced groping each other passionately. Articles of clothing and undergarments came off at record speed and were tossed recklessly aside.

Alexa decided she didn't need this lesson in lust and window peeking wouldn't gain her information for this case. She squeezed her eyes shut when Elliot yanked down the bodice of the woman's chemise and feasted on her breasts. Breathless moans and whimpers filled the room and embarrassment flooded Alexa's cheeks. She wanted to flee the scene before the grand finale of this tryst took place in the office.

Anxious to climb down the face of the wall, she clawed at the rough rocks and struggled to maintain her balance. When an unseen hand came out of nowhere to clamp around her bare ankle, she assumed the armed guard had shown up. Frantic to wrest free, she kicked out her leg—and lost her footing.

Alexa swallowed a squeal of alarm, refusing to let Elliot and his courtesan know she had been spying on them. She hoped to avoid capture before Oscar dragged her into Elliot's office to face the consequences.

When the guard jerked her back against his chest, she

elbowed him in the jaw. When he didn't let go she reached over her shoulder to rake her broken nails over his neck.

"Ouch, damn it," came a familiar voice that didn't belong to Oscar Denton. "Stop clawing me, she-cat. I'm here to help."

Alexa angled herself sideways to peer into the shadowed face behind her. She wished *Miguel* had shown up to assist her. But no such luck. *Coop* was glowering at her. Her mind raced, wondering how she was going to explain her way out of this predicament. Then she reminded herself that she didn't owe Coop an explanation. She was annoyed with him because he had arrived earlier that evening to consult privately with Elliot.

Although that incriminating visit indicated he was a traitor, she couldn't accuse him of betraying her because he didn't know that she and Mr. Chester were one and the same and she planned to keep it that way.

"You scoundrel—" she said with a hiss.

"Call me all the names you want but keep your voice down," he muttered against her ear.

Coop clamped his hand over Alexa's mouth and clutched her to him when she squirmed for release. When she gestured toward the corner of the house, he noticed her satin slippers sitting on one of the protruding stones. He snatched them up, but he didn't set Alexa to her feet so she could don her shoes. Instead he carried her through the garden to the gate.

He didn't know whether to be angry or amused by her outlandish antics so he decided to be both. But angry first. "What the hell did you think you were doing besides taking the risk of falling off a ledge and breaking your damned neck?" he demanded sharply.

Her chin came up and she refused to back down. "I was spying on Elliot. If it's any of your business, which it is *not*."

"Ah yes, one of your favorite pastimes," he murmured sarcastically. "How could I have forgotten?"

"I told you that I am determined to discover Elliot's true character, personality and expose any secrets he plans to keep from me," she reminded him as he set her to her feet.

"Nice breeches, by the way," he smirked. "Are those the latest fashion in your uppity social circle?"

She glared flaming arrows at him while she crammed her feet in her slippers.

"What the hell are you doing here? *Really,*" he inquired.

"I could ask you the same question," she countered, tossing the comment he'd made last night right back in his face. "Why did you call on Elliot during dinner this evening?"

Coop plucked up her discarded petticoats from the fence and tossed them over his shoulder. He delayed in answering her question by clutching her hand and leading her through the gate. He walked briskly toward the carriage where he'd tethered Bandit.

Alexa jogged to keep up with his hurried strides. "You haven't answered my—"

"Shh-shh-shh!" He made a stabbing gesture toward the front of the house where Oscar Denton stood as a posted sentinel.

Thankfully Alexa didn't fire more questions while he scooped her up and set her on the seat. With Bandit tied behind the carriage, Coop hopped up beside her. Before she tried to interrogate him again, he laid his finger to her lips to shush her. Then he grabbed the reins and drove off.

She waited until he'd gone a quarter of a mile before she half turned on the seat to stare intently at him. "This is far enough. I demand to know what you wanted to talk to Elliot about. Do you work for Elliot? And why are you here now?"

He avoided the first question and said, "I wanted to know why a woman, who has more money than God and as many social connections as the governor, is practically walking a tightrope outside the window. Who is in there with Webster?" he demanded.

"A dark-haired harlot, judging by the skintight red dress she was wearing before it came off," Alexa replied. "They were having a tête-à-tête and I saw far more than I wanted."

She stared accusingly at him. "You scared another ten years off my life when you grabbed my ankle. At this rate I won't last until my thirtieth birthday."

Coop decided now was the time to tell Alexa about the madam. This should be the crowning blow that convinced her *not* to marry Webster The Philanderer.

"Webster has standing appointments with Lily Brantley, the owner of Lily's Pleasure Resort," he reported. "Three nights a week, I hear. Regular as clockwork. I don't know how often they have these late-evening trysts at his office."

He expected Alexa to recoil as if she had been slapped. Instead, she cocked her curly blond head and frowned. "Lily's Pleasure Resort…" Her voice trailed off then she shook off whatever thought had distracted her momentarily and focused absolute concentration on Coop. "Do you work for Elliot?"

Coop hesitated, unsure whether he should lie or tell her the truth. He really preferred to tell her nothing at all. The less she knew about his reasons for being in Questa Springs the better off she'd be.

"Answer me, damn it," she snapped impatiently.

Her harsh language made him chuckle. "Not the Goody Two-shoes I mistook you for, I see." He clucked his tongue. "I didn't know blue-blooded ladies were allowed to curse."

She stared pointedly at his leg—the one he'd forgotten to bind up before he skulked around Webster's ranch. "Not the invalid I mistook *you* for, either, are you? Does Elliot know there is nothing wrong with your leg? How long have you been working for him and in what capacity? The same capacity as Oscar Denton? Are you one of his hired guns that he planted in town to gather information and protect him from the resentful neighbors and business competitors that he says are trying to ruin his reputation?"

Coop's brows swooped down over his narrowed gaze. He appraised Alexa astutely. He'd seen glimpses of her inner strength and depth of character during several telling moments. He was thoroughly convinced now that she was no airheaded female whose greatest aspiration was finding a man to support her in the manner she was accustomed.

"Who *are* you?" he asked flat out.

"You know who I am. I'm Harold Quinn's—"

He waved her off. "No, *who* are *you?*" he said sharply.

She crossed her arms over her full bosom and stuck out her chin. "I have no idea what you mean."

"Ha!" he burst out. "Don't play dumb with me, lady. You're anything but. First, you poison your bodyguard so you can tail Webster. Then you save Mrs. Fredericks from a thrashing, at the risk of your own injury, I might add. Now you've ditched Miguel so you can scale walls and spy on Webster and his concubine. What the hell are you really up to?"

"I told you repeatedly that I'm checking out every aspect of my prospective fiancé," she muttered. "Quit changing the subject. Does Elliot employ you or not?"

He scowled and said, "Yes."

She withdrew into herself so quickly that Coop did a double-take. She even scooted as far away as the tufted leather seat allowed. Then she stuck her nose in the air and ignored him as if he wasn't there.

Coop wanted to tell her that he was on assignment and that her father wanted information about Webster's character, morals and business ethics, in case Alexa decided to accept the wedding proposal. He wanted to expose each of Webster's faults and assure Alexa that he was looking out for her, not Webster.

However, his dealings with Mr. Chester were confidential.

He couldn't tell her anything and that tormented the hell out of him. He had to let her think the worst about him—and why she cared if he worked for Webster, Coop didn't know. Maybe because she didn't have much respect for Webster, which made Coop's association with him distasteful to her. Whatever the case, she had turned her back, refusing to look at him or speak.

Coop took his cue to climb down before her frigid reaction caused frostbite. He knew this parting of ways was for the best because he didn't need the kind of distraction Alexa caused. He was working a case, after all. Yet, he didn't want her to think the worst about him. Not that he should care, damn it.

He hopped to the ground then pivoted toward her. "Just one last question," he said, eager to satisfy his curiosity. "Why should it matter so much if I decide to work for Webster?"

She twisted on the seat to look straight into his eyes and said, "Because I expected better of you, Coop."

He frowned, more confused than ever.

"Most men don't disappoint me because I hold low expectations of them. Elliot wants my money and my connections, like so many men who ply me with false flattery and attention. I understand what makes them tick. But *you* usually don't put on airs. I thought you were honest and trustworthy. My mistake."

Before she snapped the reins on the horse's rump and trotted away, he grabbed her hand. "If I've already disappointed you then I might as well do it up right—"

She yelped when he tugged on her hand and sent her tumbling into his arms.

It was insane, ill advised and impulsive, he knew. But if this was the last time Alexa came within ten feet of him—and he figured it would be—he had nothing to lose. He had been craving a long, thorough taste of her since she had kissed him unexpectedly on the boardwalk the previous night. If nothing else, he'd have this one moment to remember.

Coop bent Alexa over his arm and angled his head down to devour her lips. He plunged his tongue into her mouth and heard her surprised gasp. One moment she was shoving the heels of her hands against his shoulders to resist him and the next instant she encircled her arms around his neck and combed her fingers through his hair. She kissed him back without an ounce of reserve, as if she were starving for the taste of him, too.

Wild, incredible sensations ripped through him. He swore he was about to black out when she strained urgently against him then thrust her tongue into his mouth to deliver a sizzling wallop of a kiss. They shared the same breath until they were forced to come up for air. He inhaled raggedly, but her alluring scent fogged his brain again. *She* was the only thought he seemed capable of processing, the only need that he craved to obsession.

When he lifted her off the ground, she wrapped her legs around his hips. He knew she could feel him hard and aching between her legs. The heat curling inside him burned like a brand. He'd never wanted a woman as desperately and urgently as he wanted Alexa at this wild, reckless moment.

"Kiss me like that again," she whispered as she tilted her head back to stare up at him. "I didn't know desire could feel like this."

He grinned rakishly. "Well, since you asked so nicely—"

Then he put all he had into their last kiss. All his forbidden fantasies. All the tenderness she deserved and he had yet to offer because unruly desire made him needy and impatient. But he vowed to take his time, to savor the intoxicating taste of her.

This was the kiss he wanted her to remember always. He seduced her dewy-soft lips as gently as he knew how. He glided his hands over her shapely hips, pressing her against his rigid length, letting her know how thoroughly his body reacted to her.

He wished they were naked, lying on a blanket beneath the canopy of twinkling stars. There and then, he wouldn't allow himself to disappoint her in any way. If he could share one intimate moment with her, he would do all within his power to pleasure her beyond measure and to restore her opinion of him.

Only God knew why the prospect of disappointing Alexa in any form or fashion tormented him. But it did. He *liked* this woman. He liked being with her. She was naturally seductive, alluring, quick-witted and sassy. Plus, he hadn't been able to get Alexa off his mind since the moment he met her. In addition, it was the first time in years that he'd looked forward to anything or to being with anyone.

His thoughts spun out of control when he brushed his fingertips over the soft skin of her breasts. He felt her arch into him as he dipped his head to flick his tongue against her taut nipple. She moved restlessly against him, as if she, too, needed much more than a fleeting embrace in the moonlight.

"Coop?" she whispered unevenly. "Sweet mercy…" Her words trailed off and she kissed him hungrily again.

His knees threatened to fold up like a tent and he wasn't sure he wanted to be held accountable for his actions tonight. His willpower seemed to have abandoned him, along with his good sense. Something about this complicated woman made him hot, hungry and irresponsible and provoked him to throw caution to the wind.

"What the hell is going on here?"

Hearing the outraged male voice explode from the darkness was equivalent to being doused with cold water. Hurriedly Alexa unhooked her legs from around Coop's hips and launched herself away from him. Miguel's voice, sharp with censure and reprimand, rang in her ears. Nevertheless, erotic sensations pulsated through her body and she staggered to keep her balance.

She glanced at Coop, wishing she could rail at him for igniting this wildfire of sensations that burned to the very core of her being. However, the instant he had clutched her to him and kissed her so thoroughly, her sanity had abandoned her. He tasted wicked and delicious and she hadn't been able to get enough of him.

If Miguel's timing hadn't been so perfect, she wasn't sure she could have gathered enough self-control to stop until they were naked in each other's arms. She and Coop might have ended up like Elliot and Lily—tossing aside garments to touch each other intimately.

The provocative thought sent a hot blush rising from her neck to stain her cheeks. She skimmed her hand over the bodice of her gown to ensure that she was properly covered. Coop, she discovered, was still staring intently at her, paying no attention whatsoever to Miguel, who was stamping toward them like an angry elephant.

"Now you must die!" Miguel snarled at Coop.

"Miguel, don't be so dramatic," Alexa said with a dismissive flick of her wrist. "Coop is not to blame. I'm the one who started this. I wanted this."

She wasn't sure why she felt compelled to rush to Coop's defense. After all, she was mad at him for working for Elliot. He was supposed to be working strictly for Mr. Chester. In addition, he had caught her spying on Elliot again and he was beginning to get suspicious of her true intentions. She would cause more complications in this case if she didn't watch out.

"*You?*" Miguel crowed in disbelief. His wide-eyed gaze bounced back and forth between her and Coop. "You're lying to protect him? *Why?*"

"It was me," Coop spoke up. "I stepped over the bounds that you and I discussed previously." He pivoted to drop into a respectful bow in front of her. "I have disappointed you a second time this evening. My apologies, Alexa."

Then, without another word, he strode around the carriage to fetch Bandit. Then he rode off into the night.

"Have you lost what is left of your mind, woman?" Miguel railed at her as he boosted her onto the carriage seat. "You are out of control! First, you send me off to town with Kate. Leaving me alone with her was all your fault and I'm laying the blame squarely at your feet."

Alexa glanced down at Miguel. She had the unmistakable feeling that her two dearest friends might have experienced the same wild desire that she had discovered with Coop.

The thought made her grin broadly.

"Don't look at me like that," he snapped as he shook his finger at her. "And I do not want to talk about it, either."

"I caught Elliot in a tryst with his paramour tonight," she said as he clambered onto the seat to take up the reins.

Miguel smirked. "Don't try to sidetrack me. I'm angry and I'm not speaking to you ever again."

So much for that vow of silence. Thirty minutes later, he was still lecturing her about her daredevil recklessness with the investigation and with Coop. He also raked her over live coals for temping him with Kate. Alexa decided he was really angrier with himself than with her. He must have discovered that he, like she, had a definite weakness.

His went by the name of Kate.

Hers went by the name of Coop.

Coop used the time it took to ride back to town to chew himself up one side and down the other. Holy hell! What was the matter with him? Why did that blue-eyed siren devastate him so completely? Why couldn't he muster the slightest willpower where she was concerned? She was his blind spot and he wasn't proud of it. Furthermore, she was everything he knew he couldn't have.

Perhaps that was the crux of the problem, he thought to himself. Maybe a sense of the forbidden had triggered this reckless behavior in him.

It sounded reasonable so he decided to go with that.

When he heard the clatter of hooves behind him, he veered off the road to let the unidentified traveler pass. Turned out it was Lily Brantley. She trotted down the road, her red skirts billowing around her while she straddled the saddle. Too bad Alexa couldn't show Lily how to fashion breeches to contain all those yards of fluttering fabric.

Coop swore under his breath, wondering if Elliot Webster was going to end up with both women in his bed. And now, having discovered how passionate and responsive Alexa could be, Coop really hated the thought of her and Webster naked together.

Moreover, he detested the thought of disappointing Alexa in any way. Yet, he couldn't think of one reason why he needed to live up to her expectations for him. After a week or two, they wouldn't see each other again. He would be off on another assignment and she would be rubbing shoulders with the crumbs in the upper crust. He sure as hell wasn't going to be pining away for her.

But still…if he'd had just one magical night with her…

"Stop driving yourself crazy," Coop burst out loud.

Bandit danced sideways beneath him. Coop sighed heavily as he rubbed the gelding's tense neck. "Sorry, old boy. I've got a woman on my mind and she won't let go."

Coop snapped to attention when he saw Lily circle behind the bordello to tether her horse. He veered across the grass to watch her scamper up the fire escape to the second story room that he presumed to be her personal quarters. Interesting. She had a private exit. He wondered if Webster used it occasionally so no one would know how often he visited the madam.

His attention settled on another lone rider who showed up five minutes later to enter the back door on the ground floor. My, the place was busier than a train depot, he noted as he studied the vaguely familiar silhouette. Who the hell was that man? It didn't look like Webster.

Lust and the need for passion were obviously in the air tonight, Coop mused as he watched the visitor scuttle into the brothel. He ought to know. He was still nursing a ravenous ache for a woman he would never claim.

On that realistic thought Coop rode away to board his horse in the livery then hiked off to sleep alone in his bed.

Chapter Six

Four days later, after having lunch with Elliot at Sawyer's Café, Alexa wandered down the aisles at the mercantile store. She cringed at the high prices Elliot had marked on several items. She could see why more customers chose to shop at Hampton, Barrett and Figgins Dry Goods Store—which sat on the southeast corner of the square. However, there were a few men milling around the shop, gathering supplies. Mostly miners, she guessed. Apparently they couldn't purchase their needed tools and supplies at the other store.

Alexa glanced sideways when she heard a disgruntled prospector grumbling while Elliot tallied the purchases.

"If the other store in town hadn't sold out of horse blankets and axes, I wouldn't be buying my supplies from you," muttered the crusty miner, who looked to be in his mid-forties. "You oughta be arrested for highway robbery, Webster."

Alexa watched Elliot shrug indifferently. When he noticed that she was watching him, he produced a dazzling smile and ambled toward her.

"Please say you'll marry me, darling. It will make dealing with grumbling customers bearable."

Apparently the prospector thought Elliot's proposal was as ill timed and unromantic as she did. The prospector rolled his eyes, shook his frizzy brown head then set a Dutch oven on the counter beside the blanket and tools. "You gonna wait on me or not, Webster?"

Elliot held her gaze and ignored his customer. "Will you marry me?" he persisted.

"I'm still thinking about it. I'll give you my answer later. This doesn't seem to be the time or place."

To her relief, Elliot returned to the disgruntled miner. Using the excuse that she wanted to shop at the local boutiques, Alexa strolled outside. Her gaze reflexively drifted across the street to the entrance of Walker Hotel and then to Valmont Saloon. Her gaze kept seeking out Coop, though she had told herself dozens of times to avoid contact with him.

Inhaling a determined breath, Alexa lifted the front of her skirts and hiked toward the town square. She had to find a way to occupy her time and thoughts until Kate arrived in town to meet her for supper. Otherwise, she was going to drive herself crazy thinking about a man who was completely off-limits!

"Lexi? You've been hundreds of miles away the past few days." Kate jostled Alexa's arm. "Where are you now?"

Alexa shook herself from her distracting thoughts. She had spent the better part of the day trying not to think about Coop and she had taken great pains not to bump into him. She had also spent the morning pretending to laugh at Elliot's *un*amusing remarks and tolerating his touch. Every time she had looked at Elliot, she had visualized him clutching Lily Brantley passionately in his home office while she peeked in the window.

In turn, the thought of that tryst triggered forbidden images of her brief but steamy encounter with Coop in the moonlight.

"Tell me what's bothering you," Kate persisted.

Alexa focused on her friend, who sat across the table from her at the restaurant. "I have a lot on my mind," she said, refusing to admit aloud that Coop was a constant distraction.

Kate smiled dryly. "Obviously. So how goes your courtship with Elliot?" She leaned close to add, "I still can't believe you find that pretentious bore interesting."

With each passing day, it became more difficult to convince Kate that she was enamored with Elliot Webster. Kate knew her better than most. They both had aversions to pretentious bores.

"I have discovered that *interesting* doesn't have to be a prerequisite for prospective husbands," she contended. "And look who's talking, Kate. You've been as distracted as I have."

Kate dodged her direct stare and fiddled with the silverware. "I have a lot on my mind, too."

You have Miguel *on your mind, you mean,* thought Alexa. Both of her closest friends had the attention span of gnats lately. They were fighting the attraction valiantly.

Alexa knew what that felt like…and how futile it was.

"Ah, dinner has arrived," Alexa enthused when the waitress set their plates on the table. Grateful for the reprieve, Alexa dived into her meal and made certain there was nothing but small talk between bites.

Forty-five minutes later, Alexa and Kate exited the restaurant west of the town square. Alexa stopped short when she heard footsteps that indicated a man walking with an uneven gait approached. She glanced sideways to see Coop coming toward them. Tormenting need riveted her when she met his gaze. He nodded mutely as he limped around her and Kate to enter the restaurant they had exited.

Kate strolled toward the awaiting carriage. "Since you quit striking up conversations with Mr. Cooper on the street you've stopped the gossiping tongues from wagging. Thank goodness for that. Word got back to Papa and he's been worrying about you."

"He can stop fretting. I've had no contact with Coop."

However, she'd had very little to look forward to. Spending time with Elliot hadn't cured the frustrating yearning. In addition, she should be inspired to work hard on this case now that Coop had practically confessed that he'd joined the enemy camp. Lord, the man was causing her so much mental anguish she was ready to pull out her hair by the roots.

Or do something else equally desperate.

"Where is Elliot tonight?" Kate questioned.

"Previous engagement at the brothel," she replied as she ambled alongside her friend.

Kate frowned disconcertedly. "I cannot believe you're letting him get away with that."

"It appears to be a common practice among the upper crust of society," Alexa remarked. "I don't have to like it, but if I accept Elliot's proposal I will have to deal with it."

Kate halted abruptly. "His proposal? When did this happen?"

"After lunch. In between the sale of a horse blanket and the Dutch oven that one of his customers purchased."

"And you said—?" Kate asked anxiously.

"I said I'm still thinking about it. But I do have other offers on the table, you know."

"Good. Take any of the other offers. I am not an Elliot Webster fan," Kate said frankly. "I have to try too hard to be nice to the man. Besides, he torments my father regularly."

You aren't the only one who has to make an effort to be nice to him! she thought. "Marriages and romance aren't all they're cracked up to be. My parents can't live in the same house. Half a country between them is barely enough of a separation to keep them civil."

"No offense, Lexi, but I don't know how anyone could get along with your mother." She glanced questioningly at Alexa. "How is Bethany managing back East with her?"

Alexa didn't want to discuss her difficulty in communicating with her younger sister without her spiteful mother's intervention. She had enough problems on her mind already. Indeed, they were about to burst inside her and she needed relief!

"Miguel?" she called out as they approached the carriage.

"*Si, querida?* I'm here." Miguel pushed away from the far side of the buggy where he had been waiting dutifully.

"Please take Kate home then come back for me in two hours," she requested. "I want to check on Selma Mae. Kate said she didn't show up for work at the ranch today."

"No," Miguel said in no uncertain terms.

"You prefer that I walk to the ranch?" she teased. "That is rather mean-spirited of you."

"Staying here without a chaperone is not a good idea," Miguel warned.

Alexa wasn't sure if his objection had more to do with his concern that she might get herself into trouble or the temptation of being alone with Kate would get *him* into trouble. Mostly the latter, she suspected.

"Nevertheless, I intend to check on Selma Mae," Alexa insisted. "I made her welfare my business when I confronted Harlan and I hired her on the spot. If she comes to harm because of my intervention, I want to know. I'll ask Marshal Henson to accompany me to her home, if that will make you feel better."

That appeased Miguel. Somewhat. Now he had to escort Kate to the ranch and deal with his attraction to her. Since misery was said to love company, Alexa took solace in knowing Kate and Miguel were fighting a complicated attraction, too. Of course, none of this fazed Coop. He'd made it clear from the beginning that what he wanted from her was physical and temporary.

Unlike the growing fascination been Kate and Miguel, she mused. They had been acquaintances and friends forever. Now their feelings had deepened and expanded over the years. Alexa had no qualms about being their matchmaker, even if Percy Hampton might object. She would worry about that obstacle later.

"I'll be back in two hours." Miguel's voice broke into her wandering thoughts. He handed Kate into the buggy then pivoted to wag his lean finger in Alexa's face. "But do not get into trouble and don't try to break up any fights. Agreed?"

Alexa offered him a snappy salute and an impish grin. "Yes, sir. Whatever you say."

"Whatever I say is always lost on you," Miguel grumbled as he bounded into the carriage to take the reins. "I'm all that passes for your conscience, and you know it. I want you to feel enormously guilty if you get into a scrape while I'm not there to help."

"Don't make him fret, Lexi," Kate chimed in. "You know he adores you."

"And I love him, too. Furthermore, I promise not to pick any fights that land me in jail," she added for good measure.

"That's what I want to hear," Miguel said, pacified.

Then off he went with Kate.

Alexa chuckled in amusement as her friends drove out of sight. Then she hiked down Main Street to Gil Henson's office. She was going to see for herself that Selma Mae Fredericks was all right. Then she was going to decide what to do about this maddening need to be with Coop.

Ten minutes later, she learned that Harlan had smashed his left hand while laying track for the railroad. Selma had stayed home to care for him. Alexa insisted that Selma take another day to tend her husband before returning to Hampton Ranch to resume her employment.

Lingering outside Gil Henson's office, Alexa stared pensively toward Walker Hotel and Restaurant. She found herself standing on a new threshold, wanting something that no other man had aroused in her. Reckless temptation put her feet in motion. Although questions about her investigation cluttered her mind, Alexa decided they could wait until morning. Right now, selfish impulse controlled her mind and body. She needed relief from the maddening ache that hounded her night and day.

Coop stepped outside the restaurant and told himself the steak he'd had for supper satisfied his appetites sufficiently. It was a lie. Need had been gnawing at him for four days—and nights. The nights were the worst and sleep didn't come easily.

He glanced speculatively toward Valmont Saloon. Polly Sanders, the calico queen who flirted with him frequently, had offered to help him scratch the itch. He should take her up on it. Coop wheeled toward the saloon and took three steps in that direction before he stopped short. He had a job to do at night, he reminded himself. He was supposed to ride fences. Webster more or less implied that he should turn his back if he saw the hired hands picking off Hampton and Barrett cattle.

Coop hadn't actually heard Webster give his men orders to swipe the cattle and rebrand them. He needed to. Plus, he wanted to inspect the livestock to determine the recency of their brands. There was also the possibility that Webster's men had been instructed to set up the neighbors by placing their brands over the *W* brand. It wouldn't be the first time a shrewd crook arranged for his neighbors to look guilty of rustling.

Reversing direction, Coop hobbled toward the hotel. He planned to remove the hindering splints and ride out to

Webster's ranch. If he were lucky, he'd see Webster ducking into the line shack or hear him give an incriminating order. Coop needed something substantial to report to Mr. Chester the following evening when they met in the canyon north of town.

The lobby was vacant when Coop entered the hotel. He assumed the clerk had taken a short break since he wasn't behind the counter. It was a quiet night in Questa Springs, he noted as climbed the steps stiff-legged.

Coop opened the door to his room—then tensed apprehensively. Scant moonlight filtered into the dark room. He knew the door had been locked, but he still felt a presence inside. He drew his pistol and stepped sideways, in case an unexpected intruder tried to shoot him. Coop had learned years ago to duck and dive to avoid flying bullets.

"It's me. Close the door, Coop."

The sultry voice, straight from his fantasies, drifted toward him. When he closed the door behind him, Alexa moved into the spray of light slanting through the window. The breath he hadn't realized he'd been holding sighed out of him as he savored the tantalizing sight of her in the trim-fitting yellow gown.

He slid his pistol into his holster while he stood, spellbound, watching moonbeams illuminate her exquisite features and shapely figure. Bedazzled, he tried to find his voice twice—and succeeded finally.

"What are you doing here? How'd you get past the locked door?" he chirped.

"I'm not completely without resources," she murmured as she moved toward him. "I brought a bottle of wine. Would you like a drink?"

Coop remembered Miguel's mysterious illness and his own vow not to eat or drink anything this siren offered him. "No, thanks. I'm already drunk on the sight of you."

"I didn't come here for flattery," she said. "I told you that I get all the empty praise I can stand from other men."

"Then what do you want from me, princess—?"

His breath gave out when she reached up to unfasten the top button of his shirt. Then the second and third buttons came undone—along with his willpower. His heart thudded against his chest so hard he thought the blow might have broken a rib.

"I've decided I want the same thing from you that you said you wanted from me," she whispered as she slid her hand inside his gaping shirt to caress the expanse of his chest.

When she touched him familiarly, a soundless *purr* rumbled through his body. His thoughts were so entangled that he couldn't figure out what she meant. Hell, he couldn't even string words together. "Uh…" was all he could get out.

She glanced up at him. The impish smile playing on her lips nearly did him in.

"I want to be naked with you, Coop. Do you have any objections to that?"

"If I were granted only one wish before I died, that'd be it," he choked out raggedly.

Her fingertips splayed from his collarbone to his belly, touching him boldly, experimentally. Driving him crazy. He wondered where she had learned that technique so he just came right out and asked her. "Where'd you learn that? It's hard to think straight when you do it."

"I saw Lily do it to Elliot… Do you like it?"

"More than you know, princess." He folded his hand over hers and brought her fingertips to his lips. "What else did you see while you were spying on Webster and the madam?"

"Clothes came off and went flying in disarray," she replied, then unfastened the rest of the buttons on his shirt. She removed the garment and stood admiring the muscled planes and contours of his broad shoulders and masculine chest.

"The Greek gods have nothing on you, Wyatt Cooper," she murmured appreciatively. He was warm and solid and touching him fascinated her, aroused her. "I've never had my way with a man before…do you mind being the first?"

He set her hands away from him and stared intently at her. "Why are you really here, Alexa? Because Webster is with his paramour again tonight? Am I your consolation prize? Is this your spiteful way of getting even with him?"

He sounded hurt. She hadn't expected that. Could it be that he actually *liked* her a little? Perhaps he did, but she refused to lie to herself and she refused to be lied to by a man. It had happened all too often since she'd come of age.

"This is only about tonight," she told him as she wiggled her hand loose to trail her fingers over the corrugated muscles of his belly, following the dark hair that disappeared beneath his belt buckle. She felt him tense and wondered if her touch aroused him. The thought intrigued her. "No strings. No promises. No further expectations."

He didn't say anything for a long moment, just stared at her with those probing evergreen eyes. "Why do you want *me* to be the first?"

"Why does that bother you? There always has to be a first time for everything," she contended.

"I've never been anybody's first time. I don't think you—"

Alexa was not going to let him talk her out of this. She already had one walking conscience. She didn't need another. Earlier that evening she had decided to act on her desire for Coop. She had passed the point of no return when she used a hairpin to pick the lock on his hotel room door and awaited his arrival.

"You made me want you, Wyatt Cooper. I've been thinking about you for four endless days, since you kissed me and I discovered how much I liked it. I have less than two hours of freedom before Miguel picks me up. I'd rather not waste precious time with explanations—"

"In that case…" he interrupted as he lowered his head to brush his sensuous lips over hers. "And by the way, I like your dress." He nimbly worked the tiny yellow buttons on the bodice. "I'd like it even better if you were out of it."

Alexa figured she'd feel self-conscious disrobing in front of Coop. But when his lips moved gently over hers again, the possessive pressure of his mouth sent her thoughts into a tailspin. She lost herself in his long-awaited kiss, breathed him in and tasted him completely. She could feel his hands drifting over her gown, freeing her from it. Having him undress her was wonderfully arousing. He kept pausing to greet every inch of her exposed flesh with his caresses, causing need to unfurl inside her until she was trembling with anticipation.

The sensations he incited made her kiss him harder, made her breathless and impatient. This was the most erotic night of her life and it could only be two hours long. She wanted to be skin to skin with Coop and she wanted that *now*.

To that end, she reached down to unfasten his belt buckle and holsters. Pistols clanked to the floor. His trousers dropped in a pool around his ankles. Boldly she wrapped her hand around his hard length, marveling at her daring and at the incredible intimacy of the moment. She loved the feel of him. He was steel and velvet and she enjoyed stroking him repeatedly.

"You're killing me," Coop gasped in tormented pleasure.

"I'm sorry. Did I hurt you?"

When she tried to pull her hand away, his fingertips folded over hers. "I only meant that your touch is worth dying for, princess. You can do whatever you want to me, with me. This is your night. But all these extra undergarments you're wearing are in my way and they have to go."

Feeling self-confident, empowered by his words, she

waited for him to cast aside her chemise and pantaloons. She amazed herself by standing there, allowing him to look his fill. His roguish smile indicated that he wasn't disappointed in what he saw. She wondered, though, if she measured up to the women he'd been with. But she decided this wasn't the time to ask. Besides, she wasn't sure she really wanted to know. It might spoil her fantasy.

"I want to see you with your hair down," he murmured as he pulled the pins from her hair and let them drop beside their discarded clothing.

He ran his fingers through the long curly strands that cascaded over her shoulders. "You are breathtakingly beautiful," he whispered as he picked her up in his arms and moved toward the bed.

Alexa remembered when Elliot had said the same thing to her. She hadn't been flattered, only suspicious of his ultimate intentions, wondered what else he'd say to get what he wanted. But she accepted Coop's comment as a true compliment, whether she should trust him or not. He had told her right from the start that lust and passion were enough to satisfy him, not the prospect of acquiring access to her wealth.

She was with him tonight because her instincts told her that Coop was good to his word. In this respect at least. She'd still like to strangle him for defecting to the enemy camp. However, she couldn't confront him with the accusations because she wasn't supposed to know that Mr. Chester had hired him.

Coop was going to answer for double-crossing her eventually, but not tonight. She wanted him to appease the nearly unbearable longing that he had instilled in her.

Her thoughts scattered like a covey of quail when he laid her on his bed then followed her down. She could feel his muscular flesh pressing intimately against her. She wondered how long it took to engage in the act of passion. She squirmed beneath him, silently telling him that she was ready and willing to discover what the intimacy between a man and woman was like.

Coop raised his raven-black head and grinned down at her. "We have two hours, not two minutes," he said, amused. "No need to rush through this."

"About how long does it take?"

He chuckled rakishly. "I don't charge by the hour, if that's what you're wondering."

Her beguiling blue eyes were wide as dinner plates and her jaw nearly dropped off its hinges. *"Charge?"*

Coop laughed softly as he shifted to lie next to her luscious body. He still couldn't believe she was here with him. He was astounded that she had selected *him* to teach her about passion. There had to be a catch. There was always a catch, he mused cynically. But he was too eager and too aroused to ask what consequences awaited. All he wanted was to memorize the feel of her supple body by taste and touch.

"Okay, you win," he teased playfully as he reached up to close her gaping mouth. "No charge for first-timers. But if there's a next time it'll cost you double."

When she realized he was ribbing her, she smiled and relaxed beside him. "So what do I do first? I'll need instruction to do this properly."

"Just close your eyes, princess," he whispered as he lowered his head. "I'll take it from here…"

Chapter Seven

$\mathcal{H}$e rubbed his mouth gently against hers and felt her surrender. He glided his hand over her breast and she arched responsively against him. Never in his life had he been so aware of a woman in his bed. But tonight his sole purpose was Alexa's pleasurable introduction to passion. In this, he refused to disappoint her. He wanted her to want him desperately when he sank into her lush body. He wanted her to welcome him, eager to savor the intimacy for as long as the moment lasted.

"Oh…my…" Her breath sighed out raggedly as he trailed his hands and lips from one rigid nipple to the other. "I didn't realize—"

Her voice evaporated when his hand skimmed over her concave belly to trace the silky flesh of her inner thighs. He cupped her mound then traced her moist heat with his fingertip. Her eyes flew open and she stared incredulously at him as she trembled in uncontrollable response. Coop held her gaze as he moved down her body—one deliberate kiss at a time. She watched him offer the most intimate of kisses and he heard her quiet moan when he flicked at her with his tongue. He suckled her gently, tasting her essence and he felt the fiery heat of need course heavily through him.

He discovered that arousing her aroused him to the extreme. He had never shared such untold intimacy with another woman, but this was his fantasy lover. This was his one mystical moment in a space of time outside the harsh reality that was his life. He wanted to know Alexa as he had known no one else before her. He wanted her to remember her first experiment with passion, as well as the man who was there with her, offering all the tenderness he had within him. He wanted this night to be unforgettable for her. Because it would be unforgettable for him.

Slowly, deliberately, he kissed and caressed until she was writhing frantically beneath his hands and lips. His name tumbled from her tongue in a panting plea to satisfy the ache he instilled inside her. Only when he felt her quiver and reach impatiently for him did he glide over her.

When she clutched at him like a drowning victim going down the final time he swallowed a triumphant smile. He couldn't recall being wanted this much by anyone, for any reason. He didn't remember caring if he was—until now, with Alexa.

As he guided her legs around his hips and positioned himself above her, he made the mistake of staring into those beguiling blue eyes. Something in her expression called out to something buried deep inside him, something that he thought had calloused over after thirty-two years of hard living.

Coop tried to stifle the unfamiliar sensation that seared the inside of his chest, but he couldn't control both his body and his heart at the same time. With Alexa, it couldn't be either physical or emotional, he realized. It had to be both—and that rattled him.

When the sweet pressure of her hand contracted around his

throbbing length, his thoughts and willpower abandoned him. Expelling a gusty sigh of need, he surged forward to claim her completely. He felt her tense momentarily, and then she accepted his masculine invasion. When she hooked her legs around him to invite him deeper, Coop's noble intentions of tenderness fell by the wayside.

She grabbed two handfuls of his hair and brought his head to hers to deliver a lip-blistering kiss. She kissed him as if there were no tomorrow. As if he was the last thing she'd ever do in life.

Not that he minded her doing him as many times, as many ways, as she pleased. He was all in favor.

Coop's pounding pulse nearly beat him to death as desire spiraled out of control and took command of his body. He moved instinctively against Alexa—harder, faster, deeper. She kept kissing him until *she* ran out of breath and *he* became lightheaded. He dragged in air but all he could breathe was her, all he could feel was her velvety warmth caressing him intimately.

Coop groaned when hundreds of intense sensations converged like a thunderbolt. Indescribable pleasure radiated through him and he swore the top of his head was about to blow off. Soundless quakes rumbled through his body and he shuddered uncontrollably as the fierce impact of passion bombarded him.

He cursed silently, wishing he could prolong the incredible moment and make it last forever. He never wanted to forget how it felt to be buried so deeply inside Alexa that he couldn't tell where his body ended and her soft, responsive body began.

For now, they were one living, breathing essence suspended in a timeless moment and all was right with the world.

The scorching jolt of rapture buffeted him and he collapsed helplessly atop of her. He gasped, struggling to draw air into his starved lungs. Then he remembered that he was crushing her into the mattress and he levered himself up on his elbows.

Tender sentiment blossomed inside him as he pressed a kiss to the damp blond curls on her forehead, then to the tip of her pert nose and finally to her dewy, soft mouth.

"Any questions?" he teased huskily.

"No. I understand now why you usually charge for love lessons," she teased back. "Very impressive, Mr. Cooper. Do most folks know that your skills with pistols are the *second* best thing you do?"

"That's a little known fact. Don't spread it around. It might ruin my intimidating reputation."

He adored her quick wit and playful sense of humor. This was no fluff-headed socialite, to be sure. But then, he wouldn't be so intrigued if she were. In fact, if she had lived up to his cynical expectations of the spoiled, pampered upper class, he could have dealt with her more easily.

Alexa reached up to comb his ruffled hair over his forehead then traced her fingertips over his high cheekbones and his eyebrows. "How much time do we have left, I wonder."

"Why? Did you have something special in mind for the remainder of your two hours?"

She smiled provocatively. "You said you'd charge double for the second session?"

When he blinked at her in surprise, she laughed softly. "You think I'm insatiable? That offends you?"

"Not hardly, but—"

"It's my nickel, right?" She moved suggestively beneath him—and felt him grow hard inside her.

"Damn, woman, you're going to wear me out."

"I accept that challenge."

Alexa didn't know what had become of her usual restraint with men. With Coop, her self-control seemed nonexistent. She experienced phenomenal need, followed by the most astonishing pleasure imaginable. She wanted him all over again, wanted to revisit that hazy realm of rapturous desire she'd discovered in his arms. She knew he was going to ruin her for all other men, but she didn't care. For whatever the reason, this was the man her heart desired and her untried body craved. She adored the power-packed feel of him, loved the hair-roughened texture and sleek muscles of his body. She savored the sensations of having him pressed familiarly against her.

"It's your nickel, princess. Whatever you want," he whispered as his hands began to work their magic with her body.

"I—" Alexa shut her mouth and gave herself up completely to the wondrous caresses and stimulating sensations that flooded over her.

She could not possibly be falling in love with a man whom she'd known for a little more than a week. She must be caught up in the newness of passion, she convinced herself. Never mind that his dry sense of humor and amazing self-reliance appealed to her greatly. Not to mention that he possessed the most incredible body a woman could ever hope to get her hands on.

Coop was everything she liked and admired. Strong, passionate, playful and yet incredibly gentle…

Alexa lost the ability to process thought when passion swept her up and away, holding her suspended in a realm of vivid sensations. Her last thought before she tumbled into rapturous oblivion was that Coop was almost everything she had ever wanted in a man. *Almost.*

Too bad he had double-crossed her—as Mr. Chester. Coop was going to pay dearly for that…as soon as she recovered from the most amazing night of her life.

Harold Quinn checked the time, grumbled irritably then paced the floorboards. He'd called a meeting with his top four advisors, but all of them were running late. Not that he was in a flaming rush to get home. He'd come to realize that he'd allowed civic duty to occupy most of his time. Time he should have spent with Alexa. Now she was gone and the place seemed empty without her.

In addition, he was curious about the progress of the investigation she volunteered to initiate in his stead. Unfortunately he'd had to distance himself from the goings-on in Questa Springs, for fear of inviting suspicion. He could only hope Lexi was overseeing the matter, from a safe distance.

"It damn well better be from a safe distance," he mumbled to himself.

"Sorry, Harold," Ben Porter said as he scurried into the office. "Unavoidable circumstances caused our delay."

Ambrose Shelton, William Trent and John Marlow followed swiftly in Ben's wake. Trent and Marlow were grinning like Cheshire cats, while Ambrose and Ben looked a mite embarrassed about the late arrival.

"Why did you have difficulty getting here this evening?" Harold asked curiously.

John Marlow's blue-gray eyes crinkled at the corners as he straightened his lopsided cravat. He parked himself in a chair at the conference table and snickered. "There was a bit of a fiasco at the bordello that Ben and Ambrose took us to."

Harold's brows shot up as he stared at Ben and Ambrose, who squirmed uncomfortably in their chairs then shot John a perturbed glance.

"You have a loose tongue," Ambrose chided sourly. "It amazes me that a man of your supposed intelligence doesn't have the good sense to know when to shut up."

"Don't take it so hard," William inserted jokingly. "Everybody is aware that a man has his needs. We just happened to be at the wrong place at the wrong time, is all."

Harold noted the flushed expression on Ambrose's face.

Interesting, he mused. Then he focused on Ben who sighed dramatically.

"We had to make a run for it," Ben reported as he refastened the uneven buttons of his vest. "Some crazed cretin was out for blood and had the entire establishment up in arms."

John took up where Ben left off. "The hothead stormed upstairs with a shotgun in hand, threatening to blow away the man who horned in on his standing appointment with his favorite harlot. We didn't see who he was, just heard him yelling to beat the band."

"Good God, was anyone hurt?" Harold asked as he plunked into his chair at the head of the table.

"No, three patrons subdued him. We weren't among them because we tried to keep a low profile," Ambrose reported as he tugged on the cuff of his shirtsleeve. "Rose makes sure her establishment is civilized and she caters to the upper class. Why that hooligan was there I don't know."

Clearly all four men had dressed in a rush and fled the scene, Harold noted.

"We thought we would while away an hour before this meeting by enjoying some pleasurable diversions," Will Trent remarked as he raked his hand through his tousled gray hair. "The police arrived to haul the rascal to jail but he was nowhere to be found. Everything should be back to normal by now."

"I'm pleased to hear that," Harold said.

"Except that we didn't have time to finish what we started," John said wryly. "I don't like to pay for services unrendered, if you know what I mean…."

"Yes, well, now that we're all present and accounted for, let's get on with the meeting," Harold insisted. "We have less than a month to renew or to offer new livestock and beef acquisition contracts for the military and Indian reservations. I have gathered information on the three applicants who have asked to be considered." Harold placed the files in front of his committee members.

Ambrose glanced up and frowned curiously. "You mentioned to the four of us a few weeks ago that you were reluctant to continue doing business with Elliot Webster. What is the problem?"

The question sounded innocent enough, but Harold didn't trust anyone until he received the results of the investigation Alexa had commandeered.

"We have to follow necessary procedure in order to provide equal opportunity to other deserving applicants who would like to be considered for this contract. We are discussing a considerable amount of money, after all," Harold reminded the committee.

Will Trent glanced at his timepiece and absently stroked his dark beard and mustache. "I suggest we save ourselves the trouble and award the contract to Webster again. Then we can adjourn to the pleasurable pursuits that were interrupted earlier."

Damn, Will was eager to grant the contract to Webster without further discussion. Why was that? "Fair is fair," Harold contended. "Other large ranches in cattle country have prime horses and cattle for sale. I'm wondering if we shouldn't spread the wealth around rather than playing a favorite."

Ambrose stared at him contemplatively. "As I recall, Webster paid your daughter a great deal of attention at the recent party. Is this your way of rejecting him and his pursuit of Alexa?"

"No, I'm trying to remain impartial," Harold said quickly. "I do not base contracts on courtships." He gestured toward the open folders. "I called you in to familiarize yourself with available suppliers. I will admit that a longtime friend of mine is on the list. I consider Percy Hampton honest and reliable.

So is Andrew Barrett. They deserve your consideration. Going over their livestock inventory shouldn't keep you too long."

An hour later, the meeting adjourned and everyone agreed to interview the three applicants before reaching a decision. On the way out the door, Ben paused to invite Harold to the brothel for a drink and a stimulating diversion.

"Don't mind if I do," Harold said.

And why not? It was lonely at home and his estranged wife was in Boston with her latest lover. She made a point of keeping him abreast of her indiscretions. And he *did* have his own needs, after all. Since Alexa was out of town, he didn't have to be as discreet as he usually was when he sought female companionship.

He wondered what his daughter was doing to entertain herself in Questa Springs this evening.

It was a good thing he didn't know or someone would've had to restrain him from going on a rampage with a loaded shotgun.

Alexa hadn't seen Coop in several days because she had made a conscious effort to avoid him—to prove to herself that she could resist temptation if she really tried.

Of course, she hadn't been able to resist the first time, she reminded herself in exasperation. It frustrated her to no end that her uncontrollable desire for Coop had overridden her distrust. It was unnerving to want a man to reckless obsession.

Tossing aside the unsettling thought, she nodded and smiled at passersby on the street as she walked alongside Elliot. He had insisted on escorting her to dinner at Walker Restaurant and she had agreed, if only to focus on something besides her complicated feelings for Coop and the disturbing feeling that he had betrayed this investigation.

Her thoughts fizzled out when she saw Coop descending the hotel steps at the same moment that she entered the restaurant that adjoined the hotel. When her gaze met Coop's, all the unforgettable sensations she had experienced during their rendezvous rushed over her like a tidal wave.

Another siege of warm tingles flooded over when he stared directly at her—knowing exactly how she looked without the bright lavender gown she was wearing. To his credit—and her enormous relief—he didn't do or say anything that implied they knew each other intimately. But *she* knew and she had lain awake the past several nights, remembering the taste of his kiss. The feel of his virile body entwined with hers.

"Excuse me a moment, my dear. Go ahead and find us a table." Elliot detached himself from her side to approach Coop. "A word in private, please."

Coop didn't glance in her direction, just followed Elliot outside. Alexa silently seethed, knowing her private detective was on Elliot's payroll, but helpless to confront him because he didn't know that she disguised herself as Mr. Chester and the midnight rider in black who prowled the darkness, hoping to catch sight of Elliot's mysterious associate.

Damn it, her feelings and opinions of Coop were so conflicted and entangled that it was difficult to sort them out. She was fiercely attracted to him. No doubt about that. At first, she'd felt guilty about deceiving him with her disguise… Until she suspected he'd betrayed her by working for Elliot.

Now it was a good thing she'd used a disguise or Coop might've told Elliot what she was up to. Since the situation was complex, she couldn't accuse Coop of double-crossing her or be completely honest with him without giving herself away. Even ignoring him after their passionate tryst would have seemed out of character.

She was stuck juggling her various charades and burying her conflicting emotions.

It was enough to drive a sane woman crazy. One minute

she was so desperate for Coop that she wanted to kiss the breath out of him. The next minute she wanted to strangle the life out of him for being a mercenary who double-crossed her—or rather for betraying Mr. Chester.

"Patience," she muttered under her breath. "You'll have your say later tonight. Then perhaps you can put this ill-fated attraction into proper perspective and be done with it."

"Well?" Elliot demanded rudely as he grabbed Coop's elbow and pulled him off the boardwalk into the alley beside the hotel. "Have you seen my neighbors swiping my cattle or horses? Have you noticed their brands on top of my brand?"

"No," Coop replied. However, he had seen Oscar Denton and a few hired hands placing the Hampton and Barrett brands on *Webster's* cattle. The neighbors were being set up as rustlers.

A potential clash between Webster and his closest neighbors worried Coop to no end because of Alexa. She was fiercely loyal to her friends and not the least bit hesitant about thrusting herself into perilous conflicts. She had planted herself squarely between Harlan and Selma Fredericks and had barely missed being thumped with a makeshift club. She would undoubtedly stand up for Kate's family if they were accused of rustling.

That would place her in a precarious predicament with her suitor. Webster was going to force her to choose sides.

"You have seen nothing at all?" Webster pressed intently. "Then what the hell am I paying you for?"

"In the first place, I wasn't particularly interested in the job that takes up most of my evenings while I'm trying to recuperate from injury," Coop countered. "So far, I've seen little activity. Plus, it's damn hard to indict men of wrongdoing if I can't at least place them somewhere in the vicinity of the crime you're accusing them of committing."

Webster scowled because he couldn't argue with that reasonable logic. "What about your word against theirs? That should count for something. You were a deputy U.S. Marshal and you're a detective. That should give you the credibility you need with the local law enforcement."

"If you want to bring formal charges then you need evidence and a crime scene. Like branding irons and burned out campfires with hoofprints nearby," Coop suggested.

Webster made a slashing gesture with his arm. "I can arrange that if *you* will investigate the area." He stared grimly at Coop. "When the time comes I better not be disappointed with your efforts on my behalf…or else."

Or else Oscar Denton will be ordered to leave me with a few bullet holes in my back? Coop silently questioned. *Probably.*

Coop limped away. He'd worry about Webster's sneaky machinations later. Right now, he had to document his findings then ride to the upper canyon to confer with Mr. Chester. The man was certainly a stickler for documentation. At least the conference would take his mind off Alexa, he consoled himself.

Quickening his pace, he headed for the livery stable to fetch Bandit. Then he returned to the hotel to write up his report for the conference. That done, he tucked away his notes and told himself that he should be satisfied with that one magical night he'd spent with Alexa. He told himself he wasn't envious that Webster could be seen with her in public and Coop wasn't allowed. Curse it, all these alien and unexpected feelings of possessive jealousy and hungry desire that ricocheted around his body and brain were maddening.

Alexa Quinn—with her high and mighty social and political connections and her potential betrothal to a man Coop disliked—was not the woman he needed in his life. Hell, he didn't need the complications of *any* female because his nomadic profession took him hither and yon constantly.

"Forget her," Coop ordered himself sharply. "Do the job you're paid to do then get the hell out of this place."

With that sound advice ringing in his ears, he mounted Bandit and headed for the hills to meet with the very particular and persnickety Yank named Mr. Chester.

Chapter Eight

"I think this is a very bad idea," Miguel complained as he watched Alexa don the Mr. Chester disguise she kept in her carpetbag.

"You're a worrywart and you think all my creative ideas are bad ideas." Alexa crammed her arms into the padded jacket then pulled the bowler hat low on her forehead. She glanced in the mirror to paste the beard and mustache in place.

"Not all of your ideas were bad," Miguel clarified, smiling reluctantly. "There were one or two." He frowned in feigned concentration. "*One* now that I think about it."

Alexa rolled her eyes at her two-legged conscience then pulled the dark breeches over the padding she had wrapped around her hips and thighs. "Mr. Chester is still a convenient go-between when dealing with Coop. He doesn't know who I am and I intend to keep it that way."

However, Mr. Chester was going to let Coop have it with both barrels blazing for turning traitor, she promised herself resolutely. She had paid good money for his loyalty and assistance and she expected him to honor the commitment.

The fact that she knew he'd likely double-crossed her by

hiring on with Webster and she still desired him was driving her nothing short of crazy. If this wasn't the dark side of lust defying all costs, she didn't know what was. Whatever flaw of character or personality had caused this lapse in good judgment must have come from her mother, she thought sourly.

"I'm going with you," Miguel said.

It wasn't an offer; it was a demand.

"No need. Mr. Chester can take care of himself."

Miguel's dark eyes narrowed on her. "I'm *going* so don't waste your breath trying to talk me out of it."

Alexa sighed heavily. Her human shadow wouldn't leave her be. "If you're afraid to stay here at the ranch, for fear of encountering Kate in the dark, because you have no will-power where she's concerned—" and Alexa was sorry to say that she knew firsthand what lack of self-control felt like "—then go to town. You can keep an eye on Elliot to see if he ends up at the bordello or the line shack tonight."

Miguel made a big production of muttering and grumbling at her remark and suggestion.

"Papa is running short of time in investigating Webster and his informant. The committee renews the government contract for meat and mounts for the soldiers and reservation Indians this month," Alexa informed him. "If you aren't helping resolve this case then you are a hindrance."

"Okay, fine," he burst out begrudgingly. "But I intend to accompany you partway to the canyon before I ride into town."

"Whatever makes you happy," Alexa retorted.

He scowled. "Nothing about this makes me happy."

With her disguise in place, Alexa scurried across the second story terrace to descend the rear steps of Hampton's sprawling ranch home. Miguel was a few paces behind her. She ducked behind a tree and waited for him to fetch the horses from the stables.

Alexa rode at full gallop until she reached the fork in the road where she and Miguel parted company. After he warned her—for the third time—to be careful, she trotted away. Honestly, her own mother hadn't fussed over her as much as Miguel had.

Obviously he liked her more than her mother did.

For years, that realization had cut her to the quick. But Alexa had learned to live with the disappointment of an uncaring mother. She had also transferred her skepticism and lack of expectations to her suitors, but one man had slipped past her defenses during her formal introduction as a debutante into society. After that, she'd vowed devoutly never to be hurt or disappointed again.

Then along came Wyatt Cooper. She'd allowed her unwanted feelings for him to take root and grow. It was dangerous, it put her heart in jeopardy and that worried her to no end.

"Just tend to business," she lectured herself as she dismounted. "Don't make this personal. It's bad enough that it has become physical, but you have no one to blame but yourself."

She continued to chant that mantra while she positioned herself beside the rippling stream that sparkled in the moonlight. She scanned the area, noting several small caverns on the outcropping of rock above her. She wondered if unfriendly beasts inhabited them. Probably.

Five minutes later Coop emerged from the stand of pine trees to the west. He'd taken the precaution of cradling his rifle over his arms, just in case a four-legged predator showed up. Alexa decided to follow his precautionary procedure and she grabbed her pistol for protection.

"Right on time, I see," she said, using a deeper voice than normal. Once again, she mimicked her mother's Eastern accent to throw Coop off track.

"Same for you, Mr. Chester," Coop replied.

"What information do you have to warrant your large monetary advance?"

"Our man Webster has a weakness for the madam at Lily's Pleasure Resort. We might try bribing the madam for information about Webster if you feel the need to dig deeper."

Alexa hadn't considered that. "What are the chances of gaining facts without being double-crossed? There seems to be a lot of that going around these days."

Coop shrugged his broad shoulders—and she wished she'd quit noting such things about him. "Fifty-fifty chance, I suppose," he said. "I don't know if Lily actually has feelings for Webster. It might not matter. Money is a strong motivating factor."

She wondered how much money Webster had offered Coop to betray her.

"I'll save Lily as a last resort," Coop decided. "There is the possibility that she is emotionally involved with Webster and that she would turn informant for *him*."

"Anything else?" Alexa prodded as she shoved the wire-rimmed spectacles back to the bridge of her nose.

"I've seen Webster at a line shack twice this week," he reported. "Once he met an associate but I haven't been able to identify him. *Have you?*"

Alexa stared warily at Coop. There was an edge to his voice that warned of trouble. "What are you suggesting, Mr. Cooper?"

"Who is your backup detective who lurks around in black breeches and a black cape? I don't appreciate the implication that I can't do my job effectively and I need reinforcement."

"And I don't appreciate being betrayed when I have paid you more than the going rate," she fired back, taking the opening he unknowingly offered. "How much does Webster pay you to double-cross another paying client? And do tell me how much a liar's word is worth. To my way of thinking I've overpaid you."

Alexa noted the look of surprise that claimed his rugged features momentarily. Then it was gone and the deadpan expression was back in place. Her resentment simmered beneath the surface as she watched him stare straight at her. Damn it, she wanted an explanation and she wanted it now!

"Is your caped crusader following *me*, too?" Coop demanded sharply.

"Yes, and with good reason. I have no respect for a man who plays both ends against the middle. You're fired. A shame that, Mr. Cooper. I will always pay better than your friend Webster."

Coop snorted caustically. "I figured out what the investigation is really about so don't spout indignation at me."

"Have you?" she challenged. "Obviously you are smarter than I gave you credit. What is it that you think is really going on here?"

"My main duty is to dig up dirt on Webster because Quinn's daughter is courting the man," Coop speculated. "Harold Quinn doesn't intend to give his blessing to this match unless Webster is squeaky clean and worthy of marrying into Quinn's blue-blooded family. *He isn't.* Take that back to your client."

Alexa set aside her irritation momentarily and grinned beneath her beard and mustache. Coop thought he was so damn smart and had it all figured out, did he? She would put him on the spot, do a little prying and satisfy her own curiosity while she was at it.

"What do you think of Miss Quinn?" she asked flat-out.

"I think she's a handful. Her father has every reason to check up on her and her latest boyfriend."

She stiffened at the comment. "You don't approve of Alexa?"

"I'm not getting paid to approve or disapprove of her."

She gnashed her teeth, annoyed at Coop's neutral tone

that gave none of his feelings away. She wanted to know if he liked her for who she was on the inside, not what her money could buy.

"Who is this elusive detective you pay to skulk around at night?" Coop demanded. "Does he have a name?"

"What difference does it make to you? All that matters is that he knows you're meeting with Webster on the sly and that you can't be trusted. He has also seen you with Alexa. And don't think I won't inform my client that you have stepped over the line."

That comment definitely got a reaction out of him, Alexa was pleased to say. Coop snapped up his head. His stance became defensive and he muttered what sounded like an extremely foul curse under his breath.

Alexa didn't ask him to repeat the remark.

"Good night, Mr. Cooper. I am no longer in need of your services. I expect to have half my money returned, too."

"Come back here!" Coop ordered when she wheeled around and stamped off. "This meeting isn't over yet."

"It is if I say it is," she threw over her shoulder as she quickened her step to reach her horse.

She yelped when Coop pounced like a cougar springing on its quarry. He grabbed her elbow and spun her around to face him. She tripped over a fallen branch and she would have landed flat on her back if Coop hadn't jerked her upright.

"It *is* Harold Quinn whom you represent, isn't it? My assignment was to check on his debutante daughter's intended fiancé, am I right?"

"Yes, you were to check on Webster, not dally with his daughter," she flung back, feeling angry and hurt.

"You leave Alexa out of this," Coop snarled at her.

"No, *you* leave her out of this and keep your distance from her." She yanked her arm from his grasp. "You are no longer in my employ and that's all that matters. You are unreliable and untrustworthy. A combination I will not tolerate."

"Webster did hire me," he admitted. "He wanted me to plant evidence that Hampton and Barrett are rustling his cattle. You can learn a hell of a lot when you're on the inside, pretending to be a friend or employee."

"He wants planted evidence?" she crowed. *"Good God!"*

The news caught her so completely off guard that she forgot to use her deep voice and her fake accent. She knew the exact moment when Coop recognized her. Cursing herself soundly, she lurched around and took off like a gunshot in the darkness to reach her horse before he could run her down.

Coop couldn't believe his eyes or his ears. One moment he was debating with the annoying Yank called Mr. Chester. The next instant he heard Alexa's voice coming from that hefty body wrapped in fashionable men's clothing. He realized that the pudgy man might be *short* for the male gender but he was *tall* for a woman—exactly Alexa's height. It hadn't dawned on him until this precise moment that she was in disguise and she had made a fool of him. That rankled!

Furthermore, Mr. Chester's written instructions had reminded Coop of fancy invitations. That was *her* doing, he realized suddenly. Plus, only *she* knew how intimate they had become. No one else could possibly have known. It all made sense now. She had used him and made him look like an idiot. That was as aggravating as it was embarrassing.

"Damn it to hell!" he spouted off as he gave chase. "Stop!"

When she defied his command, Coop dashed forward to grab her by the nape of her thick jacket. She shrugged out of it, revealing two layers of padding wrapped around her chest and abdomen. Coop launched himself through the air to tackle her around the knees, sending her sprawling facedown in the grass. She landed with a *thud,* a yelp and a curse with his name attached to it.

"You scoundrel, that's no way to treat a lady!" she railed angrily. "Let me go before I decide to use my pistol on you."

They rolled across the ground, both struggling for control of her firearm. When he shoved her to her back, he disarmed her before she carried out her spiteful threat. Unfortunately *she* made a grab for one of *his* Colts while he was disarming her.

Panting for breath, he plunked down on her hips—and found himself staring down *his* pistol barrel while she stared down *hers.* "Are you really going to shoot me?" he asked her.

"I'm thinking about it," she muttered angrily.

"Make up your mind, princess. If Miguel is out there somewhere, ready to rush to your rescue, I don't want to have to hurt him, just because his employer is a reckless daredevil who doesn't have enough sense to fill a thimble."

He figured that comment would infuriate her. Sure nuff.

"You're a bastard! And you're right. Miguel has a rifle sighted on you. Now let me up!"

Coop scanned the area. He knew Alexa had eluded Miguel's protection on a few occasions. She might have duped her bodyguard tonight, too. Seeing no one, he focused his irritation and offended dignity on Alexa.

"I want to know why you're posing as a representative for your father."

"None of your business. I told you, you're fired. Besides, how good of a detective can you be if you couldn't figure out who *I* was?"

The snide question caused him to gnash his teeth, even if she did have a point. She had fooled him completely, which didn't say much for his skills of observation. But in his defense he said, "That was a sneaky trick and you never let me close enough to tell who you were. But what matters is that you aren't going to fire me because I'm not ready to quit—"

Catching her off guard, he slammed his pistol barrel against hers. The unexpected blow knocked the weapon from her hand. She shrieked and tried to *whack* him upside the head. Coop grabbed her wrist before she could do any real damage.

"Hold still, damn it," he barked at her.

"Get off me, damn it," she muttered, and then bit his hand.

Coop shook his stinging hand and stared at the wildcat in disbelief. He kept seeing Mr. Chester's wire-rimmed glasses and bearded face superimposed on Alexa's delicate features. The contrasting images kept distracting him.

He decided to let her up before she bit a few more chunks out of his hide. He bounded to his feet then hauled her up beside him. When he jerked the beard from her face, she squawked in pain.

"Serves you right, you little termagant," he said unsympathetically as he removed her glasses and stuck them in his shirt pocket. "Does your father know what you're doing?"

"That isn't your concern," she mumbled as she rubbed her tender chin. "All you need to know is that you can leave town whenever you please. The sooner the better as far as I'm concerned. I'll handle this case myself."

Coop quick-marched Alexa to her horse. Instead of assisting her onto the saddle, he climbed aboard, and then offered his hand to her.

When she stared at his hand, as if she preferred to bite it rather than accept it, he said, "Ride or walk. You decide. Doesn't make a damn bit of difference to me."

She grumbled under her breath—calling him a few foul names, he suspected—but she took his hand and allowed him to situate her behind him on the horse. Coop moved his pistols out of her reach and stuffed them in the front waistband of his breeches. When he trotted to the place where he had tied Bandit, he plucked up Alexa and deposited her on his horse.

However, he refused to hand her the reins. He led the way through the trees and halted at the spot where oversize boulders and trees lined the river, providing protection, so he and Alexa wouldn't become sitting ducks if someone attacked.

"You and I are going to have a long talk, princess," he said ominously.

"I'm not a princess and I have nothing more to say to you," she said with stubborn defiance.

"Tough. I want to know exactly what's going on and you're going to tell me."

She made a spectacular production of clamping her lips shut and thrusting out her chin. Try as he might, he couldn't squelch a grin. She was feisty, headstrong, daring and courageous. He couldn't believe his first impression of her had been so far off the mark. She'd put on a convincing act that threw him and everyone else off track.

"I don't appreciate the fact that you purposely misled me," he complained as he pulled her off Bandit.

"I don't have to answer to you," she sassed him.

Coop blew out his breath. "I do not envy Miguel his job as your bodyguard. Where is the poor man? Did you stuff him down a well or poison him again?"

She flashed him a go-to-hell-and-stay-there glare. It didn't faze him. Outlaws had been giving him that look for years. He was immune. "I can tie you up and torture the information out of you. Or you can be nice and cooperate."

"It takes someone *nice* to bring out the nice in me," she shot back.

She wheeled around, stuck her nose in the air and ignored him. Coop bit back an amused snicker. The woman didn't know when to quit. Plus, she was blasting his preexisting perception of her all to hell. To prove that he meant business he grabbed a strip of leather from his saddlebag, walked up behind her and lashed her hands to an overhanging tree branch. She glared at him but he disregarded her expression of outraged disgust.

Careful not to come within kicking distance, Coop crossed his arms over his chest and stood with feet askance. "Now let's hear it and don't leave anything out."

"You want to hear it? Fine. I think you are a bullying brute and I rue the day I hired you," she smarted off. "I swear *you* passed around those exaggerated tales of your legendary heroics as a lawman and detective, just to drum up business. You are a liar and a cheat and I don't like you one whit!"

"Forget about your personal feelings for me," he said dismissively. "I want to know what this case is really about. Obviously it isn't about checking out Webster as possible marriage material. Now that I know the real you, I realize you have been investigating him all by yourself. You found out a lot of things you wanted to know about the bastard."

The comment seemed to please her and that surprised him. Which only proved how little Coop understood women. This one in particular. She confused the hell out of him.

Pleased though she appeared to be, she still didn't offer an explanation so Coop said, "I'm not kidding about the torture tactics." He flashed his most vicious glare and towered over her like a thundercloud. "Don't make me wring the information out of you. I don't want to hurt you, except as my last resort."

She took a long time before answering. Which indicated how little she trusted him not to betray her confidence. That hurt. He didn't want to delve into the reason why her opinion mattered. It just did.

Alexa met his stony stare. "Are you going to help Webster set up my friend's father as a rustler?"

"Hell no, but I did see Webster's men putting an *H* brand and a *B* brand over the *W* brand. I'm withholding that information to relay to Gil Henson when the timing is right.

"And even though you probably don't believe me, I figured the easiest way to come and go from Webster's ranch without drawing suspicion was to pretend to work for him."

She studied him pensively for a moment. "All right, I'll give you the benefit of the doubt…for the moment. Besides, I've been feeling guilty about deceiving you. That is, when I wasn't furious with you for what I thought was betrayal."

He frowned curiously. "Why did you deceive me?"

"Because I doubted you would have taken me seriously if I'd asked to be involved in this case and insisted that you report to me. So I became someone I thought you could take seriously." She brought his attention to her bound hands. "If you untie me I'll tell you what's really going on with this investigation," she bartered.

Coop cocked his head and eyed her skeptically. "We have a real dilemma, princess. You're not sure you can trust me completely and I feel the same way about you. I think you might shoot me if I give you an opening."

"Me?" she tittered innocently. "Really, Mr. Cooper, you give me far too much credit. We socialites just don't have it in us to do any such thing. Our only objective is to amuse ourselves constantly."

His gaze narrowed. "You can drop that fluff-headed routine with me. I know that isn't the real you. The real you is half wildcat and half crafty fox."

Alexa beamed at the compliment, although he hadn't meant it as one.

"Answer me this," he insisted as he untied her hands in a

gesture of good faith. "Who is the caped crusader I saw at the line shack and again while I was galloping across Webster's pasture looking for rustlers? Was that Miguel?"

Alexa peeled off the padding on her chest then unfastened the oversize breeches. Coop watched her reduce fifty pounds in nothing flat. Beneath the padding were trim breeches and a black shirt.

"Oh hell, it's you." He glanced suspiciously at the carpet-bag tied behind the saddle of her horse. "How many other characters are you carrying around in your luggage?"

"That's all…for this case, at least." She rolled up the Mr. Chester-disguise and tucked it into her carpetbag, along with the glasses she retrieved from his shirt pocket.

Coop shook his head in amazement. "Your father approves of this? Is he insane?"

"My father doesn't know I'm involved in the investigation." She stared threateningly at him. "If you try to blackmail me I'll make you dreadfully sorry. And Miguel will help me torture you within an inch of your life."

Coop smirked at her threat. Alexa watched him sink down on a chair-size boulder near the tumbling rapids. No doubt, he planned to use the sound of rushing water to drown out their conversation—in case someone was listening.

Coop was very thorough, she'd give him that. She would have to remember that tactic. It might come in handy.

"My pretended interest in Webster is my excuse for being in Questa Springs," she admitted. "Visiting the Hamptons makes me accessible for his courtship and my subtle investigation."

Alexa sank next to him. Immediately she became aware of the hopeless attraction that had been her complete downfall one reckless night not so long ago. "This is about the possibility of one of my father's advisors providing Webster with inside information. Government contracts for the military posts and Indian reservations will be negotiated this month. Elliot got wind that my father isn't pleased with present arrangements. Elliot has been defrauding the forts and reservations by delivering substandard food and livestock. The committee is taking other applications and Elliot is playing up to my father and to me so he can promote his own agenda."

"He wouldn't be the first to shortchange the Indian tribes," Coop replied. "Sick horses and rancid beef have been sold as prime stock to reservations in Texas, Indian Territory and Arizona for years."

"My father prefers to give the contract to one or both of Webster's honest neighbors," she explained. "Hampton is one of them and Barrett is the other. Which suggests that Webster wants to ruin their reputation as ranchers to ensure that he receives the contract."

"You think the unidentified man at the line shack might be the informant or his agent," Coop presumed. "He was here two days ago, by the way. I followed Webster that night. Short of bursting inside the shack with pistols drawn, I couldn't get a detailed description."

Alexa sighed in disappointment. "I had hoped Webster would invite his coconspirator to his home, the same way he did his concubine. So far I've only seen Oscar Denton and a few hired gunmen hovering around while I'm at Webster's ranch."

She shivered repulsively. She didn't like the way Denton stared at her when he thought she wasn't looking. It made her skin crawl. Furthermore, she preferred not to be alone with him unless she was heavily armed.

"Now that I know exactly what I'm looking for I can get better results," Coop insisted. "You can clear out of Questa Springs to rejoin your father in Santa Fe."

Alexa snapped up her chin. "I will do no such thing. I intend to prove to my father that I'm capable and worth—" She shut her mouth so quickly that she bit the end of her tongue.

Coop eyed her speculatively. "Your father doesn't appreciate you, is that it?"

"I'm sick to death of playing hostess to his social and political gatherings," she confided. "He doesn't expect more from me, but I do. He adheres to the same conventional philosophy as most men. He thinks women need to be protected, tended to and cared for. But if I'm partially responsible for exposing Webster's underhanded dealings, Papa will recognize my potential and grant me the freedom to live my life as I choose."

"All the same, Webster is dangerous, especially when threatened. If you get in his way, or if he figures out that you have been investigating him, he won't go easy on you just because you're female. I've known dozens of men like him, princess."

She shook her finger at him. "Call me princess one more time and I'll shoot both your kneecaps," she threatened. "I don't know why you resent my money so much. I don't resent *you* because you're being a complete ass."

"How forgiving of you." Coop barked a laugh. "I respect your desire to become more than a man's trophy wife and a politician's hostess. But I don't intend to put your safety at risk. You've taken enough chances already. You hired me to investigate Webster. Let me do my job."

"I want to help. I can still go places you can't," she argued. "I can enter Webster's house without being watched closely. If I can gain access to his ledgers or eavesdrop on conversations between him and Denton—"

"No. Absolutely not." His voice resounded like a judge's pounding gavel.

"Then you're still fired," she insisted.

Alexa bounded to her feet and stalked toward her horse. She could feel Coop breathing down her neck. She tried to ignore the warm tingles his closeness incited and focus on her irritation with him. It worked—marginally.

"Damn it, hellion, will you listen to reason just once?"

"At least *hellion* is better than *princess*," she said as she clamped her hand on the pommel of the saddle, prepared to hoist herself up.

Coop spun her around and grabbed her by the shoulders, giving her a quick shake. "Don't you get it? I don't want to see you hurt."

"I don't want to see you hurt, either."

"Finally something we both agree on…other than this…"

Chapter Nine

Coop couldn't help himself. He couldn't touch Alexa without wanting her obsessively. If he didn't kiss the maddening female this very moment, he swore he'd starve to death without the addictive taste of her. Obviously his emotions were in a hopeless tangle after discovering that Mr. Chester and the mysterious man in black were Alexa's alternate personalities. Plus, she kept testing his temper until it frayed—and it had.

It was official now. She'd driven him so crazy that basic instincts prevailed over common sense.

The instant Coop crushed her petal-soft lips beneath his and pulled her familiarly against him the frustrating tension coiled into a knot of flaming desire. And sure, he could list a dozen reasons to back away from Alexa but only one reason to ignore sensible logic.

He craved her. He didn't want to admit it, but he couldn't deny the truth.

It didn't help that she wrapped her arms around his neck and arched sensuously against him when she should have shoved him away. Her ardent response fueled the wildfire of desire that burned through every sensitized inch of his body.

"Why does this keep happening?" he asked no one in particular. "We need to stop, for both our sakes, Alexa. Tell me to stop."

She peered up at him with those captivating blue eyes that mystified him. Her lips were swollen from his demanding kisses. Her breath came out in ragged spurts as she traced her forefinger over his mouth.

"We'll stop…after tonight," she murmured. "But first I need to touch you in all the intimate ways you touched me. I want to know every inch of you, too, Coop. I want you to feel all the amazing sensations I discovered with you."

That wasn't what a man standing on the crumbling edge of self-restraint needed to hear. The sultry image she painted with words made his knees wobble. He watched her unbutton his shirt and felt her moist lips skimming over his laboring chest. The darkness, sprinkled with twinkling stars, spun like a kaleidoscope around him. He felt light-headed as her hands and lips drifted languidly from his belly to the band of his breeches.

Coop groaned in helpless defeat when she tossed aside his pistols then relieved him of his holsters, boots and breeches. There had been a time not so long ago that he'd prided himself on his willpower and his ability to take control of certain situations. He could face down gunmen and outlaws fearlessly.

But he was *afraid* of what this alluring siren did to him. She made him feel too deeply. She made him want too fiercely. He hadn't allowed anyone this close to him in two decades but Alexa had broken through the defensive barriers and intrigued him.

He was still reeling with the undeniable fact that she held an unstoppable mystical power over him when she urged him down to the pallet of his discarded clothes. Then she tortured him with such delicious pleasure that his body quivered and his mind melted into mush.

Her lips feathered over his belly and he moaned aloud in erotic anticipation. Her hand enfolded his throbbing length and his heart hammered furiously against his ribs. She stroked him provocatively and white-hot sensations bombarded him. Each one was like a bullet striking hard and deep and leaving him to burn alive.

Then she took him into her mouth and suckled him. Coop all but lost consciousness when infinitesimal pleasure converged on him from every direction at once. She flicked at him with her tongue, nipped him playfully with her teeth and he groaned in unholy torment. When he gasped for breath there was none forthcoming…until her lips slanted over his, sharing the taste of his own desire for her.

"Enough," he rasped when she cupped him in her hand.

"Not yet," she whispered as her lips skimmed over his chin, his chest, his abdomen. "I'm not finished getting to know what pleasures you most."

"*You* do," he heard himself say before he could bite back the incriminating words.

She lifted her head, her tangled blond hair coiling around her bewitching face in frothy curls. When she smiled at him, it was like having refreshing new life breathed into his battered heart. Allowing a woman like Alexa to know he was powerless against her was dangerous business. If he wasn't careful she would run roughshod over him—and he'd let her get away with it.

"You do, too, Coop," she replied as her free hand brushed over the muscled contours of his hips and thighs. "I think you're my greatest weakness. Good thing this is our last night together."

"Damn good thing," he agreed hoarsely. "I—"

What he was about to say—and suddenly he couldn't remember what the hell it was—fizzled out beneath his muffled moan. Her soft lips found his most sensitive flesh again. She flicked at him, teased him with evocative pleasure and stole the air right out of his lungs.

"Come here," he demanded with what little breath he had left after she'd all but devastated him.

She rose above him, holding his gaze as she removed her black shirt and breeches. Coop had never seen anything as beguiling as Alexa's lush body set against the backdrop of river rapids glistening in the moonlight. The water sparkled and rippled, sending droplets spraying through the air like diamonds dancing in the darkness. When she straddled him, Coop clamped his hands around her waist and settled her exactly upon him. She was hot and tight and the sheer intimacy of their union struck like a blow to the very depths of his soul.

This woman completes you, came a whispering voice from somewhere deep inside him.

That was not what Coop wanted to hear. He wanted a purely physical attraction. In fact, he silently chanted those very words while tumultuous sensations crashed over him. He arched into her, watching her expression change as passion overtook her, as completely as it overtook him.

"Coop…ah…" Her breath broke and she threw back her head, sending her blond hair cascading over her shoulders.

He felt her body quiver, felt her nails curl into his chest, as if to anchor herself against the phenomenal pleasure riveting her. She made him lose control in that wild instant when she convulsed around him again and again. He went over the edge with her into blinding ecstasy and he clung to her as shudder after helpless shudder pulsated through him.

When she sighed contentedly then cuddled up on his chest, Coop all but melted into the makeshift pallet. Every ounce of energy drained from him. He wasn't sure he could have mustered the strength to move, even if someone held a gun to his head.

Sweet mercy, he hadn't known passion could be so wildly devastating. Whatever he'd been doing, when he ended up in a woman's bed to appease his needs the past decade, was nothing remotely close to this!

And that worried him to no end, too. Everything about Alexa Quinn was beginning to scare the hell out of him.

Her dewy lips brushed over his mouth and her fingers speared into his mussed hair. "Now we're even," she whispered.

Then she laid her cheek against his chest and breathed his name with a contented sigh.

That was the last thing Coop remembered before he fell asleep with Alexa encircled in his arms.

Alexa eased away when she heard Coop's deep, methodic breathing and felt his arms go slack. Smiling in sated pleasure, she lightly touched her index finger to his sensuous lips then to the muscled flesh above his heart. She knew these reckless trysts couldn't continue, for fear she'd become too attached to a man who wouldn't be a part of her future. But she doubted she would ever forget the incredible way Coop made her feel. For these timeless moments of rapture, she was free to follow her most secret desires.

Rising quietly to her feet, she gathered her breeches and shirt then walked to the river to bathe and dress. Such a perfect spot for such a perfect night of passion beneath a dome of glittering stars, she mused as her gaze drifted back to where Coop slept. She studied his magnificent body while she fastened herself into her clothes. She knew him completely now and that brought an amazing sense of satisfaction.

Alexa grabbed the reins to her steed then weaved through the trees to reach the trodden path leading to the main road. When she spotted a rider cantering toward her, she ducked into the underbrush. Recognizing Miguel, she rode into view to flag him down.

Miguel drew his laboring steed to a halt then motioned for her to join him. "*¡Caramba!* I am glad to see you."

Alexa trotted her horse toward him. His tone of voice sent jolts of apprehension spurting through her. "What's wrong?"

"Nothing if you like high drama on the town square," he said sarcastically. "After Webster paid his mistress a visit at the pleasure resort, he went to fetch the marshal."

"And?" Alexa waited anxiously for her friend to continue.

"And he claims Percy Hampton rustled his cattle and he wants a posse to search the ranch." Miguel burst out bitterly. "Kate's father might not approve of *me,* but I refuse to believe *he* is involved in illegal activity."

"According to Coop he saw *Webster's* men place the Hampton brand over the original brand."

Miguel's dark brows shot up to his hairline. "He is framing the Hamptons? Does he expect Cooper to corroborate the story? Will he do it?"

"Of course not," she said, and tried to reassure herself that Coop wouldn't betray her cause. "I just don't want to put him to the test and make him one of Webster's enemies right now."

"Then how are we going to divert trouble?" Miguel questioned.

Alexa frowned thoughtfully. "I suspect that Webster is going to force me to choose sides. He'll demand an answer about the betrothal immediately and expect me to accept. If I turn my back on the Hamptons it will imply that I think Percy is guilty of rustling."

"He won't be happy if you turn him down, *querida,*" Miguel warned. "Especially if you do it tonight when he is the center of attention."

Alexa nodded in agreement. She knew this courtship was all about expecting a contract renewal and favoritism. But if she embarrassed him in front of his hometown community, his resentment and wrath would double.

Her thoughts tailed off when she saw torches blazing along the path to town. "Damn," she muttered. "He's gathered a posse."

"*Si,*" Miguel said. "He wants Hampton's herd inspected immediately to locate his missing steers."

Alexa wasted no time wheeling her steed around and racing toward Hampton Ranch. She didn't want to be caught wearing masculine garb and have to explain herself. If she and Miguel cut cross-country and rode hell-for-leather they could stable their horses and dash into the house to change clothes before the torch-carrying brigade arrived via the road.

If she wasn't on hand to intervene between Percy and Elliot, tempers might explode and gunfire could break out. Come to think of it, Elliot would probably delight in provoking a shooting contest between Percy and Oscar Denton because he knew who would win. The grim thought provoked Alexa to quicken her pace. She needed to take a position between the two men to discourage a showdown.

Coop moaned groggily and opened his eyes to find himself spread eagle atop his discarded clothing. Alexa, alias Mr. Chester and the caped crusader, was nowhere in sight. He scrubbed his hands over his face then propped himself up on an elbow. The woman had damn near killed him with passion.

But what a way to go.

Coop smiled rakishly as he came to his feet. The first time and the last time with Alexa had been incredible. The last time… The thought squeezed at his heart so he walked into the cold water to distract himself.

Moments later Coop was dressed and straddling Bandit. He trotted through the trees then noticed the lighted procession of riders headed for Hampton Ranch.

"That son of a bitch," he muttered when he recognized Webster, spotlighted by a torch, riding abreast with Gil and Oscar Denton.

He knew Webster would try to set up Hampton, but he hadn't expected the shyster to strike this quickly. Coop took off cross-country at a gallop. He didn't know where Alexa was but he hoped she had tucked herself out of sight—and stayed there.

With no time to spare Alexa dashed into her room, tossed her nightgown over her head and grabbed her robe. The procession of riders approached. From her vantage point at the second-story window, she could see they were led by Elliot—who was bookended by Oscar Denton and Gil Henson. She darted down the hall to rouse Percy and Meg Hampton.

Percy answered her insistent knock and blinked like an awakened owl. "Something wrong, child?"

"Get dressed quickly. The marshal and a posse are outside with Webster."

Percy's gray brows swooped down into a flat line over his eyes. "What does that scoundrel want?"

"According to Miguel, who was in town earlier this evening, he has come to accuse you of stealing his cattle."

"Why, that is preposterous!" Percy howled before shutting the door in her face to dress quickly.

Kate poked her head around the edge of her bedroom door. "What's going on?"

Alexa explained hurriedly.

Kate muttered a few unflattering remarks about Webster then said, "It is beyond me how you can continue to keep company with that devious weasel."

"It isn't easy," she confided as her friend wrapped a modest robe around her nightgown.

Kate jerked up her head and stared intently at Alexa. "Then why have you been doing it?"

"Long story."

"I have all night now that I'm awake," Kate insisted. "What the blazes are you up to?"

Alexa dodged the probing question by hurrying downstairs. Kate and her parents were a few moments behind her. She stepped onto the covered porch before Gil could dismount and knock on the door.

"Rather late for a social call," she said. "At least in Questa Springs. Of course, in Santa Fe the soirees—"

"Alexa my dear, this is a serious matter," Elliot broke in impatiently. "You have aligned yourself with a criminal."

"That is absurd." Alexa flicked her wrist dismissively. "I've known the Hamptons for years. They have all the proper social credentials and connections."

"Marshal, do your duty," Elliot demanded the instant Percy Hampton stepped into view.

"Elliot, really," Alexa inserted as she strategically planted herself in front of Percy. "I haven't heard you use that tone before. It is not becoming."

"Neither is rustling cattle," Elliot snapped.

She tried to look flabbergasted by the harsh accusation. "You must be mistaken. Why, Percy wouldn't do such a thing."

"Move aside and stay out of this, Alexa." Elliot fixed his narrowed gaze on Percy's tall, lean figure. "This isn't women's business."

Percy, who was in his mid-fifties, thrust back his shoulders and stuck out his chest, as if he were a pugilist preparing to go several rounds with his opponent. "I wouldn't want your cattle, Webster. Their quality doesn't compare to mine. Your livestock is no match for years of dedicated breeding. Same goes for my stock of race horses."

"We can clear up this matter within a few minutes," Gil declared before reining his horse around. "We'll start by checking the livestock penned in your corrals, and then we'll look at the cattle in your pastures."

"You are wasting your time and we're missing needed sleep," Percy called out to Gil.

Alexa wanted to tell him that he had been set up, but that would invite too many questions that she didn't want to answer. She had no idea how to settle this matter without Percy suffering the humiliation of being locked in jail.

Damn that Elliot Webster! He was going to pay—somehow—for using the Hamptons to further his own cause.

She wished Coop would magically appear, but involving him would cause him to lose his edge with Webster. If he did in fact have an edge, she mused warily. And he better not have lied to her or she was going to rake him over live coals to vent her fury.

Alexa watched the posse reverse direction to check the corrals. She wanted to call them back but she couldn't dream up an excuse to keep them at the house without arousing suspicion.

From the hill overlooking the stone ranch house, Coop grabbed his field glasses from his saddlebag to watch Alexa step onto the porch to confront the posse, which was comprised mostly of Webster's gunmen. A backdrop of light from the doorway and windows silhouetted Alexa while she stood like protective armor in front of Percy Hampton so he wouldn't be shot.

Coop cursed her daring, but he couldn't say he was surprised to see her stand up to the riders. He admired her for being a champion for whatever noble cause needed her immediate attention. But damn it, if she got herself shot he'd never let her hear the end of it.

Pensively he surveyed the group of riders then the corrals that sat a quarter of a mile from the house. He wondered if Webster had some of his men plant the rebranded cattle in Hampton's pen earlier tonight. That had to be what this evening confrontation was all about.

Coop blew out his breath in frustration and his thoughts ran in a dozen directions at once. He had told Alexa what he thought Webster was planning, but she was in no position to blurt out the information to Gil without drawing Webster's suspicion. Coop doubted Webster would take it kindly if he discovered the woman he hoped to marry, to obtain more wealth and political influence, was actually here to investigate his unlawful activities.

Webster would become vindictive, Coop predicted. Which was why Alexa needed to clear out and let him handle a case that was becoming more complicated with each passing minute.

"First things first," Coop murmured as he took another sweeping appraisal of his surroundings.

He needed a distracting diversion to counter Webster's scheme. Inspiration struck and Coop twisted in the saddle to retrieve a box of matches. Nothing like an unexpected fire to grab attention and send Webster dashing off to prevent the flames from consuming his property.

Dismounting, Coop jogged to the fence line that separated Hampton's property from Webster's pasture to the north. In a matter of seconds, he had ignited the tumbleweeds that were tangled in barbwire. In another moment smoke rolled from the dry grass beneath the fence. The south breeze sent flames dancing across Webster's pasture.

As he'd hoped, the fire caught the attention of the posse. Coop bounded onto Bandit's back to circle toward Hampton's ranch house. With any luck, Webster would dispense with the search for rustled cattle and save his pasture.

Sure enough, the riders aborted their intended inspection of the corral and thundered toward the flickering flames while Coop raced off to avert disaster.

"Coop," Alexa whispered to herself when she saw the unexpected flames illuminating the darkness.

She wanted to hug him for his quick thinking. He had managed to send Webster's hired guns riding off in the opposite direction before they could descend on the stock pens. Wheeling around, she dashed into the house to dress. She was up the steps in nothing flat. She wished she could don her breeches, but she didn't want to explain her unconventional attire, in case someone saw her.

"Lexi? Where are you going?" Kate questioned as she breezed into the bedroom.

"To prevent a range war, I hope," she said as she darted onto the terrace. "Make sure your parents stay in the house."

"Why?" Kate demanded as she followed in Alexa's wake.

"Just do it," Alexa said shortly.

Kate opened her mouth to fire another question, but Alexa waved her off as she jogged toward the back steps.

"Miguel?" Alexa called out.

"I'm here." He stepped from his covert position by the side of the house.

Alexa noticed that he carried a rifle, just in case shooting started. She was thankful it hadn't…yet.

"Fetch the horses, pronto. Coop should be here any minute."

"I'm already here," came the deep voice from the shadows of the trees. "We need to—"

"—I know," she cut in as she hurried toward him. "You saved the day. I could kiss you for your ingenuity."

She could see a flash of white teeth in the shadows. "I'll collect later. And thank you for not getting yourself shot when you faced down the posse. I would have hated to have to kill someone on your behalf."

She could tell by the tone of his voice that he was displeased by her attempt to block Percy from view and spare him from being gunned down. But she had done what she felt she had to do to prevent bloodshed. They could argue about her methods later, if he were so inclined, but definitely not now.

Miguel scurried forward, holding the reins to two unsaddled horses. Alexa grabbed the nearest horse. When Coop leaned away from his mount to give her a boost she grabbed his arm and pulled herself up.

"Can you ride bareback?" he questioned skeptically.

Miguel smirked. "Of course she can, *gringo*. I taught her. She can handle a pistol and knife expertly, too."

Coop glanced at Alexa then frowned at Miguel. "So you are responsible for the way she is."

Miguel scoffed as they trotted their horses toward the corral to check for planted cattle. "Have you ever tried to tell this woman no? She is relentless when she makes up her mind to do something."

"I see your point," Coop conceded.

In the moonlight, Alexa could read Coop's expression and hear the subtle change in the tone of his voice. He was referring to how she'd had her way with him during their tryst. She had made a thorough, erotic study of his masculine body… and he had allowed it.

She was grateful that the darkness concealed her blush, for her face pulsated with heat and her mind stumbled over the remembered sensations of their passion. Willfully she pushed aside the thought and concentrated on removing damaging evidence so they could clear Percy Hampton's good name.

"There." Miguel pointed out three head of cattle sporting fresh *H* brands.

"Here are two more," Coop reported. "That accounts for the ones I noticed recently." He glanced over his shoulder. "Alexa, open the gate so we can sort off the cattle."

She bounded to the ground and hurried over to let the men into the corral. When the five steers had been cut out then herded into the pasture, Alexa secured the gate and used the fence rail as a makeshift ladder to climb back on her horse.

"No, you stay here," Coop ordered when she tried to rejoin him. "If Webster circles back tonight it will look suspicious if you aren't here."

Alexa couldn't argue with that logic. She *wanted* to, though, because she wanted to remain involved in this case.

As the two men rode away she heard Miguel say, "You won one, *gringo*. How'd you do that?"

"I think she let me win," Coop replied.

She smiled at Coop's comment then rode off to return her horse to the stable.

Chapter Ten

When Alexa bounded up the back steps to the terrace a few minutes later Kate was primed and waiting for an explanation.

"What is going on and where the devil have you been?" she asked without preamble.

Alexa whizzed past her curious friend. "I can't tell you."

Kate grabbed the hem of her dress and hauled her back to the terrace. "You *will* tell me," she demanded. "Have you forgotten that I was your partner in mischief for years? Don't try to pass me off as one of those prissy socialites we met in school. This involves my father's reputation and I demand to know what is going on so I can help!"

"Keep your voice down," Alexa said with a quiet hiss.

"Start talking. Now."

Alexa sighed in defeat then pulled Kate into the bedroom. She secured both doors and the window. "If you breathe one word of this to anyone, it might endanger my life, Miguel's life and Coop's."

"You know perfectly well that I wouldn't do anything to hurt you or Miguel." She stared curiously at Alexa. "But what does Coop have to do with this?"

"He and I are investigating Elliot Webster's shady business practices for my father."

Kate's brown eyes nearly popped out of her head. "You and Mr. Cooper are working together?" she croaked.

Alexa nodded as she motioned for Kate to sit beside her on the edge of the canopy bed. "He is following Elliot to monitor all his activities. My supposed interest in him as a potential husband provides me with an excuse to enter and leave his home and mercantile store without drawing suspicion."

"My, isn't that something. I can't believe your father agreed to this…" She smiled wryly as she appraised Alexa. "He doesn't know, does he?"

"No, he is unaware of the extent of my involvement." She gave Kate the evil eye. "You aren't going to tell him."

Kate sniffed in offended dignity. "Of course, I'm not. Did I tell him that I was your companion for your daredevil escapades at school? Did I mention the late night rides, dressed in men's clothes, when you claimed you needed a breath of fresh evening air? I certainly didn't tell anyone about the mountain climbing expedition that nearly got us washed away in the flash flood during a storm."

Alexa grinned conspiratorially at her friend. They had enjoyed several exhilarating adventures that most women hadn't experienced and didn't intend to. Kate was still a bit of a daredevil at heart herself.

Alexa's expression sobered when her thoughts circled to the precarious situation at hand. "Elliot planted his recently *re*branded cattle in your stock pen and showed up here tonight with the marshal in tow to accuse your father of rustling." She paused momentarily to allow Kate to gasp and mutter in outrage. "If not for Coop's quick thinking we wouldn't have been able to remove the steers from the corral before the marshal saw them."

"I want Elliot's head," Kate said vengefully.

"So do a lot of people. You'll have to get in line."

Kate expelled an exasperated breath and squeezed Alexa's hand appreciatively. "Thank you for what you've done. Sometimes my father can be stubborn and hidebound when it comes to his expectations for me, but he is an honest man. I don't want his reputation ruined by Webster's underhanded manipulations. And thank God you aren't considering that shyster as a husband. I've been thinking you've lost your mind."

"Believe me, I only want Elliot to receive his due," Alexa assured her. "Which is why it's vital that you keep this information in strictest confidence. An unknown informant in my father's political circle is passing privileged facts to Elliot. We want to catch him as well."

Kate nodded determinedly. "I will help you any way I can. I can provide an alibi for you if you need to be two places at once. I can pass information to Miguel or Mr. Cooper, if necessary, too."

"Thank you, Kate. I must admit it has been a strain trying to keep this from you since we've never kept secrets. Also, if your father decides to retaliate against Elliot, you can try to talk him out of it. In addition, you can forewarn us so we can head off another volatile confrontation."

After Alexa changed back into her gown and robe, she and Kate descended the stairs to watch the mounted posse return from stamping out the grass fire.

Elliot pointed an accusing finger at Percy. "More of his doing!"

"He was standing here when the fire started," Gil pointed out reasonably.

"Nonetheless, I suspect he was the mastermind behind the scheme." Elliot flapped his arms in expansive gestures to gain attention. "Let's check the cattle pens and see if my livestock are there."

Alexa swallowed a chuckle as Elliot, Oscar Denton and the other hired guns raised their torches to look over the cattle. She was pleased when Gil called an end to the futile search and announced that he was returning to town. However, she was concerned when Percy mounted up and called upon some of his cowboys to escort Elliot and his hired guns to the boundary line between their properties.

"Kate and I will come along," Alexa called out, startling the men on horseback.

"Stay here, Alexa," Elliot ordered sternly.

She mentally thumbed her nose at the sneaky sidewinder and strode to the stable to have a horse hitched to her carriage. Although Percy strenuously objected to his daughter's involvement, Kate bounded into the buggy. They joined the procession and Alexa made certain that she and Kate remained directly in the middle, shielding Percy from Elliot's heavily armed entourage.

Clearly Elliot was perturbed with her, as was Percy. But she pretended to be blithely unaware of the tension. There would be no range war or bloodshed on her watch, she silently vowed.

"Tomorrow we need to have a serious talk," Elliot said to Alexa as he lingered beside the pasture gate.

"I shall look forward to it," she replied with false enthusiasm. "I'm glad Kate and I came along. It is a lovely night for a ride."

"I would have preferred that you remain at the house," Elliot grumbled.

"At least we were able to clear up that silly misconception about my dear friends. Cattle rustling? Indeed!"

Alexa swallowed a grin when Elliot's face puckered in a sour scowl. When he rode off to rejoin his men Alexa breathed a gigantic sigh of relief. Another disaster averted. Trouble would continue, however, if she didn't ferret out the informant from Santa Fe and expose Elliot's unethical business methods.

"I wish I knew what his next strategy might be," Alexa murmured as she and Kate drove back to the house.

"Maybe we could just shoot him, and then we wouldn't have to worry about it," Kate suggested.

Alexa glanced disconcertedly at Kate who shrugged and said, "I'm just saying…"

"Appealing as it sounds, taking the law into our own hands might earn us a life sentence. I don't think our jailer would permit midnight rides when the need for adventure and fresh air strike us."

Kate sighed heavily. "I suppose you're right. But I still think Elliot deserves a good shooting."

"I couldn't agree more," Alexa murmured as she headed for the stable.

"I am paying you good money to set up situations like the one *I* had to arrange," Webster growled at Cooper, who had been summoned to the back office of the mercantile store during his lunch break. "Where the hell were you last night?"

"Doing what you asked," Coop replied calmly. "I was riding the fences between your place and Andrew Barrett's."

Webster waved him off while he paced back and forth across his office. "It's the Hamptons that I've decided to focus on exclusively. Even though they're both being considered—" He stopped short. "What I mean is that I want my future fiancée to realize that she should align herself with *me,* not the Hamptons."

Coop knew that both of Webster's neighbors were being considered for the government contract but he kept his expression carefully blank. "Is Miss Quinn easily managed? Will she do as you request?" As if he didn't know.

"No, damn it," Webster muttered. "She's a bit too independent minded to make a subservient wife but time and relentlessness will tame her down."

Coop seriously doubted it. Her irrepressible spirit refused to be stifled. If Webster dared to lay a hand on Alexa to force her into submission Coop would give him a taste of his own medicine.

"I want Alexa away from Percy's influence." Webster wheeled around to pace in the opposite direction. "That nuisance of a man needs to have a conveniently timed accident that incapacitates him…at the very least."

"I don't arrange accidents," Coop let him know immediately. "Besides, it's too soon after your confrontation."

Webster huffed out his breath then raked his fingers through his tawny hair. "Forget I said that."

Coop shrugged nonchalantly. "Okay. Anything else?"

"Yes." His brows furrowed pensively. "The owners of the mercantile shop in the town square should at least run into a little bad luck. Hampton, Barrett and Figgins need to suffer the setback of a fire because they're stealing my customers by undercutting my prices."

Coop silently cursed. He suspected that his grass fire inspired the idea of burning out Webster's competitors. Damn it, Webster would become suspicious if someone overtook his henchman before he could torch the store. "I wouldn't advise that right now, either," Coop replied. "Considering your unfounded accusations of rustling last night, you will be the prime suspect for arson, too. Then *your* reputation will be in tatters and you might find yourself under arrest."

Webster mumbled and grumbled as he went back to his pacing. "Curse it, you're right. I'd need a time delay for that. I think Hampton was a mental step ahead of me last night. He must have been waiting for me to show up so he could make me look like a fool. He, or one of his men, must have spotted the rebranded cattle and removed them from the pen."

"Did you locate the missing livestock?" Coop asked, although he knew the answer already. After all, he and Miguel had tucked away the cattle for safekeeping.

"No, and Hampton better not be holding them for evidence." He checked his timepiece then shooed Coop toward the back door. "I have a dinner engagement with Alexa. I'm going to convince her to take a room in the hotel so she won't be in the middle of my ongoing feud with Hampton."

Coop just listened, careful not to give himself away. He didn't want Alexa taking sides, for fear she might be hurt. However, he knew she would always vouch for a friend. Hell, she even stood up for *him* the night Miguel caught them wrapped in each other's arms near Webster's house.

"I'll swing by your home later if I have something to report," Coop offered as he limped away.

"Don't bother. Alexa will be with me. I don't want any interruptions tonight. I intend to get her to accept my marriage proposal, one way or another."

The thought of Webster coercing Alexa into a betrothal by forcing himself upon her turned Coop's mood sour. He reassured himself that Alexa was quick-witted and capable of handling Webster. Still, if Webster overpowered her, Coop refused to let him get away with it, even if it meant blowing this case wide-open and exposing his real purpose for being in Questa Springs.

Damnation, he thought as he hobbled off on his supposedly gimpy leg. He needed to convince Alexa to hightail it back to Santa Fe so he wouldn't have to fret over her safety and whereabouts while trying to do his job.

He wondered if she would figure out who was behind her sudden abduction if he hired someone to haul her back to her father. Coop grinned. He predicted that he'd be able to hear her ranting and raving at him all the way from the territorial capitol.

Alexa had been dreading her dinner with Elliot since his message arrived early that morning. She had dressed in her best silk gown, one that she usually saved for her father's special political functions. Selma Mae had ironed the expensive garment and laid it out carefully so it wouldn't gather wrinkles. Then she helped Alexa with her coiffure before going home for the night.

Miguel had driven her into town a quarter of an hour earlier and she had ambled down the boardwalk for a few minutes before entering Webster's mercantile shop. She was especially pleased to note that no customers were on hand. They had gathered at the southeast corner of the town square in his competitors' dry goods store.

Obviously the citizens had heard about Webster's false accusations the previous night and were boycotting overpriced merchandise. Good for them.

"Yoo-hoo, Elliot!" she called out in a singsong voice. "Are you in here?"

"Coming, my dear."

She manufactured a cheery smile when Elliot appeared. She had secretly hoped he'd dropped off the edge of the earth during the day. No such luck.

He halted in front of her and Alexa pirouetted around, allowing him to survey the rose-colored gown that displayed her figure to its best advantage. The streaming colors of sunset poured through the window, spotlighting her. She had his attention. Too bad she couldn't hypnotize him and get him to divulge the name of his mysterious informant.

"You look positively enchanting," he breathed appreciatively. She twirled in another circle, smiling as if her greatest aspiration in life was to become the goddess of high fashion. "Do you really think so, Elliot?"

He swaggered forward to bow over her hand. "Your beauty puts all other women to shame, Alexa."

She resisted the urge to jerk her fingertips from his grasp before he slobbered on them. Pretending to preen beneath his flattery, she batted her eyelashes and tittered. Inwardly, however, she compared Elliot to Coop and found him sadly lacking in every way imaginable.

Alexa allowed Elliot to escort her from the store. She scanned the street while he locked up shop. Miguel was leaning casually against the carriage that he'd parked in front of The Collins House, the hotel next door to Webster's store. Miguel had volunteered to keep an eye on the other dry goods store after Coop informed him of Elliot's spiteful scheme to smoke out his competition. Hopefully, the scoundrel took Coop's advice and didn't start any devastating fires this evening.

"I know I put you in an uncomfortable position last night," Elliot remarked as they strolled down the boardwalk. "I was upset when my cattle went missing and some of my men thought they had seen Hampton's cowboys on my property."

"I do hope you locate your missing cattle," she replied with just the right amount of concern in her voice. "But I still cannot imagine my friends being involved." She flicked her wrist and smiled. "But that is over and done and we shall forget all about it."

"If it were only that easy," Elliot countered. "You cannot wave your arm and magically clear the air. I'm afraid you will have to pick sides, Alexa." He halted to bow over her hand again. "I'm hoping you will choose me. You know how fond I am of you. And I'm anxiously awaiting your answer to my proposal."

Alexa inwardly tensed. "I shall make my decision soon. I promise. But let's just enjoy our evening, shall we?"

"Whatever you wish, my dear," he said smoothly. "I want to spend the rest of my life making you happy."

Alexa smiled brightly, even though she knew what a liar and cheat he was. She sat at the table and ordered the most expensive item on the menu. The man was going to pay for all of his transgressions eventually. In addition, sharing her company was going to be expensive. Her first preference, however, was to dump a plate of food on top of his blond head and storm off.

Coop stepped from Valmont Saloon in time to see Webster and Alexa stroll across the town square to reach Donovan's Café. Lord, she was lovely, he thought admiringly. Her rose-colored gown, trimmed with pearls and lace, made her appear surreal. The pastel colors of sunset seemed to form an aureole around her that captivated and beguiled.

Possessive jealousy stung like a wasp.

Coop cursed himself soundly. He was too emotionally attached to Alexa and that made him vulnerable. She symbolized everything he wasn't—well educated, well connected and well accepted. Plus, she was all tangled up in his personal and professional life and he couldn't separate one from the other because of his intense feelings and obsessive desire for her. He'd never had that problem before.

"Buy you a drink, *gringo?*" Miguel questioned.

Coop cursed his preoccupation with Alexa. Ordinarily he was attuned to his surroundings and to potential danger. But he hadn't heard Miguel walk up beside him. Worse, Miguel knew what had distracted him because he glanced pointedly from Coop to Alexa then smiled wryly.

"Not to fret," Miguel murmured as he sauntered down the

street toward one of the many saloons. "You are not the only man who has trouble thinking straight when Lexi is in the vicinity. She has scores of hopeless admirers in her social class."

"I know where I belong," Coop assured him. "So don't preach."

"So do I, *gringo*. I believe a man is much happier if he accepts his limitations and restrictions. Don't you agree?"

"I'm not sure happier is the right word," Coop replied. "Maybe the best a man can hope for is to accept what cannot be changed."

"I'll drink to that," Miguel said before he entered the swinging doors of the saloon.

"Dinner was delicious," Alexa gushed as she and Elliot trotted off in the carriage toward his ranch. "For such a small community, the cuisine is amazingly good."

"If you don't mind, I'd like to discuss a more serious topic," Elliot said, glancing at his watch.

"Yes, of course, how silly of me, going on about the meal." She offered him a contrite smile, for appearance's sake. But she knew what was coming. It wasn't too difficult to second-guess Elliot.

"You were placed in an awkward situation last night because of your loyalty to Kate," Elliot commented. "Whether you believe it or not, Percy lacks integrity and I don't trust him."

Alexa yearned to tell Elliot that she thought *he* was the un-trustworthy scoundrel who lacked integrity, but she held her tongue and played her role.

"I don't want you placed in potential crossfire again so I want you and your bodyguard—" he glanced over his shoulder at Miguel, who trailed a short distance behind them in the rented carriage "—to take rooms at the hotel. I couldn't bear it if you were injured."

"But how will I explain that to my dearest friend without hurting her feelings?"

Elliot checked his watch again. "I'm sure you'll think of something appropriate to say. You have years of experience in dealing with such matters since you've been your father's hostess. You can be diplomatic if need be."

Alexa gnashed her teeth. Her hands curled into fists. She wanted to tear into this arrogant chauvinist. However, it was his narrow-minded perception that enabled her to outsmart him so she kept silent. For now.

"You're right, of course," she patronized him. "When I have time to sit myself down and think about it, I can come up with a logical reason to move into town. But I still don't believe Percy—"

"Believe it," he interrupted harshly.

Alexa feigned a startled gasp. "Really, Elliot, I'm not sure I know you as well as I thought. Perhaps my consideration of your proposal should be postponed a while longer."

The comment forced him to change his tune, as she knew it would.

"So sorry, my dear Alexa," he cooed. "Last night's unpleasant incidents, and my concern for your safety, have put me on edge. Forgive me?"

Alexa patted his arm. "There, there, it's all right, Elliot. I know you care about me." *Care about my money and connections,* she silently amended.

"Then perhaps you will put me out of my misery and end the suspense. I would like to announce to all of Questa Springs that you have agreed to be my wife."

Alexa had planned to accept. Temporarily. But the ruggedly handsome image of Coop popped to mind and refused to let her agree. Heavens, it wasn't as if she and Coop had a promising future together. She had assured herself a dozen times that she didn't need a man to lead a productive, rewarding life. Her father had managed to function without a woman since her mother boarded a train for Boston and never looked back.

"Alexa?" Elliot prodded.

"You know I am fond of you, too." She forced the lie from her lips and manufactured a smile to go along with it. "Nothing would make me happier than to live nearby Kate. Of course, if there is a long-standing feud between you and Percy that might put a strain on our friendship."

"You have to choose, Alexa," Elliot insisted. "Me or them."

Alexa sighed dramatically. "Well, I suppose the time will come when Kate takes a husband and moves away from the area. So I cannot rely too heavily on my friend indefinitely."

"No, you cannot. I'm the one you can rely on to take care of you, to support you," Elliot purred.

"All right then, Elliot, I will send a telegram to my father after I move to the hotel." Staying in town would make it easier to come and go without the Hamptons's servants and cowboys seeing her, she reminded herself. "If Papa gives his consent we'll announce our betrothal…."

Her words trailed off when Elliot leaned over to kiss her full on the mouth. His scent, his taste, the feel of his thin lips were all wrong. It was all she could do not to shove him backward and send him cartwheeling off the seat.

"Then it's settled," Elliot proclaimed triumphantly then checked his watch—again. "I know your father will approve because I told him of my interest in you when I attended your party in Santa Fe. We can arrange a town-wide celebration and you can see to all the details."

"That will provide me with the perfect excuse to stay at the hotel," Alexa said with more enthusiasm than she felt—which was none whatsoever. "I do love to hostess parties. We shall invite everyone."

"That's a grand idea. Perhaps the party will assure my neighbors and customers that I don't want last night's incident to divide our community and drive off my business."

"I have so much to do and to arrange that it's giving me an instant headache. I do hate to cut our evening short, Elliot, but I'll have Miguel take me back to the Hamptons to inform them of my change of plans. I'll move into town tomorrow."

Before he could accept or reject her plans, she twisted on the seat to wave at Miguel. He pulled up beside them immediately. She made a mental note to see that he received a monetary bonus for preventing her from spending another moment with Elliot.

"Yes, Miss Alexa? Is there a problem?" Miguel asked.

"I have a headache."

Miguel's discreet glance indicated that he could see why that might happen, given the company she was keeping. "Shall I take you back to the Hamptons' now?"

"Please do." She stood and waited for Miguel to jockey the carriage beside Elliot's buggy so she could step easily across from one to the other.

After she listened to Elliot carry on about what a memorable evening it had been, she urged Miguel to rein toward Hampton Ranch.

"What the devil was that all about?" Miguel murmured confidentially.

Alexa pulled a face and whispered, "I was forced to accept his marriage proposal to shut him up."

"Congratulations. You're betrothed to a despicable sidewinder," he teased. "That should make you happy."

"Of course, what woman wouldn't want to wed a snake?"

Five minutes later, while they drove down the path, Alexa

reached beneath the carriage seat to retrieve her carpetbag then began rooting into it.

Miguel groaned in dismay. "Now who is coming out of hiding? Mr. Chester or the midnight rider?"

"Mr. Midnight," she replied. "Elliot has been keeping track of the time all evening. He has a meeting with either his informant or his harlot. I will be at his house to take advantage of his absence."

"Oh, no, you won't. Not if I have anything to say about it!"

Alexa and Miguel jumped simultaneously when a deep voice boomed like thunder in the darkness.

Chapter Eleven

"At long last," Miguel said, grinning. "The voice of reason."
He glanced at Alexa. "By the way, Coop told me last night
that he knows who Mr. Chester and Mr. Midnight really are."

Alexa glanced disparagingly at Coop. "That goes to show
how well you can keep a secret, doesn't it?"

He shrugged lackadaisically. "Since we're all on the same
side, what does it matter?"

"None, I suppose. And I guess I should inform you that I
was forced to take Kate into my confidence last night."

Miguel scowled. "If she becomes as daring and inquisitive
as you, I will never be able to stop worrying about her safety
and welfare."

"Then why don't you go check on her safety and welfare
right now," she suggested flippantly. "Coop and I will keep
surveillance on Elliot."

"*We* will?" Coop smirked. "There is no *we* in Cooper Investigations. It's just me. I thought I made myself clear on that
point last night."

Alexa bounded from the carriage with carpetbag in hand.
"No, you'll have to explain it to me again, after I change into

my disguise. If Elliot ventures out for the evening I intend to search his office for incriminating evidence."

"Damn it, Alexa—"

She ducked into the bushes before he could read her every line and paragraph in the riot act.

Coop blew out his breath and glanced at Miguel for support. But the Mexican shook his head and shrugged.

"You try being her conscience for a change, *gringo.* I'm going to check on Kate. Alexa corrupted her when they were roommates at boarding school in Albuquerque. Kate has a few adventurous tendencies herself and I don't want her involved in this fiasco."

A few minutes after Miguel drove off, Coop was still waiting for Alexa to change into her masculine disguise. "I'm considering leaving you afoot if you don't hurry up," he called out impatiently.

"Go ahead and leave me here," she called back, undaunted. "I'll swipe one of Elliot's horses from the stable after I sneak in the office window to check his financial ledgers."

"Last time you peeked into his office you nearly fell flat on your face," he reminded her as he mounted his horse.

"That didn't count. I was dressed in a cumbersome gown at the time." She stepped into view, garbed in form-fitting breeches and shirt that accentuated her alluring curves. "Now I'm appropriately dressed as Cooper Investigations's top-notch detective."

Coop ground his teeth. "*You* hired *me,* remember? Let me do my job."

She halted beside Bandit and stared up at him. "I also fired you, remember?"

He leaned out to grab her arm and hoist her up behind him. Then he twisted sideways to kiss her. He'd wanted to do that since he'd watched Elliot kiss her earlier and jealousy had taken a vicious bite out of him.

"What was that for?" she asked after he faced forward once again. "You have the darnedest way of ending an argument. And thank you. Short of eating dirt, I didn't know how to rid myself of Elliot's repulsive taste and scent."

Coop smiled as he trotted Bandit through Webster's pasture. It didn't dawn on him until a few minutes later that, instead of sending her packing, she had him doing her bidding. "You're too smart for your own good, woman," he muttered.

"Which should prove that I am good detective material." She slid her arms around his waist and trailed her hand provocatively over his belt. "You're lucky to have me."

Desire coursed through Coop and he made a mental note to pick up a white flag while he was in town. It looked as if he'd need one. Hell, he couldn't seem to say no to this adorable, but maddening, female—and make it stick.

"While I'm checking Elliot's financial ledgers you could follow him and see where he goes," Alexa suggested as she opened the garden gate then made a beeline toward the office window.

"I'm not leaving you here alone," Coop insisted sternly.

Alexa smiled to herself. She let him win this argument because she liked working with him. Besides, he was the expert in such matters and she wanted to learn what she could from him.

She gestured toward the elevated window that had given her fits during her previous surveillance. "Any suggestions?"

"Give me your foot and I'll boost you up."

She placed her foot in his cupped hands. He lifted her up so she could peek inside. "The coast is clear."

Coop heaved her up higher and she stood upside down on her hands momentarily before tucking and rolling across the carpet. When she opened the window wider, Coop's head and shoulders appeared. Then he thrust a leg over the sill and came agilely to his feet.

"I'll stand watch while you search the desk." Coop tiptoed back and forth between the window and door while she checked each drawer.

"Find anything interesting?" he asked a few minutes later.

"Two love notes from Lily," she reported. "Wait! Here's something curious…Norville Thomas…" She frowned pensively, trying to recall if she remembered the name from previous guest lists at dinner parties or from somewhere else. "The name sounds vaguely familiar but I can't put a face with it."

Alexa picked up the handgun in the top drawer, emptied out the bullets and tucked them in her pocket.

Coop smiled approvingly. "Good thinking. You do have a knack for detective work, after all."

Alexa wanted to hug the stuffing out of him for the compliment. At last, someone realized she had potential beyond making party arrangements and seating assignments.

Her thoughts trailed off when she found a note in the bottom right drawer. "Sure enough, Elliot is expecting a conference meeting at the line shack. Eleven o'clock."

"Which means he is probably enjoying Lily's company until his rendezvous," Coop predicted. "We should have enough time—"

His voice dried up when footsteps echoed through the foyer. Alexa and Coop dived to the floor behind the desk. A moment later, Oscar Denton's husky form filled the doorway. He scanned the dark room then lurched around to lumber down the hall.

"Let's go," Coop whispered in her ear.

"I'm not finished."

"You are for now." He surged to his feet, dragging her along with him. "I'll go out the window first, then I'll help you down."

Coop crawled silently through the opening. He hung by his fingers on the windowsill until he secured his feet on the stones protruding from the outer wall. Alexa glanced longingly toward the desk. She knew there was more to learn about Elliot's activities. If she could have gotten her hands on his ledgers, she might have discovered all sorts of interesting facts for the investigation.

"Come on," Coop demanded impatiently.

Alexa slung her leg over the window casing. Then she lowered the window to the same position she'd found it. She let go when she felt Coop's hand on her rump and the other one round her ankle. He carefully lowered her to the ground.

"Thank you for the help." She looped her arms around his broad shoulders and kissed him soundly.

"You're welcome." He grinned and kissed her back. Then he grabbed her hand and weaved around the shrubs and flowers to reach the garden gate.

This partnership was working splendidly, she mused. She had found her true calling and she had engaged in the kind of action and adventure she had craved. She wished this could be the beginning of her career in Cooper Investigations. But Coop insisted that he didn't want or need a partner. She would have to strike out on her own after she gained experience and guidance from her mentor. She glanced discreetly at Coop and smiled to herself. Unless she found a way to convince him that he needed her a lot more than he thought he did.

A half hour later, Coop tethered the two horses in a grove of trees near the line shack. He smiled reluctantly at Alexa who scurried ahead of him to find the perfect lookout position. He had never met a woman so anxious to involve herself in the danger and intrigue of investigation. Alexa didn't shy away from difficulty. What she lacked in experience she more than compensated for with intelligence, ingenuity and enthusiasm.

"When all is said and done, I hope your father appreciates your efforts," Coop remarked as he scanned the empty shack.

"I hope to make a good impression," she replied. "I want him to realize that I have useful skills and talents so I can begin a career in which I can make a positive difference in people's lives."

"Are you competing with a brother or sister for your father's approval?" he asked curiously.

Alexa shrugged nonchalantly. "Yes and no. When I was ten my mother took my younger sister, Bethany, and returned to Boston to live with my grandmother."

Coop frowned, bemused. "Why didn't your mother take you, too?"

He saw her stiffen, as if battling down long-held resentment. She didn't change facial expression, but he heard the emotion filtering into her voice. "Because she said I was my father's daughter and she'd had more than enough of both of us. She was tired of the lack of social opportunities in the West and of my father, who was making his way up the ranks of the railroad echelon at the time. We had to move from one new railhead to the next while he organized work crews, inspected construction sites and dealt with the legalities of land permits and right of ways."

She smiled fondly. "Bethany was only six the last time I saw her. She has my mother's dark eyes and dark hair. By now, at eighteen, I'm sure she is so attractive that she's the toast of the town, as my mother was before she married an upstart and went with him to connect one side of the nation to the other by rail." Her smile faded as she stared into the distance, as if gazing through a window to the past. "I haven't been allowed to see my sister in twelve years. Neither has my father."

Coop wondered if Alexa had battled feelings of rejection since her mother chose one daughter over the other. Most likely so. No doubt, Alexa had devoted herself to her father and attempted to prove her worth to the one parent who hadn't cast her aside because of her blond features and her strong-willed personality.

"Since we are trading dark secrets, while keeping surveillance, tell me what made you the man you are," she suggested. "What of your family? Brothers or sisters somewhere? Where are your parents?"

Coop rarely spoke of his past. He had put it behind him long ago. "There's not much to tell."

"Come on," she insisted, giving him a nudge with her elbow. "We're partners now and—"

"We are not..." His voice fizzled out when he noted the look of rejection on her bewitching features. Considering her mother's abandonment, he didn't have the heart to protest too long or too loudly. "Okay. Partners...temporarily. For this one case," he stipulated. "But don't start making plans to have your name printed on my office door in Albuquerque."

She threw her arms around his neck and nearly squeezed him in two. "Thank you, Coop. I know I have a lot to learn but I'm eager for you to teach me what I need to know so I can become a good detective." She stepped back a pace, still grinning from ear to ear. "Now tell me about your family. Please? I'd really like to know."

Coop found himself staring off into the darkness, too, fighting emotions that he swore were buried and forgotten a lifetime ago. "My mother died of complications two weeks after giving birth to my younger brother, Phillip. My father owned a small farm in Kansas. He stayed busy working the land and planting crops. It was my job to do the domestic chores, tend to our livestock and watch over my brother."

He felt the tension rising inside him, as if it had been months rather than years since disaster struck and tore his world apart. "I was fourteen when confederate raiders descended on our farm to take what little food and livestock we had. They shot my father, even when he made no attempt to resist them."

"Oh, Coop, I'm so sorry for your loss," Alexa murmured as her fingertips glided comfortingly around his clenched fist.

"Phillip panicked. Before I could grab hold of him, he dashed from the cabin, yelling and screaming my father's name. They killed him, too."

She sidled closer, as if to bear the burden of pain and anger he'd carried with him for almost two decades. There had been no one to turn to. Now he found solace in Alexa's strength and presence. He wrapped his arms around her and confided things that he had never told another living soul.

"I made a solemn pact that day while I buried my father, brother and staked a grave for myself beside them. I promised a reckoning for those cutthroats who murdered and raided," he gritted out. He looked down at her grimly, knowing he was about to invite her disgust and disapproval, because she would know what kind of man he'd become that fateful day.

"I learned to handle a knife, pistol and rifle and I practiced faithfully every spare moment. I went after the four men who were responsible for taking my family away from me. For three years I followed in their wake of death and destruction through Missouri, Arkansas and finally to their hideout in Indian Territory. By then I had learned to survive efficiently in the wilderness. I had become exceptionally skilled with weapons and I learned to track and hunt like an Indian warrior."

He stared bleakly at Alexa and said, "My father and brother weren't the raiders' only victims. There were eight others. Two of them were young women who were held captive for the men's pleasures before being disregarded heartlessly.

"It was deep in the Ouachita Mountains that I picked off the raiders one by one. I made certain none of those ruthless bastards survived to rape, murder and steal again. Then I took another name and began a new life as a peace officer, a deputy U.S. Marshal, a bounty hunter, a gunfighter and a detective."

Coop expected Alexa to withdraw from him after he confided that he had blood on his hands and had resorted to vigilante justice to avenge his family and the other innocent victims.

Instead she lifted her hand to limn the taut features of his face, as if to soothe away the guilt and resentment that still tormented him, despite his best efforts to leave it behind in his previous life.

"I wish I could have been there so you didn't have to suffer through that awful tragedy alone. My heart goes out to that young boy who had to become a man long before his time—"

Her voice evaporated when the sound of an approaching rider caught their attention. "There's definitely something familiar about this man, but he isn't dressed right," she murmured.

He frowned, bemused. "What the devil does that mean?"

"Just that his bulky jacket, tattered breeches and shiny boots don't strike me as his usual attire. But this must be Norville Thomas. Curse it! I wish I could recall where I've seen him."

"He looks vaguely familiar to me, too," Coop whispered. "But how and when did we both see him, other than while you were disguised as the midnight rider, keeping watch at this shack?"

Coop scowled when Alexa tried to sneak up to the window after Norville Thomas scurried inside. He grabbed her arm and directed her attention to the second rider who raced toward the shack. "Rule Number One," he stated. "Have patience. No sense getting yourself shot or captured if you can avoid it."

She nodded and smiled. "Good advice. It's just that I'm so

anxious to find out who betrayed my father that I'm champing at the bit."

Coop didn't bother to mention to her that, if she hadn't been with him tonight, he'd have been lying in wait for Norville Thomas—or whoever he was—inside the shack so he could take Webster by surprise, too. Coop wasn't afraid of trouble and danger because they were commonplace in his life. But he didn't want his overanxious, inexperienced protégé injured.

"That is definitely Elliot," Alexa murmured as she monitored his staggering stroll to the cabin. "I'll sneak up to the window so I can overhear—"

"I'll go," he cut in.

She stared him down. "Not without me, you won't."

"Are you always this stubborn?" he ground out.

"No, I'm usually worse. You caught me on a good night."

Coop swallowed several pithy curses when Alexa darted ahead of him, hiding inconspicuously behind one tree and then another to reach the window. With both pistols drawn—just in case trouble erupted—Coop followed her silently.

"Winning Harold Quinn's loyalty is going to cost you," Norville said to Elliot.

"Hell, it has cost me plenty already," Elliot mumbled begrudgingly. "But now that his daughter has agreed to marry me I'll be in a solid position to get the government contract."

Alexa felt Coop's intense gaze boring into her when he overheard Elliot's comment. Since this wasn't the time or place to explain why she'd had to say yes to the betrothal, she simply leaned over to place a kiss on his cheek.

She wanted to surge to her feet so she could peek directly into the window and identify Elliot's cohort. However, as Coop said, a good detective had to be patient and cautious. Those two traits didn't come naturally for Alexa. Giving her presence away right now would prompt Elliot to change his habit of making contact with his cohort at the line shack and complicate the investigation. Her only recourse was to eavesdrop.

"Harold Quinn has called another meeting for the end of this week," Norville reported. "By then he will know of your betrothal and that should be the end of your problems. Your neighbors will be turned down for the military contracts again and you'll be secure for another year."

"I still plan to discredit my neighbors and rebuild my mercantile business. If I can coerce my new bride into giving financial backing I might even run for public office so I can make my own arrangements."

When Coop glanced at her again, she shrugged indifferently. She had already told him that she understood why men like Elliot Webster pursued her. If Coop thought the comment hurt her feelings, he was mistaken. She was accustomed to being used and she was very aware of the tactic.

"I'll need my expense fee right now," Norville prompted Elliot. "Riding the rails back and forth to Santa Fe so often is costly. Not to mention that the trips are taking considerable time away from my usual duties."

What usual duties? Alexa wondered. Who the devil was this man? Again, the urge to bolt to her feet for a closer look nearly overwhelmed her. Coop must have sensed her eagerness for he clamped his hand around her elbow, in case she gave way to temptation.

"Fine, here's your money. By the end of the week, when my plans fall neatly into place, you can go back to your usual duties."

"I'm looking forward to that," Norville remarked. "My lucrative side business is suffering because of this extra traveling."

What lucrative side business? Alexa wondered. She was more confused and frustrated than ever by her inability to place Norville Thomas—if that was his real name. Or maybe it was an alias he gave to Elliot.

When Coop tapped her on the shoulder, silently ordering her to skulk away from the window before the men exited, she went reluctantly. Barely a minute later, Norville Thomas strode outside, looked this way and that, and then walked swiftly toward his horse. Alexa paid particular attention to the mount, wondering if Norville had rented the horse in town or from one of the nearby stage stops between Questa Springs and Socorro. If Norville stayed the night at one of the local hotels, she intended to find out which one then follow him.

After Elliot exited and rode toward his ranch, Alexa mounted her horse then reined toward town.

"Where do you think you're going?" Coop demanded as he hitched his thumb over his shoulder. "Hampton Ranch is the opposite direction."

"I'm following a hunch," she said as she trotted off.

"You aren't experienced enough as a detective to have hunches yet," Coop said caustically.

"Then call it women's intuition."

She heard him sigh—loudly—indicating that he wasn't pleased with her plans. "Look, Alexa, I appreciate your enthusiasm and dedication in this case, but it's nearly midnight."

"A detective's work is never done," she declared.

"Who the hell told you that?"

She grinned at his exasperated scowl. "No one. It's my new motto."

Although Coop muttered and grumbled, he kept pace beside her. Together they remained a safe distance behind Norville Thomas so he wouldn't know he was being followed. A quarter of an hour later, Alexa was surprised to see that Norville veered around to the back of Lily's Pleasure Resort.

Lily's… The name whispered through her mind as it

had several times the past two weeks. She kept trying to attach some significance to the concubine but she kept drawing a blank.

"That must be where I saw him," Coop said. "I saw a man enter the back door shortly after Lily returned from Webster's ranch last week."

The elusive thought that niggled Alexa's brain tormented her again but she couldn't put her finger on exactly what disturbed her. "There must be a connection here," she mused aloud.

"Either that or our friend Norville Thomas has a penchant for one of the ladies, as does your *fiancé*. Congratulations, by the way," he added mockingly.

"You sound like Miguel. He already teased me unmercifully because I had to agree to a betrothal so Elliot wouldn't resort to another method to gain my father's favor." She twisted in the saddle to stare at Coop in the scant moonlight. "If you don't know me well enough to realize that I'd rather suffer the ten plagues of Egypt than wed a man like Elliot then you don't know me at all."

"Now that you mention it, princess, I know you exceptionally well."

When a rakish grin spread across his sensuous lips, a warm tingle skittered down her spine. Mercy, why did this one man have the power to affect her so intensely?

"There you go then," she murmured.

"You must have good reason for accepting Webster's proposal, I suppose."

"Excellent reason," she declared. "I'm stringing along that devious scoundrel until you can arrest him for fraud and whatever else you can pin on him that will keep him in the penitentiary for years to come."

"It will be my pleasure," he assured her.

"Then trot into Lily's Pleasure Resort and get a closer look at the man we think is Norville Thomas," she requested. "I'd do it myself, but that would look highly suspicious."

Pleasure Resort... Alexa frowned pensively. Something about that name struck a hazy cord of memory, just as Norville Thomas's silhouette did. She knew she was overlooking something important, but confound it, she didn't know what it was and it was driving her crazy!

"If I walk into Lily's place I'll have to select a harlot to escort upstairs or *I'll* look suspicious," Coop reminded her. "Would that bother you?"

She inwardly winced. If she said yes, she would imply that she wanted exclusive rights to Coop. If she said no, it would imply that her liaison with him was purely physical. And that was a bald-face lie, unfortunately.

"Well?" he prodded.

Alexa blew out her breath. "I don't want you to be with anyone else while we're working this case together."

"Fine, if it makes you uncomfortable then I won't. But you need to know that I'm not entirely happy with your betrothal and whatever display of affection you feel is necessary to bestow on Webster for a convincing charade."

And so, without offering a binding verbal commitment that made either of them vulnerable they agreed to temporary exclusivity. For some reason Alexa found their pact reassuring. Day by day, she was learning that she could trust and depend on Coop. That was a comforting realization because she didn't feel that way about any other men except her father and Miguel. For entirely different reasons, of course.

"I think we've had a productive night so we can conclude our surveillance," Coop said, breaking into her thoughts. "I'll check the livery in the morning to see if Norville's sorrel mare is stabled there."

"I'll check the pen behind the brothel on my way into town

tomorrow morning. Elliot insists that I take a room at the hotel, because of his ongoing feud with Percy Hampton."

"Webster mentioned that to me this afternoon, but I'm not sure that's a good idea," Coop replied.

She arched a challenging brow. "Why? Are you afraid to allow me to take a room at your hotel? Too close for comfort?"

"Too close for temptation," he clarified as he reined north. "I'll escort you to the ranch before I head into town."

"That isn't necessary. I'll be fine," she insisted.

"Of course you will," he agreed, though he continued to ride alongside her. "But since we're partners…temporarily…I have your back."

She shot him a disgruntled glance. "You're using that against me," she accused. "You sneaky rascal."

She saw his white teeth flash in the moonlight and decided she felt anything but offended by Coop's protective company. No doubt about it, she was going to miss him like nobody's business when he concluded this case and he went his own way.

Chapter Twelve

"I don't care what that damn Elliot Webster says about anything," Kate muttered resentfully the next morning. "I'd feel better if you remained at our ranch instead of taking a room at the hotel."

"You have to admit that we can cover more bases if we spread out," Alexa said reasonably, as she folded her clothes then placed them in her trunk. "You can keep an eye on what's going on beyond your fences and you can protect your livestock. In the meantime, I can monitor Elliot's activities and that of his cohort's without having to explain coming and going from here. I'll have Miguel assist you whenever possible."

She watched Kate spin around to fidget with the garments Alexa had neatly packed. "Something wrong?" As if she didn't know.

"Nothing," Kate said all too quickly, and without glancing in her general direction.

Alexa let the matter drop, but she had the inescapable feeling that Kate and Miguel had failed the same test of temptation that Alexa had failed with Coop.

After breakfast, Alexa and Miguel loaded the luggage in the

carriage and left the ranch. Her suspicions about her best friends' involvement were further confirmed when Miguel kept silent—a rare occasion—during the jaunt to town. Alexa left him to his thoughts while she made a mental list of tasks she wanted to accomplish that day. She had to compose a telegram to her father—not the one Elliot expected, but a discreet contact to assure him that Elliot would be arrested inevitably and that Hampton and Barrett were good candidates for the government contracts. Then she had to figure out how to keep Selma Mae Fredericks occupied to earn her salary. Alexa also wanted to work in a short nap so she would be alert this evening while she kept surveillance on Elliot, Lily and Norville.

"As soon as we return to Santa Fe I am resigning from my job," Miguel announced out of the blue.

Alexa's jaw dropped open and she gaped at him, bewildered. "Good Lord, why? How will I function without you? Surely I'm not *that* difficult to chaperone and escort, despite your mumbling and grumbling…am I? Papa pays you well and I will be only too happy to supplement your salary if—"

Miguel waved her to silence as he drove toward the edge of town. "I've complicated Kate's life, not to mention my own," he said grimly. "The best course of action for me, and everyone concerned, is to leave the territory."

"You are overreacting," Alexa insisted.

He stared at her, his dark eyes tormented. "You have no idea what I'm reacting or overreacting to."

She scoffed at him. "Give me a little credit, Miggy. I'm not entirely stupid. In addition, your place is in this territory. Your brothers and their families are in Santa Fe and Albuquerque. Besides, Kate is here."

"That is the problem," he burst out. "*¡Caramba!* What have I done?"

"It's not the end of the world," she reassured him.

"No?" His black brows swooped down into a self-deprecating frown. "I should be shoved in front of a firing squad and shot."

"Right. We should all shoot each other for our lack of self-restraint. That will make everything better." She smirked.

Miguel jerked to attention. "You and Coop? Hell and damnation!" he exploded.

"Calm down," she insisted. "It was my doing."

"Your father will not approve, just as Percy Hampton won't. *Gringo* and I are from a different class of people. Now I will have to shoot him and, damn it, I like him!"

"I like him, too, so shooting him is out of the question."

Alexa glanced sideways, noting they had reached the red light district. She gestured for Miguel to veer east so she could inspect the corral. The sorrel Norville Thomas rode the previous night was not penned up with the other horses. She wondered if he had stayed in town and stabled his mount at the livery. If so, where had Norville taken a room? Or was he on his way back to Socorro to catch a stage that took him to Albuquerque to ride the rails to Santa Fe.

Miguel set aside his misery momentarily and asked, "What are we looking for?"

"The horse used by Elliot's contact, the man who met him again at the line shack last night," she explained. "I haven't gotten get a clear look at him yet, but his name is vaguely familiar. Norville Thomas. Does that ring any bells with you?"

Miguel became pensive then shook his head. "I'm afraid not. But then lowly servants don't travel in your social circle."

Alexa rolled her eyes in annoyance. "Stop feeling sorry for yourself. Honestly, I think I liked you better when you were my worrywart of a conscience."

"You should have been my nagging conscience when I needed one desperately," he sulked.

Alexa demanded his full attention by shaking her finger in his face. "Do you love her or not? I mean really love her. Or did you take advantage of her weakness for you?"

When Miguel puffed up like an offended toad Alexa had to bite her tongue to prevent laughing at his expression.

"I would never—" he tried to protest.

She waved him to silence and gestured toward Walker Hotel, urging him down the street. "Stop beating yourself black and blue, Miggy. Kate is a grown woman with a mind of her own, as I am. You can sort this out after we solve this case. Right now, you aren't going in front of a firing squad and we need to rent rooms. By the way, I volunteered you to escort Kate at night. She will be keeping surveillance on Elliot's cowhands to ensure they don't plant evidence of stolen cattle again."

"Escort her?" he crowed. "That's what got us into—"

"Shh-shh-shh!" Alexa gave his arm a shake. "We don't need to attract attention."

He clamped his mouth shut and drove to the hotel.

"Bring in the luggage, please," she requested. "I'll rent our rooms."

"Make sure mine is on the third floor so I can throw myself out the window," he mumbled.

Alexa cast him a withering glance then alighted from the buggy without his assistance. She could see that Miguel wasn't going to be a bit of help until he came to terms with his affection for Kate.

Good thing Alexa and Coop didn't have that problem, she mused. They were only working together and enjoying a few temporary benefits—or so she tried to tell herself.

Alexa composed her carefully worded telegram to her father then stepped onto the boardwalk. Elliot was there to follow her around the corner of the town square to make sure she contacted her father.

That was another of Elliot's personality flaws that annoyed her. He was so determined to manipulate her into marriage that he relentlessly dogged her steps to the telegraph office.

"It shouldn't be long now, my dear," Elliot said confidently as he strutted alongside her. "We can plan our town-wide celebration for this weekend."

"That is much too soon," she insisted authoritatively. "Trust me, I have scheduled functions and activities for years. I will need more than a week to make all the necessary arrangements." She opened the door then turned back to Elliot. "I will be back outside shortly."

When she exited the telegraph office a few minutes later, she spotted Selma Mae walking toward Miguel, who waited in front of the hotel. "Yoo-hoo!" she called out.

When she waved her arms in expansive gestures, Selma Mae spun toward her. The older woman smiled in welcome, but her expression sobered when she noticed Elliot.

"We'll serve free food at our soiree," Alexa told Elliot, after noting Selma Mae's lukewarm reaction.

"I'm not sure the extra expense will be necessary," Elliot remarked.

"Of course it is," she enthused. "If you want to acquire friends and customers you must feed them." Especially in Elliot's case. He wasn't a popular personality in town.

Alexa more or less dismissed Elliot in favor of speaking to Selma Mae. After he swaggered back to his store, Alexa explained Selma Mae's new tasks. The older woman pulled a face.

"Writing invitations for a celebration to announce your betrothal to Webster might be better suited to someone else," she said in her thick Swedish accent. "Begging your pardon, missy, but you know I have no regard for that man. You can do so much better."

"Nevertheless I am placing you in charge of speaking to the newspaper office about printing invitations."

It was at that exact moment that Coop ambled from the café. Instant longing hit Alexa like a blow to the chest. Every time she stared into those vivid green eyes and that suntanned face, her heart flip-flopped.

This isn't fair, she mused irritably. She had come here to help her father and to prove her worth. Nevertheless, the sight of this ruggedly handsome, raven-haired gunfighter never failed to distract her.

"Missy?" Selma Mae gave her a nudge to gain her attention.

Alexa dragged her gaze from Coop. "Yes?"

"I asked if you had set a date for this celebration."

After Coop limped past her with barely more than a nod of recognition, as was expected of him, Alexa managed to turn her attention to Selma Mae. "It will be a week from Saturday. We can cater food from all the restaurants, so as not to offend anyone."

"Clever," said Selma Mae, smiling reluctantly.

"We'll need the marshal's permission to cordon off the street around the town square for dining and dancing. I'll check on that before you order the invitations. We'll need musicians, too."

"There are two bands who play for holiday celebrations," Selma informed her.

"Then we'll hire both of them and they can perform on opposite corners of the square."

Selma Mae smiled approvingly. "You are very good at this, missy. I can't imagine what you have forgotten."

"Tables and benches," Alexa told her. "I'll have Miguel purchase planks and sawhorses from the lumberyard. We must contact the bakery to make several cakes and pies. The local saloons can provide wine."

"My goodness, so much to do." Selma Mae blinked, clearly overwhelmed.

Alexa patted her arm as they walked down the street. "No need to fret. We have several days. I'll check with Marshal Henson for permission to hold the party then visit the restaurant owners while you order the invitations and contact the musicians."

As Selma Mae marched off, taking her duties quite seriously, Alexa smiled impishly. If her luck held, this town-wide celebration would take place at Elliot's financial expense and he would view it from *inside* a jail cell.

This was the first party in years that Alexa actually looked forward to organizing.

Alexa found Marshal Henson at his desk shuffling papers. He smiled cordially when she swept into his office.

"How may I help you, Miss Quinn?" Gil asked as he rose respectfully to his feet.

"I'm here to ask permission to seal off the street around the town square for a city-wide celebration set for a week from this Saturday," she requested of the golden-eyed peace officer whose reddish-blond mane was sorely in need of clipping.

Gil was a rugged-looking man who reminded her of Coop. No doubt, they had battled the elements in the wilderness as often as they had clashed with thieves and cutthroats.

He grinned wryly and crow's-feet crinkled the corners of his eyes. "Why? So you can step into the crossfire during another explosive feud?" He gestured toward the empty chair then took his seat behind the desk. "I hope you realize that you took a terrible risk during the confrontation at Hampton's ranch."

Alexa fluffed her dress and pretended to flick at a piece of lint on her puffy sleeve. "I couldn't let Elliot and Percy shoot each other over a few silly cattle, now could I? Besides, it was all so dramatic and exciting that I couldn't help leaping into the fracas. It is one of my worst faults, you see."

Gil leaned back in his chair, steepled his fingers and regarded her thoughtfully. Alexa mustered her most charming smile and flicked her wrist to dismiss whatever thought Gil was mulling over.

"The thing is, Elliot and I want to invite the entire town to dine and dance the night away in celebration of our betrothal."

His expression fell like a rockslide, indicating that he wasn't pleased by the news, either. "Are you sure you wanna do that, ma'am?"

"Have a party? Why, of course. I live for parties, you know."

"No, I'm referring to the betrothal," he clarified. "I don't want to see you hurt unnecessarily. Maybe it's not my place to tell you, but someone needs to. Webster's reputation in town isn't as good as he probably led you to believe. Also, he pays regular visits to the district north of town. In case you haven't heard, Elliot is very friendly with Lily, the tainted flower, who runs one of the houses of ill repute. She and her two sisters own establishments in the territory and they do a thriving business." He stared meaningfully at her. "I wouldn't hold high expectations of fidelity for Webster if I were you."

She arched a challenging brow. "Why, Mr. Henson, I was not aware that you moonlighted as a marriage consultant. Or is this one of your duties as a law officer? Is this an ordinance that applies exclusively to Questa Springs or the entire county?"

Gil chuckled and shook his shaggy head. "Are all debutantes as witty and clever as you? Or are you the exception?"

"I have no idea what you mean." She gave him her best impression of a dense stare. "But I would like permission to host a party at Elliot's expense. May I go ahead with my plans?"

He perked up immediately. "Webster is footing the bill, you say?"

"Right down to the last penny," she assured him.

"All right, then. It's your life and your engagement. I suppose I should congratulate you on your upcoming wedding."

"It would be the polite thing to. It's much better than lecturing me on my choice of a husband." She surged to her feet. "But I forgive you. And you are personally invited to attend the celebration."

"I'll be there with bells on," Gil said.

Alexa glanced over her shoulder to appraise the marshal. She had the inescapable feeling that she had exposed her true personality to him one time too many since her arrival in town. He had been on hand when she clashed with Harlan Fredericks and then he had escorted her through town when she checked on Selma Mae after she'd missed work. In addition, he had seen her thrust herself between two feuding ranchers to stop a senseless range war.

Halting at the door, Alexa pivoted to face Gil directly. He seemed an honest sort and Coop was certain that his former associate and friend wasn't on Elliot's payroll. "In case things go badly at some point in the near future, I ask that you avenge me, Gil Henson. I would be honored to call you friend."

His thick brows rose to his hairline. "Ma'am?"

Alexa grinned wryly. "Don't play stupid with me, either. I'll see you at the party with your bells on."

When Gil chuckled in amusement, Alexa spun to exit. The door opened unexpectedly, jerking the knob from her grasp. She glanced up to see a military officer poised in front of her. While he looked her up and down, she did a quick appraisal of his crisp-looking uniform, his sheathed sword, pistol and polished boots.

"Excuse me, miss." The officer dropped into an exaggerated bow. "May I accompany you to your next destination?"

"No need, sir," she said, flashing the coy smile men expected from her. "But thank you for your kind offer."

"Miss Alexa Quinn, may I introduce Lieutenant Arnold Gunther from nearby Fort Stanton. I contacted him after the clash between Webster and Hampton…just in case more trouble arises."

"It is my pleasure to meet you, Miss Quinn," the tall, trim lieutenant murmured as he doubled at the waist to brush a kiss over her fingertips. "I was unaware that we had such a lovely addition to this community."

Alexa tired of his fawning flattery immediately. He reminded her of the men she knew in Santa Fe. She frowned when she noticed his shiny boots for the second time. They had been polished until they glistened. She wondered what other fetish plagued the officer, besides a preoccupation with his footwear.

"Please excuse me, gentlemen. I have several errands to attend," she said, withdrawing her hand from Gunther's clinging grasp. "Good day."

And off she went, leaving Gil with the self-important military officer who could have been Elliot's brother, for all his airs and posturing. The encounter made her appreciate men like Coop and Gil even more. There was never any pretense with Coop. Well, except for the fact that Coop had taken a new name and made a new life for himself after vindicating his family and other hapless murder victims.

But that didn't count, she thought dismissively. Even if Coop was an avenging angel with one wing in the fire, at least he treated her like an individual who had a brain in her head, not like a trophy to present to the world. Lieutenant Gunther was a reminder of what she had to look forward to when she returned home to Santa Fe.

The thought nearly soured her reasonably good mood.

* * *

Harold Quinn stepped onto the street in Santa Fe then discreetly checked his clothing to make sure he was buttoned properly. Since Ambrose and Ben had invited him to the Pleasure Palace previously this week, he had visited the establishment again. He had definitely taken advantage of Alexa's absence.

The thought of his absent daughter put a fretful frown on his face. He strode off to the buggy he'd parked a good distance from the bordello. He'd hoped to hear from Alexa by now. The scheduled meeting was four days away and he needed justifiable reason for canceling the contract with Webster.

"Hello there, Harold, I wasn't expecting to see you out and about tonight."

Harold glanced up when he recognized Ambrose Shelton's voice. Although he felt a mite self-conscious about being seen by one of his constituents, when exiting the brothel, Harold nodded a greeting.

Ambrose climbed down from the carriage then glanced speculatively toward the establishment down the street. He cracked the semblance of a smile. "I assume you just left the place where I'm going."

Harold shifted awkwardly. "Er…yes. With Lexi away from home I have spare time on my hands and I've grown… um…lonesome."

"Ah, yes, speaking of your daughter." Ambrose dug into his coat pocket. "Here it is."

Harold frowned warily when Ambrose produced a telegram.

"I was at the telegraph office sending a missive before supper and this one arrived for you," he explained. "I told the agent I'd deliver it to you. I was planning to drop it off after I paid a visit to my friend down the street."

Unease settled over Harold as he accepted the missive that

Ambrose *just so happened* to intercept when he *just so happened* to be in the telegraph office. Now Ambrose was on his way to the Pleasure Palace. It was almost as if his associate had been monitoring his activities and knew where he'd be. He wondered if the man had also read the telegram before passing it on.

"Thank you, Ambrose."

"Think nothing of it."

Harold thought *a lot* of it. Surely this wasn't a coincidence. There was an unidentified informant among his trusted colleagues and now Ambrose was the most likely candidate.

Harold waited until Ambrose waddled off before he climbed into his buggy. He watched his associate veer into the upscale bordello where lights beamed like beacons in the night. He wondered if Ambrose, a sworn bachelor, was a regular customer who preferred one female in particular or if he made the rounds to visit all the ladies of the evening.

Discarding the curious thought, Harold grabbed the reins and trotted the buggy home so he could read the telegram in private. A quarter of an hour later, while ensconced in his favorite chair in the parlor, he opened the missive that read:

> Having a grand time. A productive one, too. You must give high praise to both the Hamptons and Barretts. Webster proposed but he won't have much time for courting by week's end. Miss you, Lexi.

Harold sank back in his chair to read between the lines. Obviously, Alexa had gathered evidence that suggested Webster had indeed conspired with someone to gather privileged information. Furthermore, she recommended that he grant the contract to both neighboring ranchers. Although Harold had hoped to offer concrete evidence at the meeting, Alexa implied that the hired detective had enough evidence to charge Webster of wrongdoing.

He expelled a sigh of relief then sipped his drink. Alexa was all right so he could stop fretting about her. She would return early next week and his household would be back to normal. Of course, he would have to find Lexi another challenge to occupy her time. She'd suffered growing pains and he'd been too busy to notice that his spirited daughter needed more excitement in her life than he'd previously supplied.

"I'll figure all that out later," he said before he swallowed his nightcap. He'd eased his needs and he'd heard encouraging news from his daughter. Now he could rest easy.

Content for the first time in days, Harold strode off to bed.

The next evening Coop returned from the livery, wondering what had become of Norville Thomas's horse. The man and his sorrel mare had vanished without a trace, much to Coop's chagrin.

Halting on the boardwalk, Coop held his timepiece up to the streetlight to see it clearly. It was half past eleven. While scouting the area earlier, he'd seen Miguel and Kate on horseback, checking for small campfires that indicated illegal cattle branding. The fact that Miguel had left Alexa to her own devices worried him. She had a history of striking off on her own without Miguel to discourage her from her daring misadventures.

Coop entered the hotel and nodded a silent greeting to the clerk. His first stop was Alexa's room, which was on the opposite end of the hall. He didn't expect her to answer his knock because he figured she was in disguise, tracking her *fiancé*. Coop didn't know why that rankled so much but it did. She assured him that she had no interest in Webster. And certainly, he and Alexa had no future. Not with his checkered background and her elevated social status. But still…

His troubled thoughts trailed off when she opened the door and he saw her dressed in her frilly cream-colored robe and nightgown. Desire hit him like a freight train. He had to brace a hand on the doorjamb to steady himself against the onslaught of fierce attraction.

"Did you find Norville and his sorrel?" she asked.

"No, they're gone with the wind," he said, distracted.

"Is there another problem for us to resolve tonight?" she questioned as she grasped his arm and towed him inside her room.

"Absolutely."

"What is it?" she asked anxiously.

"It's *you*, princess."

Coop did what came naturally when he was within kissing distance of this alluring female. He swept her off her feet and claimed her lips—until he was forced to come up for air.

"You've become a problem yourself," she rasped as she locked her fingers around his neck and leaned familiarly against him. "How am I to keep my mind on this investigation when I can't see past you?"

"I'm glad I'm not the only one," he murmured as he caressed her hip and trim waist. "I'm not used to this kind of distraction."

"Neither am I."

Coop was needy as hell, and she looked so tempting and inviting that he couldn't think past his compulsive desire for her. "You are fast becoming an obsession to me, princess," he confided between kisses.

"I thought I asked you not to call me that," she said as she tugged impatiently at the buttons on his shirt.

"It serves to remind me that we hail from entirely different backgrounds. But right now, I can't remember anything except how much I want you. Hell, I can't even remember when I *didn't* want you...."

Chapter Thirteen

Suddenly Coop was kissing her again, and without one ounce of reserve. He tried to make himself slow down and be gentle. It was a wasted thought because Alexa seemed to be as hungry for him as he was for her. With a groan of defeat, he accepted his maddening obsession for her and reminded himself that even Napoleon had his Waterloo.

This woman was Coop's downfall. It was as simple and as disturbing as that.

He glided his hand over her thigh, tunneling beneath her robe and nightgown so he could touch her intimately. He found her warm and responsive and that knowledge turned him hard and aching in the batting of an eye. When she reached down to free him from the placket of his breeches, he struggled to draw breath. Desire was eating him alive.

"I've never wanted anything the way I want you," she admitted raggedly.

"Same goes for me," he replied hoarsely as he backed her against the wall and guided her legs around his hips. "Damn, Alexa, you deserve better than this, but I've been having this fantasy—"

When she arched upward, her hand closed around his throbbing shaft. Coop lost the ability to speak. He felt the warmth of her body encompass him as he surged helplessly toward her. He looked into her enchanting face and felt that uncontrollable wave of fiery emotion flood through him—as it always did when he was one with her. He moved instinctively against her, setting an erotic cadence. He watched her vivid blue eyes glitter as desire overtook her at the same instant that it seized him. He clamped his hands on her hips, loving the feel of her satiny skin beneath his hands, savoring the intimacy of being buried deep inside her as they moved in perfect rhythm.

His pleasure intensified when she cupped his face in her hands and kissed him thoroughly, ravenously. He heard her breath catch as he plunged deeply inside her, burying himself to the hilt. Then he withdrew to plunge again and again.

He swore he was no more than a shell of flesh that housed seething need. For the first time in his life, he understood what it meant to be on fire for a woman, understood mindless desperation. He savored the feel of the passionate tremors that rippled through Alexa then vibrated through him. The incredible sensations left not one part of his body, mind and soul untouched and unaffected.

"Sweet mercy…" Coop gasped when indescribable rapture pulsated through him repeatedly and with devastating force.

He braced one forearm on the wall for support before his knees buckled and left them both in an entangled heap on the floor. He held Alexa tightly in one arm while shudder after uncontrollable shudder bombarded him. When she laid her cheek against his laboring chest and murmured his name, contentment stole over him. Coop sighed, closed his eyes and cherished the incredible moment.

When Alexa lifted her blond head a few moments later then

unhooked her legs from around his hips, the thought of how he had taken her in such a heated rush shamed him. Fantasy or not, he should have given more than he'd taken.

"I'm sorry. That was—"

He tried to apologize but she laid her forefinger to his lips to silence him. "It was good...for starters." An impish smile tripped across her kiss-swollen lips. "Spend the night with me, Coop. I want to know what it's like to have you in my bed, to lie in your arms until dawn."

Coop peeled off his gaping vest and shirt and tossed them aside. Then he thought of Miguel's overprotective feelings for Alexa and decided to barricade the door for absolute privacy.

"Did you follow Webster tonight?" he asked as he heel-and-toed out of his boots.

"Yes, but he remained at home so I couldn't search his office," she said, disappointed.

"Don't try that alone," he advised. "I shudder to think what might happen if Webster or Denton catches you red-handed and retaliates."

"There are answers in those ledgers," Alexa replied as she stretched out on the bed. "I'm itching to get my hands on them."

He smiled roguishly as he doffed his breeches. "You'll have to settle for getting your hands on me tonight, princess."

The playful *purr* that tumbled from her lips before she snuffed the lantern indicated that she wasn't all that disappointed with the change in her evening plans.

"I could get used to this," she murmured as she cuddled beside him.

"So could I." Which would make leaving her behind when he took a new assignment even more difficult, he thought to himself. "I've never spent the entire night with a woman," he confided before he dropped a kiss to her dewy-soft mouth.

"Truly?" she asked.

"You're the first." And probably the last, considering his tumbleweed lifestyle. Not to mention that she meant entirely too much to him. All other women would become substitutes for the one he really wanted.

"I'll cherish the exclusive privilege forever."

Her hand brushed over his chest and then descended across his belly. Coop was pretty sure he wasn't going to get much sleep during the night.

Sure enough, his prediction proved correct. But he didn't voice a single word of complaint.

Alexa spent the next day with a smile on her lips. Her unexpected late-night tryst with Coop kept popping to mind at irregular intervals. She wondered what it would be like to wake up beside him for the rest of her life.

The voice of reason kept shouting that wasn't going to happen. Coop didn't want or need a permanent arrangement to complicate his life. Neither did she. Her parents' inability to get along for an extended period of time had cured her romantic tendencies years earlier.

"Pay attention to business," she muttered at herself as she watched Elliot hike down the street to the bordello, after he had dropped her from their late supper.

Alexa wheeled around to hurry upstairs so she could change into her dark breeches and shirt. She was definitely going to take advantage of Elliot's liaison this evening. Despite Coop's warnings, Alexa intended to take a good look at Elliot's financial ledgers. Her father's meeting was coming up in two days. She needed tangible proof of Elliot's unethical dealings so her father could award a contract to other ranchers.

Dressed in black, a cap pulled low on her forehead, Alexa used the servants' exit to descend to the alley. She had secured a horse that afternoon and the bay gelding was more than ready to stretch its legs after being tethered for a few hours. She gave the gelding its head as she cantered from town.

Anticipation surged through her as she dismounted in the clump of trees near Elliot's house. She stared at the darkened window of the office then noticed Oscar Denton who was leaning negligently against the porch railing. A few cowboys milled around the bunkhouse that sat near the barn. Laughter and guffaws wafted in the evening breeze.

While the hired hands entertained themselves for the evening, Alexa scurried toward the garden gate. Scaling the outer wall to crawl in the window took more effort than it had when Coop had been there to give her a boost. Yet, within a few minutes, Alexa was inside the office, tiptoeing to the desk.

If she thought she could get away with swiping the ledger without Elliot noticing for a few days, she'd do it in a heartbeat. But then, he might accuse Percy Hampton or Andrew Barrett of theft and a range war might erupt. That was the last thing she wanted.

Crouching, Alexa eased open the drawer to retrieve the ledger. Despite the scant moonlight filtering through the window, she opened the book to study Elliot's expenditures, credits and notations he'd added in the margins. She was going to be sorely disappointed if she didn't return to town with conclusive evidence to present to her father.

This has to be the vital clue to convict Elliot of wrongdoing, she assured herself as she held the ledger up to the faint light.

Coop paused on the boardwalk to lean on the rough-hewn beam outside the saloon. His gaze drifted instinctively to Alexa's hotel window. Dim lantern light flickered in the darkness. He wondered what she was doing and he wished he could be there with her. Yet, he had taken a risk by staying the previous night. He couldn't make a habit of it without inviting notice and provoking Miguel's outrage.

"Would you be interested in joining me for a drink?" Gil Henson asked as he ambled up beside him. "You're buying, of course. Since I'm still on duty for another half hour you can fetch a bottle."

"You want the whiskey delivered to your office?" Coop asked as he pushed away from the post.

"Yep. I want to tell you about the visit I had from Miss Quinn recently."

"Oh?" Coop tried not to sound too intrigued but Gil had piqued his curiosity.

When Gil strode off to check the locked doors on both sides of the street Coop limped back inside Valmont Saloon to make his purchase. He dodged Polly Sanders for the umpteenth time when she flirted outrageously with him. Then he hobbled down Main Street to the marshal's office. The deputy showed up five minutes later to take Gil's place. Together they walked to the south edge of town to Gil's modest home.

"Nice place," Coop complimented as he surveyed the house.

"Thanks. It beats the hell out of sleeping on the ground and trying to stay dry during downpours," Gil replied as he led the way into the parlor. "I had my fill of battling inclement weather during my bounty hunting days."

"Private investigation is a step up, too," Coop agreed. "But I don't have a home like you, only a headquarters."

Gil motioned for Coop to make himself comfortable while he filled two glasses. "I'm inviting you to a party next weekend, compliments of Elliot Webster. The cunning son of a bitch managed to win over Miss Quinn and she agreed to marry him," he added with a distasteful scowl.

"Did he?" Coop said as he plunked down in a chair.

Gil nodded his reddish-blond head. "Apparently. But there's

something about that bewitching woman that has me baffled."
Gil downed his drink in one swallow. "I know there's more to
her than the dazzling beauty that meets the eye. Plus, I think
something's going on and I wish the hell I knew what it is."

Coop played dumb but he could feel tension coursing
through him. "Are you talking about the clash between
Hampton and Webster?"

"Partially." Gil poured another drink then stared pensively
at the contents of his glass. "I tell ya, Coop, whatever Alexa
Quinn is, she is not the flighty socialite she tries to portray in
public. I saw her withdraw into herself when Lieutenant
Gunther plied her with gushing flattery when I introduced
them. She didn't feed on it. She seemed indifferent, even perturbed by it."

"What's the other part that disturbs you?" Coop prodded.

"I think Miss Quinn is trying to keep the peace between
Webster and her friend's father," he elaborated. "But I'm afraid
it will land her in trouble because of her engagement to Webster."

Coop didn't doubt it for a minute. "Do you want me to keep
track of her unofficially?"

"That might be a good idea," Gil replied.

Coop sipped a second drink and chatted with Gil for nearly
an hour before he hobbled outside to note that Questa Springs
had more or less shut down for the night. Of course, tinkling
piano music from the dance halls and saloons still competed
with each other. Laughter and loud voices drifted from the
doorways, but no one stumbled around in the streets, shooting
out the lamplights.

Coop paused to glance at the hotel window, noting the
lantern was still burning in Alexa's room. He decided to retire
to his own quarters so he could remove the annoying split. He
wanted to conclude this case, if only to toss out the damn prop
Alexa had devised for him.

When he noticed Webster's horse tied to the hitching post in front of the mercantile store, his gaze drifted toward Lily's Pleasure Resort. His best guess was that Webster was celebrating his recent betrothal by tumbling around on the sheets with his favorite concubine.

"Anyone who doesn't take an engagement to Alexa seriously deserves to be shot," Coop muttered as he limped across the street to Walker Hotel. "I'd gladly mete out the punishment."

Come to think of it, he could resolve several problems if he had a legitimate excuse to drop that conniving scoundrel in his tracks.

A fleeting thought crossed Coop's mind and prompted him to wheel toward the street that faced the town square. Just to be on the safe side he wanted to check Hampton, Barrett and Figgins Dry Goods Store to make sure Elliot hadn't discharged his henchman to start a fire while he had his alibi set with his paramour.

Considering the comment Coop had heard Webster make at the line shack recently, retaliation was inevitable because he was the kind of man who wouldn't be satisfied until he avenged whatever injustice he thought had befallen him. If Webster did try to burn out his competition, emotions would be flying high and all hell would break loose in this quaint mountain haven.

Alexa squinted in the dim light, trying to decipher Elliot's scrawling handwriting. She did note from the tallies, however, that his business had dropped off considerably the past three years. Which was probably why he was so desperate to acquire the government contract to pay his business expenses and land a wealthy wife.

She held the ledger up to the light from the window when

she saw a documentation of payment to Norville Thomas. She frowned, bemused, when the following entries listed quartermaster supplies from the territorial commissary.

A moment later, her eyes flew wide-open. It finally dawned on her why Norville Thomas's silhouette seemed familiar yet all wrong. Her thoughts circled back to the shiny boots Lieutenant Arnold Gunther had worn when she met him recently. That's what had puzzled her about Thomas. When she spotted him at the line shack, he'd been wearing a homespun jacket and breeches with shiny boots that seemed out of place. His stature and physique reminded her of the man she'd met at a function her father hosted the previous year in Albuquerque.

"Curse it!" Alexa muttered when the images floating around in her mind suddenly fell into place. She remembered seeing the unidentified man in military uniform who had spoken to Elliot on the street after he left their party. It must have been Norville Thomas making contact with his cohort, she deduced.

At the time of the party Alexa had been fretting over the possibility of Elliot asking her father for permission to court her. She hadn't seen the significance of the connection between Elliot and Norville Thomas. No doubt, Thomas was running information from Questa Springs to Albuquerque and then to Santa Fe. More than likely, Thomas was a quartermaster who used the excuse of taking military business trips to purchase supplies for the forts and reservations. But he was serving his own greedy purposes.

That snake! The side business he'd mentioned was probably the selling of military issued supplies to civilians for a profit and delivering substandard goods to the Indian tribes on reservations. More than once Alexa had heard her father complain about the illegal practice. Cheating soldiers and reservation Indians was his pet peeve and he tried to put a stop to it. Her father would be pleased if she sniffed out another culprit.

Excitement bubbled inside her as she turned the page to note entry after entry that included Thomas's name. He was obviously a supplier and messenger. But who was passing information through this grapevine that included Webster and Thomas?

Determined to uncover the Judas on her father's staff, she tucked the ledger under her arm and crawled across the floor to the window, hoping for better lighting. Hurriedly she reopened the book and scanned the pages.

She recalled a comment that Gil Henson had made recently about the tainted flowers of ill repute. She frowned as the conversation rolled through her mind. Then suddenly the information that had been churning around in her head leaped out at her with vivid clarity. She'd been searching for the connection that tied Questa Springs to Santa Fe. Now here it was, plain as day—

Her thoughts scattered like buckshot and panic spurted through her when she heard lumbering footsteps echoing through the hall. Oscar Denton was making his rounds and she was sitting in plain sight. Her wild-eyed gaze flew to the walnut desk. Alexa clamped the ledger against her chest and scrambled awkwardly across the floor on one arm and two knees, hoping to take cover under the desk without making noise. Her heart hammered in her chest when she realized how close the footsteps were to the open doorway. Her chances of hiding under the desk before Denton spotted her were too close to call. Alexa prayed for all she was worth…all the way across the room.

Coop cursed mightily when he spotted three men slinking around in the darkness behind the mercantile shop owned by Webster's business competitors. He saw smoke billowing from the back door of the shop.

The three men dashed off in separate directions. Coop

drew his pistol and fired thrice. He dropped one man in his tracks and speculated that he'd managed to wing the other two. He sincerely hoped Oscar Denton was sprawled in the door so Coop could link him directly to Webster. Coop scowled as he watched the other two wounded men disappear into the darkness before he could identify or capture them.

Raising his pistol in the air, Coop fired off two more shots, hoping to sound an alarm that would summon volunteer fire-fighters. Then he swooped down to grab the fallen arsonist by the scruff of his shirt. Although it wasn't Denton, Coop dragged his prisoner around to the front of the store. When the injured man tried to scramble to his feet and attempt escape Coop flipped over his pistol and used the butt end to knock his captive senseless.

The smell of smoke permeated the cool evening air and the glow of flames speared the darkness. Shadowed silhouettes dashed across the town square. Men toting buckets to fill at the spring gathered rapidly. Coop heard men shouting orders to one another as the bucket brigade rushed across the street to attempt to douse the flames.

"Go around to the back where the fire started!" Coop yelled over the loud commotion.

Within minutes, the citizens had formed a line to refill buckets. Several wagons filled with barrels arrived to transport larger quantities of water to the fire.

Coop kept expecting Alexa to show up to see what was going on. She was never very far from the scene of a crisis. She always arrived to lend a helping hand. So where was she now?

When Miguel didn't show up, either, Coop wondered if the twosome were keeping surveillance at Hampton Ranch. Either that or Alexa had talked her devoted bodyguard into accompanying her to Webster's ranch to have another look at the ledgers she was so anxious to get her hands on.

Coop wanted to track her down but he couldn't leave until he turned his prisoner over to Gil. For now, he could only hope that Miguel was nearby to protect Alexa from harm.

A foul curse burst from Coop's lips when he looked through the pane glass window to see that the fire had spread from the storage area and back office to the front of the store. Thick smoke billowed from the roof and flames leaped skyward, threatening to endanger nearby buildings.

The instant Coop saw Gil jogging toward the store he waved in expansive gestures. "Throw me the cuffs," he called loudly. "This is one of the three men who set the fire."

Gil launched the metal shackles through the air. Coop hurriedly secured the downed man's wrists around the hitching post in front of the courthouse.

Gil huffed and puffed, trying to catch his breath while he stared at the smoke and flames. "Damnation."

"And then some," Coop muttered. "I recognize this man as one of Webster's hired hands. The other two are long gone and I couldn't get a clear look at them or their horses."

"The son of a bitch decided to lessen his business competition, I reckon," Gil grumbled as Coop took him aside to speak confidentially.

"Webster mentioned this possibility to me after his clash with Hampton at the ranch. This might be a smoke screen for another rustling accusation," Coop speculated. "I expect Webster will have an easier time of showing you the cattle he planted in his neighbor's herd."

Gil frowned, confused. "How do you know so much about what Webster is doing?"

"Because I was hired to investigate his activities," Coop confided. He needed Gil's invaluable assistance because the situation had become widespread in its complexity. "By the way, you're right about Alexa Quinn. She isn't what she seems. She and I are working together to gather information about Webster's illegal business practices."

Gil staggered back a pace. His eyes nearly popped from their sockets. "You and Miss Quinn?" he croaked, incredulous.

Coop nodded briskly then made a stabbing gesture toward the billowing smoke. He hoped to divert Gil's attention since he looked as if he meant to pose more questions about Coop's unexpected association with Alexa. "Webster is probably tripping the light fantastic with Lily and using it for his alibi. Bring him down here so he will know that one of his hired henchmen will survive the gunshot wound to connect him to this conspiracy."

Gil glanced at the downed man. He frowned when he noticed the bloodstains on the leg of the prisoner's breeches.

"Don't worry about him. I'll fetch the doctor. Call your deputy over here to make sure no one assassinates him to keep him silent."

Gil whistled loudly. The deputy, who had joined the ranks of firefighters, came running to take charge of the prisoner. Coop hurried off to find the physician and scowled when the splint slowed him up. When he reached the physician's home, the older man was staring out the door toward the town square. His gray hair was standing on end, as if he'd been awakened from a sound sleep.

"I wounded one of the arsonists when he tried to escape," Coop explained. "Can you tend him? He's shackled to the hitching post across from the burning mercantile building."

"Too bad it couldn't have been Webster's store," the doctor grumbled. "He charges two arms and a leg for his supplies."

The doctor reversed direction to grab his bag and Coop plunked down on the nearest bench to roll up his pant leg. Quickly he untied the straps and removed the hindering splints.

This is the end of the charade, he decided. Webster had retaliated and now evidence was stacking up against him. No need for Coop to keep up pretense. He was taking charge of this case and he didn't care who knew it.

Before the physician ventured back outside Coop jogged to the town square. There was still no sign of Alexa and Miguel. That made him extremely nervous. If indeed Webster was launching an attack on two fronts simultaneously—in attempt to ruin Percy Hampton by accusing him of rustling and destroying the store—Alexa might be caught in the fracas again. If bullets started flying, he wanted her out of the line of fire. The thought of her being injured...or worse...unhinged him.

Lurching around, Coop dashed to the hotel. He had the uneasy feeling that the lantern light flickering in Alexa's room was a ruse and she wasn't there. Damn it, he should have checked on her earlier that evening. He hoped Miguel was with her, at least. Maybe he could prevent her from thrusting herself into harm's way until Coop showed up to offer reinforcement.

Miguel grabbed hold of the reins to Kate's horse when she swore aloud and tried to thunder away. "This is not the time to expose our hiding place in the bushes," he muttered at her.

"I have to stop them," Kate said angrily. "Those hired guns are driving Webster's cattle toward our pasture. You know what will happen next. Webster will show up with the marshal in tow to accuse my father of stealing. The feud will erupt again. I have to—"

Miguel leaned out to clamp his hand over the lower portion of Kate's face. "You have to stay here and keep quiet. If you startle those gunmen they'll shoot first and ask questions later," he said grimly. "You won't do your father any good if you're dead."

Much to his relief, Kate settled her ruffled feathers. "I suppose not," she whispered begrudgingly. "But I guarantee that I'm cutting those rebranded calves from our herd as soon as those men clear out of here."

Miguel noted—and not for the first time—how much alike Alexa and Kate were. Both women were spirited, headstrong and feisty. No wonder they had become best friends at boarding school.

His thoughts trailed off when the smell of smoke drifted toward him. He twisted in the saddle to see a black cloud and glowing flames rising to the south. Icy dread froze in his veins when he recalled what Coop had told him while they were stashing the planted cattle out of sight in a nearby canyon after the first rustling accusation. Webster stated he wanted to destroy his competition by starting a fire, but Coop had discouraged him—but not for long. Webster's plan was in motion.

"Dear God, now what?" Kate grumbled when she noticed the flames.

"I need to ride back to town," he said quickly. "I'm afraid your father's store might be on fire."

"I'm coming with you."

"No, you aren't."

Miguel scowled when Kate took off without him. He glanced back at the four men who were driving the cattle toward Hampton's pasture gate. He needed to be two places at once. If he allowed Kate to go haring off alone she might encounter disaster. He couldn't live with himself if that happened.

"Damn that Webster," he hissed as he gouged his steed and took off like a discharging cannonball.

Webster was dividing his opposition, in hopes of conquering them in one fell swoop. On second thought, he and Kate *should* remain with the cattle. There were plenty of reinforcements in town to fight the fire and to track down the men who had ignited the flames.

"Kate!" he called out as he raced after her. "Forget the fire. We need to stay with the planted cattle!"

She skidded her horse to a halt and reined toward him.

"Leave the arsonists to Coop and Alexa," he insisted as he motioned for her to reverse direction. "We have an important job to do here."

Chapter Fourteen

*"W*hat the hell—?"

Denton stepped into Elliot's office the instant before Alexa managed to curl her legs under the desk and tuck herself out of sight. Even worse, she hadn't thought to grab her firearm before dashing off this evening. All she had for protection was the dagger tucked in her boot.

She suddenly remembered the pistol in the top desk drawer that she'd unloaded during her late-night search of the office with Coop. Before Denton could cross the room to grab her, she retrieved the pistol. When he clamped hold of her ankles and dragged her from the desk, she trained the empty weapon on his chest.

"Back off, Oscar, or you're a dead man," she said with the most vicious snarl she could muster.

His eyes widened in amazement. *"You?"*

The only good thing about this bad situation was that she had completely fooled Denton with her airheaded socialite persona. Now he was taking her very seriously, she noted. Of course, he'd tell Elliot and spoil her charade. Confound it, if she had been a little faster at crawling and he would've been a little slower of foot, he wouldn't have spotted her at all.

Damn her rotten luck!

"What are you doing here?" His gaze narrowed menacingly as he stared at the speaking end of the pistol.

"I'm here to find out what kind of financial trouble my fiancé is in," she said as an excuse. "I don't appreciate being used."

"The boss ain't gonna like this," Denton mumbled.

"Neither do I. Elliot's finances aren't as secure as he would have me believe. You should change employers, Oscar. Elliot won't be able to pay you when he lands in jail for fraud and embezzlement. You can come to work for me." Or so she let him think.

He smiled craftily. "That won't happen, honey. The boss has everything figured out."

Alexa felt uneasy about lying on the floor while Oscar loomed over her. Furthermore, his lecherous smiles had always made her nervous—now more than ever. One misstep on her part and he'd overpower her. Then it would be next to impossible to defend herself.

Mustering her bravado, she gestured with the pistol barrel, ordering him to step aside so she could climb to her feet. When the big lummox didn't budge from his spot, Alexa said, "If you think I don't know how to use this weapon and that I'm squeamish about the sight of you lying in a pool of your own blood, you are mistaken. *Now move.*"

Her snarling growl must have been marginally convincing because he took one step to the left. Alexa bounded to her feet and moved an arm's length away from him.

She directed his attention to the coat closet just beyond the office door. Cursing her foully, Oscar galumphed across the room. Alexa swooped in close enough to retrieve his sixshooter from his holster while he had his back to her.

Suddenly he spun around, using his bulky arms like spinning blades of a windmill. The side-winding blow to her head knocked her off balance but she managed to keep her feet. Her ears ringing and her head pulsating, she lunged forward to ram his own pistol between his eyes before he could pounce on her.

"Dare me, Oscar," she challenged through gritted teeth.

"You crazy bitch, you don't know who you're fooling with," he growled hatefully.

"Get in the closet. *Now,*" she demanded in a harsh tone. "You're exhausting what's left of my patience."

She pressed the gun barrel deeply into his flesh, forcing him to walk backward. He called her every crude name in the book while she backed him into the closet. Alexa was grateful the key protruded from the door lock, making it a simple matter to restrain him long enough for her to beat a hasty retreat.

Yet, she knew the flimsy door wouldn't hold the stout bodyguard indefinitely. Using his thick shoulders as a battering ram, he'd splinter wood and come charging after her within a few moments.

Knowing she wouldn't have much of a head start, Alexa lurched around and dashed lickety-split into the office to scoop up the incriminating ledger. She predicted that if anyone heard Oscar's call to arms they'd enter the front door. She didn't intend to use that route to encounter more hired guns. One was plenty.

Serenaded by Oscar's fists rattling the closet door and his bellowing shouts filling the air, she scampered toward the window. Heart pounding furiously, she tossed aside the empty weapon then tucked Oscar's six-shooter in the band of her breeches. She slung one leg over the windowsill, knowing she'd have to jump rather than carefully climb down the outer wall. She tossed out the ledger then followed it through the air.

Her pained *hiss* mingled with Oscar's outraged roar as she hit the ground. Her ankle throbbed something fierce when she tried to stand and put weight on it. Grimacing, she grabbed the ledger and hobbled through the garden. Behind her, she heard hinges creaking and wood splintering. Then she saw several men burst from the bunkhouse and dash toward the front door. Alexa gritted her teeth and hobbled to the bushes to fetch her horse.

She mounted the bay gelding and reined toward town, but Oscar was shouting to beat the band, ordering the men to saddle their horses and give chase. She took off like a bat from hell, praying she could outrun the horde of hired guns that Oscar had pressed into service.

As she galloped along the path, she noticed the spiral of smoke from town. Her stomach dropped and she swore under her breath. Obviously Elliot had carried through with his threat to burn out his competition. He hadn't been able to resist the retaliation, the spiteful bastard. She wondered if he'd staged another rustling incident, too.

He must be getting desperate, she decided as she raced toward town. The final vote for the government contract loomed and he wanted to blacken Hampton's and Barrett's good names. However, Elliot didn't know he was under surveillance. She'd expose him for the treacherous scoundrel he was and put him away for years to come.

A pistol blast echoed in the near distance and Alexa half twisted in the saddle to see five men—with Oscar leading the charge—firing at her. The only chance of escape was to plunge into the thicket of trees and ditch the ledger. She could retrieve it later.

Another volley of bullets resounded around her and burning pain seared through her left shoulder. She flattened herself over her horse and raced into the trees and underbrush. She jerked her horse to a halt to wedge the ledger between the thick branches of a cedar tree. Then she urged her horse to zigzag through the maze of cottonwoods and cedars that lined the shallow creek.

The sound of horse hooves pounding the ground in hot pursuit demanded her full attention again. A wave of nausea threatened to overwhelm Alexa when she noticed the shiny stain on her shirtsleeve. Numbness engulfed her arm, which dangled uselessly at her side. Blood trickled down her fingers and its unique coppery scent filled her senses.

Another shot rang through the trees. Alexa slumped forward again, dropping the reins, hoping the horse could find its way back to the livery. Muffled voices came from all directions at once in the hazy darkness that clouded her vision. Alexa tried desperately to remain conscious, but the wound drained more of her strength with each passing second. Then the world went out of focus and she sagged limply against her horse.

She wondered fleetingly if Coop would miss her if she didn't survive this ordeal. He'd warned her to let him handle this case but she'd been hell-bent on proving her worth to her father.

It didn't seem quite so important now...

That was her last thought before she blacked out.

Miguel listened to Kate mutter under her breath while Webster's hired guns planted the rebranded cattle in Hampton pastures. He clutched her arm when she tried to ride off to gather the cattle the moment after the riders left.

"If waiting another few minutes puts the riders out of hearing distance then we wait," Miguel told her firmly.

Kate sighed heavily then reached out to trail her forefinger over his cheek. "I'm sorry for being difficult. I won't blame you if you lose interest in me. I'm more like Lexi than you probably thought."

Miguel chuckled softly then took her hand to press a kiss to her fingertips. "Losing interest isn't the problem, *querida*. You know that. I don't want to lose you, but—"

"Stop right there," she interrupted. "No buts, Miguel. I love you."

"Don't say that," he murmured, tormented. "You know we can't be together."

"I'll make Papa understand," she insisted determinedly.

Miguel shook his head. "He won't allow it. You and I need to accept that."

Her chin came up. "I refuse to lose you, but we will have to hammer out the details later. Right now, we have to stash these cattle in the same place you and Coop hid the other livestock. Then we need to ride into town. I'm dying to know the extent of the fire damage at the store."

Miguel trotted from the underbrush when he determined that the coast was clear. In a matter of minutes, they rounded up the six steers from Webster's herd and drove them to the canyon to join the others he and Coop had placed in makeshift pens.

Circling through the pasture to avoid a confrontation with the gunmen, Miguel and Kate rode into town to notify the marshal and check on the store.

Coop swore colorfully when he saw Miguel and Kate ride into the town square. Alexa still wasn't accounted for and his concern for her welfare escalated rapidly.

"When was the last time you saw Alexa?" he demanded without preamble.

"I left before she joined Webster for supper," Miguel replied as he nodded a greeting to Gil, who'd had no luck tracking down Webster. "She said she planned to keep surveillance on him from a safe distance after they parted company this evening."

"She obviously changed her plans...or had them changed for her," Coop said. "I saw Webster hightailing it to Lily's Pleasure Resort, but I have seen nothing of Alexa."

Kate gestured toward the four riders who halted to survey what was left of the store. "Those men planted rebranded cattle in our herd tonight. Miguel and I stashed them out of sight. I suspect those men are here to summon you, Marshal."

Coop and Gil appraised the armed riders. "Stall them with the excuse that you're investigating the origin of the fire," Coop requested. "No sense of alerting them that two eyewitnesses saw them with the cattle and that one of their cohorts is in jail for arson."

Kate appraised the store and her shoulders slumped. "There's nothing worth saving, is there? Thank goodness the fire didn't spread to such extremes that other shopkeepers lost their businesses."

"Our firefighters managed to contain the flames." Gil patted her arm sympathetically. "I wish we could have saved your family's business." He drew her attention to the east. "Your parents arrived a few minutes ago and they're speaking with the Barretts and Figgins, if you want to see them."

While Miguel and Kate walked over to join her parents, Coop ambled away before the four riders dismounted. Sure enough, he overheard the men insist that Gil check the Hamptons's pasture for stolen livestock.

"I have bigger problems than rustling accusations," Gil said as he hitched his thumb toward the collapsed building.

The men grumbled about the delay but Gil promised to follow up their accusations when time permitted. He sent them off to grab buckets to soak the hot spots where flames threatened to flare again.

Coop kept expecting Webster to show up and plead ignorance about the fire. But minutes ticked by and neither Webster nor Alexa appeared. Finally Coop couldn't tolerate another minute of suspense. He needed to find Alexa before his concern for her safety drove him completely crazy.

"I'm going to fetch Bandit and have a look around the area," Coop told Gil. "Alexa should be here. That Webster hasn't shown up, either, has me worried."

"I'll stay here, in case she shows up," Gil informed him. "Send word to me if you need help."

Coop strode swiftly across the town square then jogged down the street to the livery stable that sat on the edge of town. He saddled Bandit then led him outside—and stopped in his tracks when a darkly clad body, draped over a bay horse, appeared in the distance. His heart missed several vital beats when he saw tendrils of blond hair protruding from the rim of the cap.

"Son of a bitch!" Coop dropped Bandit's reins and took off at a dead run to reach the approaching horse.

When he clutched Alexa's hand, he felt the blood on her fingers and smelled the telltale scent that clung to her. Rage boiled through him, catapulting him through time to relive the same helpless fury and murderous revenge he'd endured when his family had been taken needlessly from him.

For years, Coop had maintained a cautious emotional distance from friends and clients. He'd refused to let anyone close enough to resurrect the torment he'd suffered as a teenager. But Alexa had gotten past his guard and she'd come to matter too much. Just seeing her hurt nearly drove him to his knees. Not knowing the extent of her injuries was killing him, inch by excruciating inch.

"Alexa? Sweetheart?" he whispered as he cupped her chin in his hand and tapped her lightly on the cheek.

She didn't respond.

Coop pulled himself up behind her on the steed, grabbed

Bandit's reins and headed toward Main Street. When he reached the town square, he scanned the area quickly, hoping to locate Dr. Robinson.

"*¡Caramba!* What happened to her?"

Coop glanced sideways to see Miguel and Kate sprinting toward him. Then he searched the crowd to locate Gil. "Find the doctor!" he called to the marshal. "Alexa has been shot."

"*Shot?*" Kate skidded to a halt and her face turned as white as salt. "Is she going to be all right?"

"I don't know," Coop said grimly. "I'm taking her to her hotel room. Send over the doctor as soon as possible."

When Coop reversed direction, he heard Miguel swearing in Spanish. Obviously he felt personally responsible, too. Coop kept telling himself that he should have kept close tabs on Alexa because he knew how daring and independent she was. Not to mention how determined she was to prove her capabilities to her father by solving this case.

Damn it, if something happened to Alexa he would never be able to forgive himself. It would be like losing his family all over again and having to suffer all that mental anguish. It had been painful enough the first time. Now it would be worse.

Coop battled to keep a firm grasp on his roiling emotions as he halted the horse at the hitching post outside Walker Hotel. Carefully he eased Alexa's limp body from the saddle and held her in his arms. Her head rolled over his arm and came to rest against his chest. When he looked into her ashen face another flashback from the past robbed him of breath. She looked deathly pale and as lifeless as his father and brother…

Coop clenched his jaw, pushed aside the morbid thought and strode into the empty lobby. It seemed everyone was in the town square, discussing the destructive fire. Everyone except Webster and his paramour, Coop thought bitterly.

Out of breath from hurrying up the steps with Alexa in his

arms, Coop pivoted toward her rented room. The locked door didn't slow him down much. With a full head of steam, he used his shoulder like a battering ram. The lock and doorjamb gave way on the second hit. Then he kicked the door shut with his boot heel.

Coop grabbed a towel from the commode. Then, balancing Alexa's motionless body over one arm, he peeled off her bloodstained shirt.

He nearly collapsed in relief when he discovered the bullet wound was on her shoulder, not her chest. He determined that she had a fighting chance, as long as she hadn't lost too much blood. Hurriedly he blotted a damp towel over the injury so he could get a better look at it. After he laid her on the bed, he covered her modestly with a sheet.

His medical skills were rudimentary at best. He knew how to use natural remedies, while roughing it in the wilderness, but he had nothing at his disposal except a tin of poultice that he kept with his belongings.

On that thought, he bounded up to fetch the salve from his room and one of his shirts for her to wear after the doctor treated her injury. He was back in a flash to dab the pasty substance over her jagged flesh.

"Mr. Cooper? It's Doc Robinson."

Coop never took his eyes off Alexa's peaked face for even a moment. "Come in."

She'd been so vibrant and active, he mused as he stared at her. It seemed unnatural for her to lie there, bleeding all over herself…and it tormented him to the extreme.

"What happened to the door?" the doctor asked on his way past the lopsided slab of wood.

"I had to unlock it the hard way."

The gray-haired physician cracked a smile as he sank on the opposite side of the bed. His expression sobered when he got his first look at Alexa. When he inched down the sheet, noting Alexa was bare to the waist, his brows furrowed. "Did you remove her clothing? I'm not even sure you should be here while I examine her, much less while I prepare her for possible surgery."

Coop stared at the doctor as intently as he'd stared down countless outlaws. "She's my responsibility and my partner. You can try to convince me to leave, but you'll waste valuable time."

The physician was the first to break eye contact. Clearly he wasn't an expert at showdowns or staring contests. "Well then, let's get her stitched up," he murmured. "You can guard the door. Her friends are only a few minutes behind me."

Elliot Webster scowled irritably when an interruptive knock rattled the door to Lily's spacious, second-story suite in the brothel. "Who is it? This damn well better be important!"

"It's me, boss…and it is important," Oscar Denton called from the other side of the door.

Swearing crudely, Elliot leaned away from the bed to grab his trousers. Lily snatched up a frilly robe to cover herself.

"Stay here," Elliot demanded. "I'll speak to him in the sitting room."

He stepped into his breeches on his way to the door. "What's so damn important? You know I didn't want any of my hired men in the vicinity on this particular night."

"Things got complicated," Oscar muttered as Elliot clamped hold of his elbow and jerked him into the sitting room.

"This can't be about the fire because I could see the flames and smell smoke from here," he said impatiently. "So what is it? A problem with planting the stolen cattle for the marshal to see?"

"No, it's about your fiancée," Oscar replied.

Elliot frowned, bemused. "What about her?"

"You got more than you bargained for, I'm afraid. I caught her in your office, dressed in men's clothes. I pulled her out from under your desk. She'd been snooping before I noticed her."

"What?" Elliot howled incredulously. "Alexa?"

"She ain't your usual bit of fluff," Oscar assured him. "She stuffed a pistol between my eyes and then backed me into the closet so she could escape. Me and some of the men chased her and fired shots. I don't know if a bullet found its mark because she plunged into the trees beside the creek. It was hard to track her in the dark."

Elliot's head spun like a carousel, trying to assimilate the startling facts with the socialite he thought he knew.

"She claimed she was checking your finances to make sure you were what you appeared to be before she married you."

Elliot's eyes widened in horror. "She saw my ledger?"

Oscar shrugged his buffalo-size shoulders. "Don't know about that, boss. I was too busy trying to figure out how to disarm her without getting my head blown off. Then I had to break down the door because she locked me in the closet."

Dozens of worrisome scenarios rushed to Elliot's mind. His grand visions of gaining financial, political and social prominence, by riding Harold and Alexa Quinn's coattails, were flying out the window. Alexa had duped him and had acquired incriminating information that would ruin what was left of his reputation and strip him of his dwindling wealth.

The thought sent wild desperation and panic coursing through him. He had to do something—and quickly!

"I have to silence her," Elliot mused aloud as he paced from wall to wall. "All the better if you managed to shoot her. Maybe she's lying on the ground somewhere. We have to find her and dispose of her." He lurched around to face Oscar. "Send one of the men to the town square. I need to know what rumors and speculations are spreading about the fire and about

Alexa's whereabouts. That Mexican bodyguard who follows her around like a devoted pup should know something."

Oscar spun on his heels. "We'll see what we can find out."

"I hope the hell you do a better job with this than you did of apprehending my cunning fiancée," he said darkly. "You can be replaced at a moment's notice, you know."

The moment Oscar closed the door Lily stepped into view. Apprehension etched her milky-white features. At least *she* cared what happened to him, Elliot consoled himself. That devious bitch of a fiancée didn't care. She was out to get him and he had to stop her before she ruined his life.

"Damnation, everything is going to hell," Elliot burst out.

Lily rushed forward to smooth the agitated frown from his face. "Don't fret, darling. I can make the necessary contacts if the situation here spirals out of our control."

"Ha! A hell of a lot of good your contacts have done thus far," he muttered resentfully. "I've done everything imaginable to set us up for life. Now that wily bitch is ruining us."

"We'll find her," Lily assured him. "You can still use her to your advantage, but in a different way than you did before. Don't let anger confuse your thinking. We can figure a way out of this if we don't panic."

The prompt relieved Elliot's outrage and jolted him back to his senses. "You're right. All isn't lost," he told himself while she bobbed her head in agreement.

If worst came to worst he could always leave home, change his name and make a new start. However, he needed capital and a head start to prevent being caught.

"You are far too clever and intelligent to let that prissy blonde outsmart you," Lily encouraged him. "I know I can depend on you to work through this temporary setback."

When she lowered her hand to cup the placket of his breeches then rubbed against him, the feverish need she never failed to arouse had the power to energize him. He craved her bold advances, the erotic passion she instilled in him. He'd wanted Alexa's money and connection, but he'd always lusted after Lily's ample curves and her unabashed sexuality.

"I'll turn this to our advantage somehow," he whispered before he kissed her—hard, hungrily.

"I'm counting on you, darling," she whispered back. "I know I can always depend on you, Elliot."

Chapter Fifteen

The moment Miguel and Kate reached Alexa's room, Coop was there to turn them away so the physician could finish stitching her back together.

"Is she going to be okay?" Kate and Miguel asked simultaneously.

Coop nodded. "Doc is finishing up right now. Fortunately for the little daredevil, the bullet passed through her shoulder and didn't lodge against bone. But she lost a considerable amount of blood during the time it took her to reach town from wherever she was tonight."

"Webster's place is my guess," Miguel said, and scowled. "As soon as she gets better I'm going to kill her for scaring me half to death."

Coop smiled for the first time in hours. "My sentiments exactly. You stab her and I'll shoot her a couple of times."

"I'll bring the poison," Kate volunteered. "We'll make sure she doesn't make us fret like this again."

Coop glanced back at the doctor. "I'll be back in a minute."

He stepped outside then requested that Miguel open the door to his adjacent room so they could speak privately. "It is your responsibility to notify Harold so he'll know about Alexa's injury," Coop insisted. "Harold doesn't know that I know who hired me and we don't need to complicate the problem right now."

Miguel grimaced. "I'm dreading the telling."

"I'll do it," Kate spoke up. "This certainly isn't Miguel's fault. I love Alexa dearly, but she spent the past two weeks trying to ditch Miguel in her effort to single-handedly solve this case and prove to Harold that she's more than a hostess for his political engagements."

"But she's still my obligation," Miguel insisted. "I'll send the telegram."

"In the meantime, I'll find Webster," Coop declared. "With any luck, he still thinks I'm on his payroll and that I'm not a threat to him."

Miguel smiled wryly. "Are you planning to wrench a confession by force? I'd like to be there to help, *gringo.*"

Coop had to admit that if he managed to get his foot in whichever door the bastard was hiding behind, he'd be tempted to exact immediate revenge. But he needed more evidence to convict Webster. Coop had to maintain a professional detachment. He'd have to satisfy his personal vendetta later.

"Tell Harold that Alexa was injured and that giving her time to recuperate will delay her return to Santa Fe," Coop instructed. "We won't worry him with the whys and what fors of a gunshot wound since we don't know the particulars ourselves."

Nodding agreeably, Miguel and Kate hurried off together to inform Alexa's father of the mishap. Coop inhaled a calming breath and prepared to face Alexa. Until the day he died, he'd never forget the alarming pallor of her skin and the excessive amount of blood that stained her arm and chest. The image triggered too many painful memories from his past.

"We're all set now," Doc Robinson announced when Coop

reentered the room. "She awakened momentarily and asked for you. Although I offered to relay the message, she's very determined to speak privately with you." He handed Coop a bottle of laudanum. "Give her another dose after you speak to her."

The physician exited, promising to return first thing the next morning. Coop sank on the edge of the bed, waiting for Alexa to wake up. He speared his fingers through her silky blond hair, combing it away from her waxen face.

"You drive me crazy, princess. You know that, don't you?" he murmured before he kissed her gently.

To his surprise she whispered, "I know and I'm sorry if I've worried you."

He was so relieved to know she was conscious that he grinned at her. "I hope that whatever you were doing to earn this souvenir-of-an-injury was worth the pain. The only positive point for me is knowing you're going to be flat on your back in bed recuperating, rather than flitting around on horseback endangering your life again."

"You think this piddly little ole gunshot wound is going to slow me down?" she rasped, and smiled impishly.

That was Alexa through and through, he knew. "Apparently the doctor couldn't find a way to remove your fighting spirit before he stitched you up," he remarked as he helped her slip into the loose-fitting shirt he'd brought for her earlier. "So tell me, princess, what the hell happened tonight and who do I have to kill for shooting you?"

Kate gasped in alarm when an unseen hand shot from the dark alley, jerking her sideways. Miguel had no time to react before the woman he loved was trapped in Oscar Denton's bulky arms. The sight of the knife at her throat sent rage bubbling through him. He growled a curse when Elliot Webster stepped up beside Denton.

"You're in on this betrayal, aren't you?" Webster sneered at Miguel. "You helped that wily bitch you work for play me for a fool, didn't you?"

Miguel's anxious gaze darted back and forth between Kate and Webster. He silently calculated his chances of attacking Webster and forcing him to release Kate—or lose his own life. Unfortunately he hesitated to take the risk when Kate's life hung in the balance.

"What do you want, *señor?*" Miguel gritted out begrudgingly.

A goading smile thinned Webster's lips. "I'm glad you have enough sense to admit defeat." He inclined his head toward the boardwalk. "I want you to trot down to the telegraph office and send Harold a message. Tell him to grant me the government contract to deliver horses and beef, plus a sizable bonus—or else."

"Bonus? A ransom, you mean," Miguel muttered bitterly.

Webster shrugged carelessly. "Call it whatever you want, but ten thousand will prevent your friend, Kate, from dying a tormenting death."

Frustrated fury assailed Miguel. He shifted his attention to Kate, who didn't flinch at the threat. She was too damn much like Alexa, he reminded himself again. Beautiful, courageous, loyal. She would make the supreme sacrifice if it ensured that Webster hanged for killing her and for trying to discredit and ruin her father.

"I want the money left in a water bucket dangling inside the well behind Harold's stables. My courier will pick it up day after tomorrow at eight. If he's detained, Kate will suffer fatal consequences."

"And where will I retrieve Kate?" Miguel asked sharply.

A sinister grin curled Webster's lips. "If Harold doesn't meet my demands, it really won't matter, will it?"

"Where…will…she…be?" Miguel snarled succinctly.

Webster flicked his wrist. "I'll drop her off near her father's ranch. You'll find her sooner or later."

Miguel tarried, weighing his chances of slitting Webster's throat and then burying his dagger in Denton's heart so Kate could go free. But she was watching him very closely, silently willing him not to risk his own life to rescue her.

"Do as he says, Miguel," she insisted.

"Indeed," Webster seconded. "And be quick about it." He gestured for Denton to back into the shadows of the alley.

Fury marked Miguel's steps as he stormed down the street to send the telegram. No matter how confident Webster felt, surrounded by his armed guards, he'd better not harm a single hair on Kate's reddish-gold head...

Miguel's spiteful thought evaporated when it occurred to him that he had to convey this unfortunate complication to Percy and Meg Hampton. He swore first in English then in Spanish, but it didn't help. The Hamptons were already upset about the rustling accusations and fiery destruction of their store. Learning their daughter had been kidnapped might be too much for them to bear.

"I'll ask you again, princess," Coop said sternly. "Who did this to you?"

Alexa appraised the determined expression on Coop's face as she shifted to find a more comfortable position on the bed. There wasn't one. Her shoulder hurt something fierce and her ankle was still sore. Fortunately, however, the dose of laudanum Dr. Robinson had given her a half hour earlier was beginning to take effect.

"I can see by the look on your face that you intend to avenge me," she said hoarsely. "But that isn't important now. We have to get word to my father that I have concrete evidence of Elliot's unethical practices, his connection to Norville Thomas and his method of receiving privileged information."

Coop blinked in amazement then cracked a smile. "Damn, you did have a productive evening, didn't you?" He gestured to the bandages that covered the painful shoulder injury. "Well, except for this small inconvenience. Now where the hell were you while you left a lantern burning by the window to throw me off track?"

Clearly he was annoyed by her deception, but she'd obtained rewarding results, even if they'd come at the expense of a gunshot wound. "I sneaked into Elliot's office." She paused while he scowled and muttered a pithy curse. "Elliot has not only used Norville Thomas to deliver information but he also purchased black market goods from the commissary post between Santa Fe and Albuquerque," she explained.

"After I read the inserts in Elliot's ledger I realized where I have seen Norville Thomas," she continued as she absently rubbed her throbbing shoulder. "He's the quartermaster in charge of dispensing supplies to forts and reservations in the territory. According to what I saw in the ledger, he's selling goods to people like Elliot for his own profit."

"There is too much of that going around," Coop said sourly. "The soldiers and Indian tribes suffer extensively, just to pad the pockets of greedy bastards like Webster and Thomas."

Alexa nodded in agreement then added, "Norville is also the man I saw with Elliot the night of the party in Santa Fe. I didn't get a clear look at him at the time. Also, I was distracted by the prospect of Elliot's forthcoming proposal. Now I recall that Norville was in military uniform, but he kept to the shadows to protect his identity. Although his short stature and lean physique seemed familiar, I didn't make the connection. He threw me off track when I saw him from a distance at the line shack because he wore homespun clothes and a cap."

She yawned tiredly and sighed. "I don't know when the two men made initial contact, but they've been partners for several years, if the notations in the ledger are anything to go by."

Coop smiled approvingly as he offered her a sip of water. "Good work, princess. That ledger will prove invaluable in court, especially with your testimony to go with it."

After she wet her whistle, she told him how and where she had left the ledger for safekeeping. "You need to retrieve the leather-bound book immediately," she insisted. "If it falls into Elliot's hands it will be my word against his."

"Did you figure out who is the traitor on your father's committee?" Coop asked.

"No, but I did figure out how the system works," she replied, battling the pain and exhaustion that threatened to zap what little strength she had left. "It's the flower sisters."

Coop blinked, puzzled. "Come again?"

"Gil mentioned to me recently that Lily Brantley and her two sisters ran brothels in the territory. I kept thinking there was something familiar about the name of Lily's Pleasure Resort. It dawned on me that I once overheard Ambrose Shelton and Ben Porter, two of my father's associates and advisors, discussing their mistress from Rose's Pleasure Parlor in Santa Fe. Then I recalled—"

"—Daisy's Pleasure Haven," Coop finished for her. "I remember it. It's in Albuquerque, but I haven't been in it."

"I passed by it a few times while I was in boarding school," Alexa murmured, struggling to overcome the lethargy that was steadily dragging her down. "The three sisters are taking advantage of their prestigious clients' connections and selling information."

"Obviously they've had a network operation in place for years, in addition to catering to upper-class clients," Coop added while she struggled to keep her eyes open. He bent down to brush his lips over her forehead. "I commend your investigative skills, but you never had to impress me. I can see you have the knack. Now get some much-needed sleep. I'll handle the arrests and contact your father about your recent discoveries."

"I don't want to miss out on this phase of the case," she complained. "I did all the legwork and you get to have all the fun."

"You bet, princess. And I'll take all the credit, too," he teased as he dropped a kiss to her lips. "Now get some rest. *Please.*"

A quiet rap rattled the broken door. Alexa rolled her head to the left to see Miguel enter the room.

She expected him to nag her incessantly for getting hurt when he wasn't on hand to protect her. However, he made her feel even worse than she did already when he blurted out, "Webster and Denton abducted Kate while we were on our way to telegraph Harold. They took her hostage and ordered me to tell Harold that she'd die a torturous death if he didn't give Webster the contract for cattle and horses, plus ten thousand dollars as a ransom for Kate's safe return."

"What! Ouch!" Alexa reared up—and instantly regretted her reaction. The pain in her shoulder made her light-headed and she wilted back to the bed. She clutched Coop's hand, demanding his attention. "You have to help Kate before you pursue this investigation. She's in danger because of me. Please, Coop. I'll never ask anything else of you. Ever. Just find her."

"Will you get some sleep if I promise?" he bartered.

She nodded then waited for him to give her another much-needed drink of water.

"Just rest, sweetheart," Coop encouraged as he buttoned her shirt then tucked the sheet around her. "There can't be too many places for Webster and Denton to stash Kate for safekeeping. We'll have her back before you wake up in the morning."

He sounded so convincing and reassuring that Alexa closed

her eyes and allowed weariness to overtake her. There was one man she could rely on completely, she reminded herself. Wyatt Cooper possessed the skills, the determination and the strength of character to get the job done right. Knowing that, she sank into the welcoming darkness.

"That was a tall order you promised Lexi, *gringo*," Miguel pointed out as Coop rose from the edge of Alexa's bed.

Coop stared down into Alexa's wan face and knew he'd promise her the moon—and anything else she wanted—if it helped her rest and recuperate so she could get back on her feet. He didn't like seeing her like this. She looked so weak and vulnerable that it tortured him beyond words.

"I have the unfortunate task of telling Percy and Meg Hampton about the abduction," Miguel remarked. "I'd rather take a beating."

Coop studied Miguel's glum expression. Relaying bad news was never easy and Coop sympathized with him. He couldn't imagine how he would feel if Alexa had been taken hostage. Having her shot was torture aplenty.

"I'm going to barricade this broken door from the inside after you leave then I'll exit through the window," Coop said as he sent Miguel on his way. "I'll brief Gil on what's going on then I'll check at the brothel to see if I can track down Webster."

"I'll be a few minutes behind you," Miguel insisted. "This case became personal a half hour ago."

The glitter in Miguel's dark eyes testified to the extent of his affection for Kate and the depth of his friendship for Alexa. He shared the same intensity of determination to apprehend Webster. Coop wanted that bastard dead or alive—and he wasn't particular which, as long as Kate returned unharmed.

Unfortunately Coop had handled enough abduction cases to know they didn't always turn out favorably—not without a lot of luck. However, he wasn't going to share that grim statistic with Miguel or Alexa.

Once Coop braced a chair beneath the doorknob to discourage unwanted intrusion into the room he paused by the foot of the bed to peer into Alexa's delicate features.

"Such a fascinating contradiction," he said with a grin. "Beguiling, refined features, a blue-blooded pedigree…and the heart and soul of a tigress."

Impulsively he moved around to the side of the bed to drop another kiss to her unresponsive lips. He wished that's all it took to revive her. "Sleep well, princess," he murmured before he climbed out the window using the gutter drainpipe to shimmy down to the alley.

"Kidnapped!" Percy and Meg Hampton howled in dismay as they stood beside the ashes of their once prosperous business.

"How dare that conniving bastard use my only child to force Harold to do his bidding. Is he mad?" Percy asked the world at large. "Does he think we will allow him to continue living in this community as if nothing happened here? He is deranged!"

Miguel listened to Percy rant and rave, while Meg stood quietly beside him, bleeding tears. When Percy finally wound down, Miguel requested his assistance. "Detective Wyatt Cooper is on this case," he told the Hamptons. "We plan to meet up at Webster's favorite bordello shortly. If you and your men could surround his ranch house we might be able to apprehend him before he stashes Kate in an unknown location."

"Yes, of course." Percy bobbed his head repeatedly. Then he motioned for his business partners, Andrew Barrett and George Figgins, to approach. "Webster, the madman, took my daughter hostage for bargaining power," he explained hurriedly. "I could use reinforcement in sealing off his ranch and finding Kate."

Miguel watched the men leap into action to organize a manhunt. He noticed Coop and the marshal striding swiftly around the square, apparently headed for the jail. When Miguel offered to rent Meg Hampton a room in town, she readily agreed. The poor woman nearly collapsed twice on the way to check into the hotel.

"Bring her back to me, Miguel," she begged brokenly. "She's the only child I have."

"I will do whatever it takes to get her back," Miguel promised faithfully as he escorted Kate's frantic mother to the hotel desk. "She will be back with you soon."

Miguel clamped his mouth shut, realizing that he had accepted the same kind of tall order Coop had sworn to Alexa. Damn, he hoped both of them could deliver.

"Now what's happened?" Gil asked as he hurried to keep up with Coop's swift strides down Main Street.

"Doc treated Alexa's gunshot wound and she's sedated. But Webster took Kate Hampton hostage and forced Miguel to telegraph Harold Quinn with demands," Coop reported concisely.

"Damn it to hell," Gil growled. "First the fire, then Alexa's injury and another accusation of rustling by Webster's hired guns. Now this. So much for enjoying a quiet life in this mountain haven."

"Webster purposely has us running in several different directions at once," Coop said, then gestured to his left. "Why don't you check Webster's storeroom and back office to see if he might have stashed Kate in there until he settles on an obscure hideout. I'll contact you after I check Lily's bordello. Miguel should be along in a minute to join us."

Coop and Gil parted company. Coop strode quickly down the boardwalk, drawing befuddled stares from passersby who noticed he had suddenly lost his limp. "Webster took Kate

Hampton hostage," he announced loudly. "Be on the lookout for him and contact me or the marshal if you have information."

Coop hurried on his way, passing the unusually silent saloons and gaming halls. The thought that Webster might have taken advantage of an abandoned business or storeroom prompted him to press several men on the street into service. He'd have the whole blessed town on the lookout if it helped, he decided. Webster had very few allies and that might become his downfall in Questa Springs.

The instant Coop entered Lily's Pleasure Resort his attention fixated on the painting of a nude Greek goddess lounging in a chariot pulled by two white horses. He could only imagine Alexa's offensive reaction to the painting. His gaze shifted to several soiled doves who were draped seductively over couches and chairs. There wasn't a gentleman in sight this evening. They had raced off to view the high drama of the fire.

"Where's Lily?" Coop asked without preamble.

"In her suite. Last room at the end of the upstairs hall, sugar," the buxom redhead purred as she looked him up and down. "But there's no need to look farther than right here."

Without comment or a second glance, Coop headed for the stairs, taking them two at a time to reach the landing. Pistol drawn, he moved silently down the hall to enter the room next door to Lily's suite. Then he exited through the window so he could use Lily's private entrance—in case Webster or one of his henchmen was lying in wait.

He glanced down to see a guard blocking Lily's private staircase at ground level. He inched toward the window to look inside. Sure enough, an armed guard waited by the main door to the suite. Lily sat in a tuft chair, watching the door intently. Webster, Denton and his hostage were nowhere to be seen.

Coop quietly turned the latch to slip unnoticed into the room. He drew a second six-shooter and aimed one at each occupant. Both of them recoiled when they realized he'd sneaked in on them.

"Drop it, Brenner," Coop ordered the guard that he'd seen often enough at Webster's ranch to call him by name. He pointed the other weapon at Lily. "You, too, sister. I want the derringer and the dagger you have tucked in the top of your chemise and garter."

They scowled then disarmed themselves and tossed the weapons on the bed as Coop demanded.

"Where's Webster? He owes me money and I'm having trouble tracking him down, what with all the excitement in town and accusations coming his way. I'm getting out of here while the getting is good." Or so he let them think.

"Elliot isn't here," said the sultry brunette. "I haven't seen him in hours."

Coop cast Brenner a steely glance. "What about you? Are you telling the same tale or are you going to show some originality?"

The brawny guard sneered hatefully and made a rude suggestion as to what Coop could do with himself.

"Kind regards to you, too, friend," Coop said mockingly then directed Brenner to lie facedown on the floor. When Brenner raised his stubbled chin in defiance and spit at him, Coop backhanded him with the butt of his pistol. The guard dropped to his knees and covered his bloody lip with his hands.

"Get down," Coop snarled. "You've tested my good disposition for the last time and forced me to deal with you the same way I handle other ruthless criminals who choose to defy my authority."

He glanced at Lily, who didn't look as smug and confident as she had a moment earlier. "Tie him up and be quick about it."

When he tossed her several leather strips Lily begrudgingly secured Brenner's hands and feet to the bedpost. Then Coop lashed Lily to the chair and used her frilly undergarments to gag both of his captives.

"Tell Webster I'm looking for him and I expect to be paid," Coop said before he exited by the same roundabout route that he'd used to arrive.

Chapter Sixteen

Coop hurried from the bordello then jogged back to Webster's mercantile shop. Gil and Miguel were waiting for him.

"He isn't here," Gil reported. "Any luck with you?"

"No, afraid not. Lily and the guard that I left bound up in her suite insist they don't know where Webster is."

"And you believe them?" Miguel asked skeptically.

Coop nodded. "Yes, I do. I think Webster and Denton are playing this hand close to the vest so no one can betray them."

Coop arched a curious brow when Hampton and his men rode through town, headed north.

"I asked Percy to keep watch on Webster's place," Miguel informed him. "It should keep him from going crazy by doing something worthwhile instead of stewing over Kate."

"Good thinking," Coop praised then frowned pensively. "From what Webster told you when he captured Kate, it seems he's planning to pull up stakes and raise money for a new start."

"I agree," Gil spoke up. "Webster has burned too many bridges in Questa Springs, especially with these last two schemes. I wonder if he's taking Lily with him when he leaves."

"I wouldn't be surprised," Coop replied. "According to

Alexa's findings, the Brantley sisters have an information network established. Unless we shut them down completely, Lily will likely set up her business elsewhere. Maybe all three of them will pull out when they discover we are aware of their unethical practices."

Coop pushed away from the supporting post then glanced at Webster's store. A grin spread across his lips, drawing Miguel's and Gil's bemused stares. "Seems to me, Marshal, that compensation is due the victims of tonight's fire. Although I'm not the local law official, I'd be inclined to offer Hampton, Barrett and Figgins the use of Webster's building and transfer the remaining inventory to them."

Gil snickered. "Hell of an idea. I was just getting ready to think of that myself."

"I'm going to swing by Alexa's room to see if she's still resting comfortably," Coop declared. "Then I'll check the line shack to see if Webster might have taken Kate there."

"I'm coming with you," Miguel insisted.

"I better wait here," Gil told Coop. "Several of the men you sent to check the alleys and storerooms for signs of Webster's occupancy haven't reported in."

With Miguel keeping pace beside him, Coop strode toward Walker Hotel. He could tell that his new friend was fretting about Kate. And rightfully so. She was in grave danger. No doubt about that. It appeared Webster was preparing to flee. Unless he deemed Kate useful as a shield of protection during his hasty escape, she'd become dispensable.

Coop refused to discuss that possibility with Miguel. He figured the man would arrive at the same bleak conclusion eventually. Coop didn't know the extent of Miguel's emotional involvement with the attractive young woman, but he suspected that losing her would devastate him.

Tossing aside the grim thought, Coop veered onto the side

street to reach the alley behind the hotel. "I'm going to use the same route to reach Alexa's room so I can remove the barrier from the door without disturbing her sleep. You can enter through the lobby if you prefer. I'll open the door for you."

Miguel studied the drainpipe, and the handholds and footholds available at irregular intervals. "The climb will help me expend my frustration. Standing and pacing haven't helped."

Coop grabbed the brace board above his head then clamped his legs around the drainpipe. The climb up demanded more strength and energy than shimmying down. He was slightly out of breath by the time he crawled through the window...

What he saw in the dark room ripped the last breath of air from his lungs.

"Damn it to hell!" he panted when he could breathe again. Still staring at the bed, he stepped aside to allow Miguel to crawl through the window.

"*¡Dios Mio!*" Miguel gasped in disbelief.

The barricaded door stood wide-open. The chair he'd braced under the knob had been knocked on its side. Instead of Alexa sleeping peacefully in bed, Kate lay blindfolded, bound, gagged and tied spread eagle to the bedposts.

When he noticed the note lying on her abdomen, he hurried over to snatch it up.

> Change of plans. Change of hostage. Tell Harold Quinn things have become more personal. I want twenty thousand dollars in ransom for his conniving daughter rather than ten for her friend.

Coop staggered back, as if he'd been sucker-punched. Seeing Alexa bleeding and injured earlier that evening had been difficult enough. Knowing she'd been abducted, when she didn't have the means or the energy to defend herself, drove him over the edge. And *he* had bribed her to take laudanum to knock her out completely. Now she didn't have a fighting chance.

She's going to die, just like my father and brother. The horrifying thought sent helpless fury coiling like a knot inside him. He stood there, paralyzed by overwhelming terror, visualizing all the terrible scenarios that might befall her.

Suddenly he'd traded places with Miguel in an emotional nightmare and there was no way out.

"Kate!" Miguel rushed over to remove her blindfold and gag and cut her free. "Are you hurt?"

"No, but—" Her voice broke as she surged upward to throw herself into Miguel's arms. "Oh God, I'm so worried about Alexa! That awful man, Denton, told me how he'd found her in Elliot's office, searching the desk for information. He cursed her for getting the drop on him and for locking him in a closet so she'd have a head start. He and the other hired guns shot at her and all of them claimed to be the one who found his target. Now—"

Kate burst into sobs. She buried her tousled red-gold head on Miguel's shoulder and struggled to regather her composure. Miguel held her close, murmuring words of solace and support.

"Lexi was too sedated to realize those bastards captured her," Kate continued shakily. "They jerked her up, without the slightest consideration for her injury. Then they rolled her in the quilt and carried her down the back steps."

Coop listened, feeling another corner of his world crumble, imagining the pain Alexa was suffering. "Did they transport you by horses or a wagon?" he asked grimly.

Kate lifted her tearstained face to Coop and wiped her cheeks with the back of her hand. "They brought me here in a wagon bed, covered with gunny sacks of feed to make sure I couldn't roll off. They carried me up the back steps. When they broke open the door, the loud noise didn't bring anyone upstairs. Most folks must still be at the town square."

"I have to hand it to Webster," Coop muttered resentfully. "He's set up smoke screens to cover his tracks. Did he give the slightest indication where he was taking Alexa?"

She shook her head miserably. "None whatsoever. He and Denton ruled out the ranch house because they expected it's the first place everyone looked. The second place was the brothel, but Elliot said too many people knew he was a regular at Lily's."

"Where did they stash you until they transported you here?" Miguel asked as he stroked her hair and held her reassuringly against his chest.

"In the wagon bed," she reported. "I have no idea where it was parked because I was blindfolded and gagged the moment you left to send the telegram to Harold."

"We have to inform Alexa's father of the change immediately," Coop said.

"We'll go," Kate volunteered as she climbed off Miguel's lap and surged to her feet.

"I'll tell Gil what happened on my way to the telegraph office," Miguel offered.

His gaze locked with Coop's. "If we don't find Alexa quickly her condition might become so aggravated when left unattended—"

"—I know," Coop interrupted. Hell, he imagined the worst possible scenario already. He didn't need his deepest fears translated into words.

Left alone, Coop plunked down on the side of the bed. Elbows on knees, head bowed, he cursed himself up one side and down the other. He'd failed Alexa when she'd needed him to protect her because she was weak and vulnerable. He'd fallen for one of the oldest tricks in the book, because his emotional attachment to her had made it impossible to keep a clear head.

Webster had used Kate as a decoy for the real hostage he wanted. He had the whole damn town in a tailspin with the rustling accusations, the fire and Kate's abduction. But Webster had been biding his time, waiting for the marshal and Miguel to organize a search. Then he'd located Alexa and kidnapped her.

Coop ordered himself to get up and get moving. Criticizing himself for not anticipating Webster's scheme wouldn't help Alexa. She was out there somewhere and she needed his help desperately if she were to survive.

A bleak expression tightened his lips, wondering if that lovely firebrand still thought investigation was her true calling. Whether it was or not, Coop prayed this case wouldn't be the death of her. He couldn't imagine the world without that blue-eyed beauty out there in it—somewhere.

Alexa's muffled groan of pain mingled with the creak of a wagon and clatter of horses' hooves. She had no idea where she was or what was weighing oppressively upon her. She felt too sluggish to think and she was too weary to care one way or another.

The jostling wagon caused her to grimace. Then she heard Elliot's voice and realized she was in serious trouble. She wondered if her captor was transporting her to the same location that he had stashed Kate.

"This is far enough," Elliot announced, alerting her that he wasn't alone. "You can hole up in one of the caves until I plant the wagon as a false clue and circle back with saddle horses."

"My pleasure. I have a grudge to settle with this bitch."

Alexa cursed silently when she recognized Oscar Denton's voice. Apparently he planned to punish her for getting the drop on him earlier that night. She inched her arm upward to determine the extent of her pain and mobility. Her shoulder hurt like hell, but she figured the threat of abuse and probable death would provide the incentive to work with the limited resources. Which wasn't much, except the element of surprise that she had regained consciousness.

Although how *surprise* would help when she'd been bound up like a mummy she didn't know.

When one of the men shoved aside the feed sack that held her down, she went completely limp. She had to bite her tongue to prevent howling in pain when she was dragged off the edge of the wagon bed.

She could tell by the bulk of the man's body that Oscar had tossed her over his shoulder. While he carried her uphill, Alexa heard the sound of rushing water. She speculated that he and Elliot planned to stash her in the upper canyon north of town.

Not that the information would do her any good, either. At least she knew the terrain—if and when she escaped.

This was where she'd first met Coop, she recalled. Coop... Alexa wondered if she'd ever see him again. She really hadn't expected to see him after she'd been shot. But she'd awakened to see him hovering over her while she lay in bed. She should've come right out and told him that she'd fallen in love with him, even though she'd tried not to become involved.

Now she might not have the chance to tell him that he was the only man she'd have liked to spend her life with. Not that he returned her affection, but she still wanted him to know he had her heart.

Now here she was, an injured hostage whose hours were numbered. The fact that she'd gotten Kate—wherever she was—into this mess made her feel decidedly worse. Her bleak thoughts scattered like buckshot when Oscar, huffing and puffing for breath, dropped her in an unceremonious heap on the rock-hard floor of a musty cavern. Alexa gritted her teeth and silently endured the pain shooting through her arm and chest.

"It might take a while to gather horses and supplies for our cross-country trip." Elliot's voice echoed around the cavern. "I'll have Lily pick up what we need."

"Don't know why you need to bring her along," Oscar mumbled. "One whore's as good as another in my book."

"Well, we obviously don't read the same book, do we?" Elliot retorted sarcastically. "Besides being a prize piece, she has connections you don't know about. Those connections will help us get set up elsewhere."

Oscar might not know about those clever connections, but Alexa did.

"Just don't forget I'm up here," Oscar demanded. "You try to double-cross me and the citizens in town won't be the only ones out for your blood."

"Settle your ruffled feathers, Denton." Webster's voice faded as he exited the cave. "I'll be back as soon as I can. All three of us will be riding off to California or Oregon to start our new lives."

When Oscar kicked her hip with the toe of his boot, Alexa continued to play possum, even though it hurt like the devil.

"You're no fun," he muttered. "But you will be before I toss you in the river and let you drown."

Now there was some encouraging news, she mused as his lumbering footsteps receded. Abuse and drowning. That didn't leave her much to look forward to.

Refusing to dissolve into tears and give way to disabling fear, Alexa pictured Coop standing beside her. Ah, how she wished he were here to boost her spirits. She'd give anything to possess his strength, experience and ingenuity.

Unfortunately she had to rely on her own creativity, although her mind was clogged with the aftereffects of the sedative Coop had crammed down her throat. Listening intently, Alexa concluded that she was alone in the cave. She heard no one else squirming about. Wherever Kate was, she obviously wasn't in here. Unless she was no longer breathing…

The grim thought threatened to reduce her to tears. Alexa inhaled a steadying breath and prayed that Kate was still among the living. Then she tried to figure out how she could get the drop on that bully when the odds weighed heavily in his favor.

Harold was still reeling from the shocking telegram that informed him that Webster—the crazed bastard—had taken Kate Hampton hostage and that Alexa had been injured. How? The message hadn't explained.

It had been a disastrous evening in progress already, what with his attempt to host the social gathering without Alexa's expertise. He had no idea how organized and efficient she was until he tried to plan the event and make it run as smoothly as Alexa did.

"Harold? Something wrong? You look a mite distressed," Ben Porter observed as he poured himself a drink from the bar in the study.

"He's right," Ambrose Shelton chimed in. "You look ill."

Harold feared that if he didn't share the disturbing news with someone he might pop. Unfortunately both men were on his list of possible informants so he needed to keep his trap shut. On second thought, he might be able to determine who was involved by gauging their reactions to the news.

"Webster, the crazed maniac, took my daughter's best friend hostage to force me to give him the contract and ordered me to pay a ransom. Plus, I received news that Alexa was injured, thanks to Webster, too, no doubt."

"What!" both men chirped in unison.

Their response caught the attention of the other six men

who were in the study, helping themselves to Harold's fine stock of liquor.

Harold gnashed his teeth. He stared into Ben's hazel eyes then fixated on Ambrose's slate-gray ones. He'd hoped he could tell who faked shock and who didn't. But damn it, he wasn't sure which one might be the culprit.

"How much ransom?" Ambrose asked.

"If you need funds I'll help you raise it," Ben quickly volunteered.

"Ten thousand."

Again, he tried to gauge the sincerity in the two men's expressions. He wondered if Webster's cohort was trying to find out if the scoundrel had added more to the ransom so he could keep extra for himself. But confound it, Harold couldn't tell if one or both men looked guilty.

"Ten?" Ambrose hooted. "Does that bastard really think his scheme will force us to give him the government contract?"

"Sounds desperate to me," Harold replied before he downed his drink in one swallow. His third, but who was counting?

"So what do you want us to do, Harold?" Ben asked. "Pay him or call upon every gunfighter and bounty hunter in the territory to track him down? I hear Wyatt Cooper from Albuquerque is the best in the territory. I can contact him."

"A young woman's life hangs in the balance," Harold replied, trying to imagine how upset Percy and Meg Hampton must be. For sure and certain, he'd be devastated if Alexa faced such grave danger.

"So we will pay," Ben presumed. "I will see to the arrangements for you…"

Ben's voice fizzled out when the same courier, who had delivered the telegram earlier that evening, materialized at the study door. Icy dread trickled down Harold's spine, fearing that Kate hadn't survived the calamity. He stared hesitantly at the folded missive the courier placed in his hand. When he read the telegram, he plunked down in the nearest chair to prevent collapsing on the floor.

"Dear God!" he howled in dismay.

Ambrose scurried toward Harold. "What now?"

Harold handed him the note. The room spun furiously around him and he struggled to draw a breath.

"Alexa has been kidnapped," Ambrose read aloud, drawing the gasp of every man in the room. "Who would dare?"

Harold suspected Ambrose was involved and fear and desperation over Alexa's safety overwhelmed him. Outraged, Harold exploded from the chair like a discharging cannonball. Chaos broke loose when Harold, in a wild rage, accidentally slammed into Ben and sideswiped two other men on his way to wrap his fingers around Ambrose's thick neck.

Ben yelped when he banged into the end table, tripped over his own feet then kerplopped on his backside. Bodies tumbled like bowling pins as Harold slammed into Ambrose's barrel-shaped torso, sending them both crashing to the floor.

"Harold, damn it, have you gone mad?" Ambrose choked as he tried to pry Harold's fingers from his throat.

"Here now, Harold, get hold of yourself!" John Marlow yelled as he bounded back to his feet to grab Harold by the nape of his jacket. "Get off Ambrose and calm down!"

"What in the world is going on in here?" came an unexpected voice from the doorway.

Stunned to the bone, Harold released his grip on Ambrose's neck then he pushed himself upright on the floor. His eyes nearly bugged out of their sockets when he stared at the new arrival. "How?" he croaked. "Why are you here? Sweet mercy—"

Shock, excitement and fear got the best of Harold. His eyes rolled back in his head and he passed out on the imported rug.

Coop reined Bandit toward the edge of town then halted abruptly. He couldn't decide where to search first. He heard the *clip-clop* of hooves behind him then twisted in the saddle to see Miguel and Gil approaching.

"We turned this town upside down but there's no sign of Alexa," Gil reported somberly.

"Where's Kate?" Coop asked Miguel.

"Since I rented a room for her mother at the hotel earlier, I took her there to rest. Then I sent a message to Percy so he'd know that his daughter is safe."

"Any idea about where Alexa might be?" Gil questioned Coop.

If he could think straight, he might come up with a few ideas. Unfortunately the image of Alexa bound, gagged and blindfolded, while suffering agonizing injury, was tormenting him to no end. "I guess I'll check Lily's place first," he said finally. "If she isn't there we can presume that she joined Webster in hiding out."

The threesome headed for the private entrance to Lily's second-story suite. Coop didn't expect the madam still to be tied to her chair. Sure enough, she wasn't. Brenner, the gunman, wasn't hog-tied on the floor and the posted guard, who kept watch at the back steps, wasn't around, either.

"I'll check with the other women," Gil offered. "Maybe they know where Lily went."

Coop surveyed the room, noting the ornate trunk at the foot of the bed stood open—and empty. "For sure she left in a rush with as many of her belongings as she could cram into carpetbags," he said, calling Gil's attention to the trunk. "Find out if any of the women saw Webster in person."

"Will do." Gil hurried off to question the harlots.

"I'm worried as hell," Miguel confided as he glanced around the dimly lit room.

"That makes two of us." Coop wished he could shake the unnerving dread that hung over him like a dark cloud of doom. "Where would Webster and Denton take her? It would have to be a natural fortress because no one in town will offer refuge to that conniving bastard."

"High ground," Miguel speculated. "Somewhere with plenty of cover to hide, in case this turns into an all-out man-hunt. Someplace where you can see someone coming from a long distance so they can't get the drop on you."

"My thoughts exactly," Coop agreed. "The upper canyon is a perfect hideout. Water is readily available. There are trees and underbrush for protective cover. When I was there, waiting to meet Mr. Chester, I noticed a few hollowed-out caves that could serve as a fortress."

"*Si*, that is exactly where I would stash a hostage," Miguel said excitedly.

When Coop rushed onto the small terrace at the back entrance of the suite, he noticed a wagon stashed in a lean-to on the far side of the corral. "There." He pointed, drawing Miguel's attention. "My guess is that Webster or Denton returned to retrieve Lily."

"They probably exchanged the wagon for horses," Miguel predicted.

Gil hurried through the room to join them on the terrace. "Webster was here about a half hour ago to fetch Lily," he reported. "She did leave in a rush and didn't say if or when she'd be back. One of the girls said Webster promised to give her money to move the wagon and park it behind one of the saloons, but since he didn't pay her in advance she didn't bother with it."

"They could be planning to skip town to pick up the ransom in Santa Fe," Coop mused aloud. He stared grimly at Gil. "Miguel and I are headed to the upper canyon. We think that's where Denton is keeping Alexa. I need you to send another telegram to Harold Quinn, telling him to leave shredded newspaper rather than bank notes for the ransom."

"You don't expect Lexi to survive, do you?" Miguel said bitterly. "Why bother with real money, right?"

Coop endured the mutinous glare Miguel directed at him. "My policy is to handle all hostage ransoms the same. You don't reward a cutthroat for disposing of his hostage and collecting a hefty payment. Isn't that right, Gil?"

The marshal nodded somberly. "That was our practice when we worked together."

Miguel swore ripely. "I was beginning to like you, *gringo*. But turns out your heart is made of solid rock. We're talking about *Alexa*. I know you care about her so don't try to deny it."

He had cared about his father and brother, too, but that hadn't changed the outcome of the tragedy, he mused as he descended the steps.

"Paying Webster and his informant won't guarantee we can reach Alexa in time," Coop told Miguel, and then turned his attention to Gil. "After you send the telegram, join us in the canyon with as many posse members carrying torches as you can round up on the spur of the moment. We'll mount an extensive search to locate Alexa."

Gil darted off, but Miguel was still glaring holes in Coop's back as they jogged toward their horses.

"I care about Alexa," Coop admitted. "A lot. But that doesn't change my policy of dealing with heartless outlaws. Webster and Denton included. You expect the worst from them. Always. That way you're never caught off guard."

Miguel expelled a sigh as he mounted his horse. "In case

things don't turn out for the best, you should know that I think Lexi cares deeply for you. She never gave any other man her affection, only cordial attention and common courtesy."

That should make Coop feel better, knowing he was special to Alexa. But it didn't. Nothing would pacify him except having her safe in his arms again. He knew from previous experience with hostage situations that her chances of survival were slim to none.

And that scared the living hell out of him.

Chapter Seventeen

❧❧❧❧❧

Alexa could hear Oscar thrashing around outside. His muttered oaths reverberated around the inside of the cave. She had unintentionally dozed off and didn't know how long she had slept. She wondered if Oscar had calculated the time required for Elliot to fetch Lily and the horses then decided he had been left holding the hostage. Either that or Elliot had been spotted, captured and wasn't returning at all.

Alexa sincerely hoped the latter was true.

No matter what had happened to Elliot, she predicted Oscar would come storming inside to take out his anger and resentment on her. Which meant she had better find a way to get loose or her future would be short and extremely unpleasant.

Alexa patted the band of her breeches with her bound hands then swore quietly. The pistol she had tucked away after she escaped Oscar at Elliot's office earlier that evening was long gone. She presumed that Coop or the physician had removed it before stitching up her wounded shoulder.

The disappointing realization gave way to an encouraging thought. She had tucked a dagger in her boot before riding off to sneak into Elliot's office. If she were lucky, no one had noticed it.

A relieved smile pursed her lips when she inched her knees up so she could reach down to check her boot. The dagger was where she had left it. Elliot and Oscar hadn't bothered to check her for weapons since she had been injured, sedated and easy to abduct.

Although pained seared her arm, she used the dagger to saw through the rope that encircled her ankles. Hopeful anticipation rose inside her as she clamped the dagger between her knees to steady it while she cut the rope on her wrists.

Once free, she rolled to her knees to rearrange the quilt and rug to look as if she were still sleeping. She tested her ankle, thankful that she could put weight on it after she'd landed wrong when she leaped out Elliot's office window. She tiptoed to the exit and craned her neck around the jutting stone wall. Oscar stamped back and forth in the moonlight. He paused at regular intervals to stare downhill, waiting impatiently for his cohort to show up. After spouting a string of crude oaths, Oscar lurched around and stalked toward the cave.

Alexa flattened herself against the wall and held her breath, in hopes of being overlooked. She was counting on Oscar's eyes taking a moment to adjust to absolute darkness in the cave. Sure enough, he moved blindly toward the motionless form he had deposited near the back wall.

"Your time has come, bitch," he boomed loud enough to wake the dead. "You're about to find out the only real purpose a woman is born to serve."

His voice was still ricocheting off the stone walls when Alexa slipped outside and scanned the area hurriedly, trying to determine the most effective escape route. She decided to climb upward so she could keep an eye on Oscar, who would exit like a snarling grizzly, when he realized she had somehow eluded him.

Wincing in pain, Alexa scrabbled uphill, using tufts of grass and boulders to steady herself. A moment later Oscar's roar of rage belched from the cave. She sank behind a boulder when he stormed out to survey the area.

"You cunning bitch! You'll pay in spades this time," he bellowed hatefully.

He commenced pawing and slashing at nearby shrubs in an effort to locate her. Alexa didn't want to give her position away so she inched uphill backward, moving as quietly as possible. Oscar, the imbecile, was making so much racket during his temper tantrum that he couldn't hear her moving up the rock ledge above him.

Things were going better than expected. She was slowly but surely placing more distance between her and her vicious captor—

The gratifying thought scattered like buckshot when her foot slipped on loose pebbles near the base of a boulder. Her leg shot out in front of her, causing a cascade of stones and pebbles to tumble over the overhanging ledge, giving away her location.

Oscar whirled around and grabbed his six-shooter. "I'll shoot both your legs out from under you!" he snarled. "I'll use you as my private whore before I put a bullet through your blue-blooded heart."

His scare tactics worked, she was sorry to say. Especially when he began firing off shots that whizzed so close to her head that she swore she could hear the angels playing their harps in heaven above. Below her, Oscar scrambled uphill, spouting all sorts of ruthless threats. He fired off another shot that slammed into the cedar tree near her left shoulder. He swore crudely when he lost his footing, causing his next shot to go astray. Yelping and cursing the air blue, he landed spread-eagle on his backside.

Alexa bounded to her feet, latched onto a stripling for balance and heaved herself upward. Then she prayed for divine intervention—because she knew she didn't have the strength and stamina to escape without assistance.

She ran for her life—and hoped her guardian angel could spare the time to lend a helping hand.

Coop snapped to attention when he heard a roaring voice roll down the canyon like an avalanche. He dug his heels into Bandit's flanks, urging the horse into its swiftest gait. The terrifying sound of a discharging pistol reverberated off the V-shaped walls of the canyon. Coop's heart stalled in his chest. He kept picturing Alexa pelted with more gunshot wounds. Outrage and fear for her life burgeoned inside him.

He'd ridden fifty yards into the canyon before he reminded himself to exercise caution and cunning. Unfortunately, speculating on all the awful pain Alexa might be suffering made him wild and reckless. It took sheer will to rein in Bandit and think rationally—because there was nothing sane or rational about the emotions that bombarded him.

When Miguel skidded to a halt beside him, Coop noted the same panicky concern in his expression that was eating him alive.

Think, damn it, Coop ordered himself. He dragged in a restorative breath and reminded himself that Alexa's life was on the line. He had to respond sensibly, immediately.

"I'll circle the hillside," Coop said decisively. "You continue straight ahead."

"You should know I'll be shooting to kill, *gringo,*" Miguel ground out vengefully.

"Wouldn't have it any other way myself, so stay the hell out of my line of fire while you're shooting uphill and I'm shooting down."

Another shot rang out, followed by another enraged bellow. Coop went one way and Miguel went the other. Forcing Bandit to lunge up the steep embankment, Coop scanned the moonlit terrain. From his vantage point, he spotted the smoke and sparks from a discharging pistol. He hoped Alexa had somehow managed to arm herself, but he doubted it. He remembered setting aside her firearm when he removed her shirt to check her injury. He certainly hadn't done her any favors by leaving her unarmed.

If she hadn't managed to confiscate Denton's weapon then he was the one shooting at her. Yet, Coop couldn't risk going with that assumption by firing into the underbrush where a trickle of smoke drifted skyward.

"Come here, you stupid bitch!" Denton bellowed in the distance.

Coop glanced around, hoping to detect movement but he couldn't locate Alexa and he didn't want to expose his position to Denton. Coop snapped to attention when Denton shot from the underbrush like a cannonball. He heard a pained yelp that he knew belonged to Alexa. Coop was off his horse in a single bound, racing through the bushes, praying for all he was worth that he arrived before it was too damn late to save her.

Alexa hissed in pain when she banged her tender ankle on an oversize rock then stumbled off balance. She tried to brace on her injured arm but it gave way and she fell flat on her face. Frantic, she scrambled back to her knees, knowing Oscar was nearly upon her.

He came out of nowhere like a charging bull, knocking her backward so hard that air gushed from her lungs in a *whoosh*. Her neck whiplashed then she hit the ground with a *thump*.

"I've been itching to have you," he growled triumphantly as he stood over her.

Head spinning, she tried to lever herself up, but he back-handed her. Stinging pain throbbed in her cheek and stars twinkled before her eyes. When she tried to rise again, he struck her, vowing to beat her into submission. Fury boiled through her veins, providing her with the strength needed to respond. When he dropped onto his knees atop of her and reared back his arm, she struck him before he could strike her again.

Hissing in outrage, she stabbed the bullying bastard in the chest with her dagger. An instant later, a gunshot rang out. Oscar swayed unsteadily above her, as if suspended in a realm of pain and astonishment. His eyes widened in disbelief as he glanced down to see the handle of the knife protruding from his chest then he stared uncomprehendingly at the shiny stain that quickly spread across the shoulder of his shirt.

When his bulky body swayed toward her, Alexa braced her good arm against his belly before he collapsed on top of her. To her stunned surprise, Denton launched backward through the air and landed with a thud.

Coop towered over her, a smoking gun in his hand. Even in the moonlit darkness, she could read the concern in his ex-pression as he took inventory of her condition. She wanted to bound to her feet, throw herself into his arms and bawl her head off. Yet, she didn't want to appear weak and helpless to a man who exemplified strength, skill and perseverance.

So she raised her good arm, silently requesting that he assist her to her feet, and said, "It certainly took you long enough to find me, partner. I thought I was going to have to save myself."

Coop glanced over his shoulder to note the dagger protrud-ing from Oscar's chest. Then he holstered his six-shooter. "Looks like we had him coming and going. A damn shame the son of a bitch is too dead to stand trial or testify against Webster."

Coop folded his hand around hers and gently drew her to her feet. When her legs wobbled beneath her, Coop curled a supporting arm around her waist. She smelled musty, as if she had been stuffed in a cave. But he nuzzled his cheek against her neck nevertheless. Knowing she was the worse for wear but alive came as a gigantic relief.

He noticed the welt on her cheek. "You okay, princess?" he murmured as he pulled her close, savoring the pleasure of holding her and of knowing he hadn't arrived too late to lend a helping hand.

"More or less," she murmured. Then her breath hitched and he knew she was trying exceptionally hard not to allow the horrifying ordeal to get to her while he was on hand to witness it.

"Which one? More or less?" he teased as he dropped a kiss to her forehead.

"Less," she finally admitted. "I was wondering if I might have the rest of the evening off this case. I'm feeling a little light-headed."

"Sure, but I wish you'd stay where I put you for once," he replied as he picked her up in his arms and turned toward Bandit. "It isn't easy tracking you after dark."

She managed a faint smile, though he couldn't imagine how, considering her weakened condition and her harrowing emotional experience. But that was Alexa, he reminded himself. She was too determined and spirited to quit. As long as there was a breath of life left in her, she refused to give up. Coop admired her greatly for that. He knew men who didn't hold up as well in a life-threatening crisis as this blue-eyed hellion.

"We needed to solve this case quickly so Papa can tear up Elliot's contract and toss him in jail," she insisted.

"*¡Dios mio!*"

Coop glanced over his shoulder to see Miguel appear from the shadows. His wide-eyed gaze landed on Denton's knife wound then swung to the gunshot wound on his shoulder.

"That was too damn close!" Miguel muttered as he quickly appraised Alexa. "You look like hell."

"Thank you. That makes me feel so much better about myself," she mocked as she rested her head on Coop's shoulder.

Not that he minded. He needed the reassurance that she was alive and reasonably well.

"Have you found Kate yet?" she asked.

Miguel bobbed his dark head. "Webster exchanged Kate for you. He left her tied to your bed at the hotel. She is fine, except that she's fretting over you."

Coop felt Alexa sag heavily in relief. "Come on, princess. Let's get you to town so you can recuperate."

He carefully deposited her on Bandit's back. When she swayed slightly, Miguel reined his horse over to hold her upright while Coop climbed up behind her. When he settled her securely against his chest and wrapped a protective arm around so she wouldn't topple off the horse—if she lost consciousness—Miguel led the way downhill.

"One last thing," Alexa murmured against Coop's shoulder.

He brushed his cheek against hers and thanked the powers that be that she possessed the ingenuity and intellect to elude Denton. "What's the one last thing, princess?" he whispered.

"I was afraid I wouldn't have the chance to tell you. Almost didn't."

She sounded so exhausted and felt like a rag doll propped up in his arms. "Tell me what?" he asked as he pressed a kiss to her neck.

"I love you. I didn't want to, tried not to, but I do…"

Her head rolled against his arm and she slumped motionlessly against his chest.

Coop agonized over her quiet confession. He knew a wild pendulum of emotion prompted her words. She had suffered fear, injury, shock and relief in the course of a few hours. She probably thought that she should love him since they had become intimate. But that was just emotional turmoil speaking for her. Besides, she didn't fit into his rough-and-tumble world. And certainly, he didn't fit into her privileged lifestyle.

As Miguel kept harping at him, a man needed to know his place in society without harboring unrealistic expectations. Nonetheless, a part of him thrilled to her muffled confession, even if she'd probably prefer to take it back after she recovered from her injuries and returned to an even keel.

His conflicting thoughts trailed off when he saw the posse, carrying torches, moving up the canyon trail. To Coop's dismay, Gil reported that Webster and his paramour were not in custody. That slippery bastard had double-crossed Denton and had escaped. Fortunately Webster didn't know that his hostage was free. Coop planned to be the one to tell him—face-to-face.

Coop eased Alexa's unconscious body onto Miguel's lap. "Take good care of her, my friend."

Miguel blinked, startled. "Where are you going?"

"To Santa Fe. This investigation isn't over yet and we're running out of time." He glanced down at Alexa's lovely but battered face and smiled. "Ask her to fetch the ledger she hid, when she feels up to it. I'll see that she receives full credit for ferreting out the information needed for evidence." He reined sideways then halted. "Have my belongings sent to my office in Albuquerque."

"As you wish, *gringo*. I'm sure you'll see that justice is served."

Coop headed north, following the Indian trail that topped the mountain ridge. Leaving Alexa behind was the single most difficult task he'd ever undertaken.

Their partnership was officially dissolved, he told himself. He never would have met her at all if she hadn't wanted to prove her potential to her father. He should be grateful for the precious time he had spent with her.

Harold would take her seriously now, Coop assured himself. Especially if he sang her praises to high heaven. And he would, too. It was the least he could do for Alexa. Harold wouldn't hold her back, not after he'd nearly lost her. No one would hold that free-spirited female back now, Coop predicted.

Alexa was vibrant, full of life and eager to spread her independent wings. She'd be fine.

He couldn't say the same for himself because there was a big empty hole in his chest where his heart used to be.

"He left? What do you mean he left?" Alexa howled at Miguel. "You couldn't have told me that *before* you crammed more sedatives down my throat sometime in the past twenty-four hours? Damn it, Miggy!"

"I told you she wouldn't take it well," Kate reminded Miguel, who had drawn the short straw and had been required to deliver the news.

"Coop went to Santa Fe," Miguel continued. "He told me to tell you that he would wrap up the case and assure Harold that you played the dominant role in acquiring the facts."

"I damn well intend to be on hand when Elliot tries to grab the ransom and head for the hills."

Her voice fizzled out when she tried to stand up abruptly. The room spun crazily, forcing Alexa to sit or fall.

"See there?" Kate chastised her. "You are not healthy enough to endure a lengthy stagecoach and train ride. Coop can handle the situation in Santa Fe. You said yourself that he's the best there is in the detective business."

Alexa wilted back to her pillow. Despite what her dearest friends thought, *she* knew the real reason Coop had left in a flaming rush. She had made the crucial mistake of telling him that she was in love with him and it had scared him off.

Nothing much scared Wyatt Cooper, but that had done it. He'd decided to get out while the getting was good. Alexa knew that he could have sent a telegram to the Santa Fe police department and had them swoop in on Elliot or Norville Thomas—or both—when someone came to pick up the ransom money. This was Coop's subtle way of telling her that he didn't return her deep feelings. He had told her from the beginning that he didn't want a permanent business partner. So that was that.

"Besides, you can't leave Questa Springs yet. You promised the citizens a town-wide celebration," Kate said with a wry grin. "Selma Mae forged ahead with your previous arrangements and turned it into a thank-you party for your part in ridding the community of Webster and his hired guns."

"Exactly right," Miguel chimed in. "At Coop's suggestion, Gil offered the abandoned mercantile store to Kate's father and his partners to compensate for Webster burning them out. You and Coop are heroes in these parts. One of you needs to be the guest of honor for the celebration."

Alexa didn't want to be hailed as a hero. She wanted Coop back. If she had kept her trap shut, he might still be here. Given time to wear him down, he might have agreed to let her assist in one more investigation. Followed by another. And then another. Before he knew it, they might have become permanent partners.

But now he was gone and soon he'd be off to who-knew-where to investigate who-knew-what. She wouldn't have the opportunity to see him for months. By then, any concern and sympathy he might have felt for her would fizzle out and it would be difficult to talk him into any future arrangements.

Damnation, it had taken her a while to convince him to let

her become his *temporary* partner. *Permanent* would be out of the question if she didn't act quickly.

"I'm not going to make your travel arrangements for sooner than the day *after* the celebration," Miguel announced.

"I'm not in a festive mood," Alexa said grouchily.

"You will be by Saturday," Kate assured her cheerfully.

Alexa glared at her smiling friends. "I want it known that I'm only attending under protest."

"Point noted," said Kate, swallowing an amused snicker. "Nonetheless you will be our guest of honor. Instead of *marrying* that weasel, Webster, you are instrumental in having him *jailed*. That makes you one of the most popular personalities in town."

Alexa set aside her disappointment over Coop's absence for the moment and glanced speculatively between Miguel and Kate. "And what, I would like to know, are you two going to do about your situation?"

Both of her friends looked everywhere except at her. Miguel appeared tormented by the direct question and Kate looked miserable.

"I'm going to accompany you back to Santa Fe," Miguel said belatedly. "That is my job as your chaperone and bodyguard."

"That is easy to solve," Alexa said with a dismissive flick of her wrist. "You're fired. I can take care of myself."

Miguel smirked mockingly. "Of course, you can. That's why you're lying in bed, nursing a gunshot wound, a tender ankle, a bruised cheek. Compliments of a couple of near brushes with catastrophe. You call that taking care of yourself?"

Alexa flashed him a challenging stare. "But I solved the case…partially…didn't I?"

"Yes, and you're still alive, thanks to Coop's educated guess as to where to find you. And you'll notice that he's the last man standing, not you." Miguel doubled over to brush a brotherly kiss over her brow. "Rest now, *querida*. You need to be the perfect party hostess, come Saturday."

When her friends exited so she could catch a nap, Alexa expelled a heavy sigh. Coop had only been gone for a day and she missed him terribly. If she gave up on these intense feelings of affection, how long would it take to get over him? Two months? Two years? Two decades? Never?

Never was probably closer to the mark, she decided as she closed her eyes and prayed that she would awake feeling revived and rejuvenated. She was not going to lie flat on her back with her arm in a sling for too long a time. She needed activity to thrive and survive. But most of all she needed Coop to make her happy.

That was her last thought before weariness claimed her and she fell asleep, wishing for the impossible.

Chapter Eighteen

◦◦◦⚬⚬⚬

From his hiding place inside Harold Quinn's stable, Coop watched a now-familiar silhouette scurry toward the well where the ransom pouch had been deposited a quarter of an hour earlier. Coop had ridden hell-for-leather to reach Santa Fe, with just enough time to spare to pose a few questions at the territorial commissary and to brief his client. The arrangements for the ransom pickup had been made and carried out according to Coop's specifications. Except for one exasperating detail.

Coop glanced over his shoulder at Harold who, like his daughter, thought he needed to be in on the action. *Must run in the family,* Coop decided. After meeting Harold, and realizing he was sincere and determined to resolve the situation, Coop knew this wasn't a publicity stunt. The man simply wanted revenge for being scared half to death when he learned the culprits had captured Alexa and demanded ransom money, along with the absurd demand to renew the government contract. Plus, there was no question in Coop's mind that Harold was exceptionally fond of his daughter.

"That two-faced, devious son of a bitch," Harold said with

a hiss. "If I had known then what you found out at the commissary about Norville Thomas being Elliot Webster's stepbrother, I might have figured out that he was involved in embezzling military and reservation supplies and selling them for profit."

"That's why they tried to keep it quiet," Coop murmured.

Alexa had mentioned to him that she hadn't made the connection that initially led to the partnership between Thomas and Webster, though she was the one who tied the two swindlers together through notations in the ledgers. Coop had asked around the military supply post until he uncovered the truth.

Now Coop would make it his mission to see that the cunning stepbrothers could spend more time together—by occupying adjacent cells at the penitentiary.

When Harold saw Thomas squatting to draw the bucket from the well, he tried to bolt forward. Coop rammed an elbow into his chest to hold him in place.

"You stay here," he demanded. "Having one Quinn injured during this case is one too many. Let me do my job."

Harold sighed audibly. "Fine, but I have a few choice words to spout at the dishonest bastard."

"You can spout at him all you want once I have him in custody."

Coop slipped out the door and moved stealthily along the outer wall. With both pistols drawn, he crept toward Thomas, who had his back to him.

"Drop the pouch and your pistol," Coop ordered sharply.

Thomas half turned to smirk haughtily at the command. "Apparently you weren't informed of the demands. If I don't walk out of here with the money then Alexa Quinn won't survive. Depend on it."

Coop shrugged carelessly. "That isn't my problem, Thomas. You're the one with the serious problem." He smiled sardonically. "You need to figure out how you're going to walk out of here alive when you have to deal with me."

"Who are you?" Thomas asked insolently.

"Wyatt Cooper of Cooper Investigations."

"Oh hell," Thomas muttered as he raised his pistol into firing position.

Coop's first shot sent sparks flying off Thomas's pistol. It flipped over his wrist and tumbled to the dirt. Howling in pain, Thomas grabbed his bloody hand and tried to take off at a dead run. Coop's second shot hit him in the back of the knee, causing him to stumble forward. Coop pounced, forcing Thomas facedown in the grass. In a flash, he fastened the cuffs in place.

"Good work, Coop," Harold panted, out of breath from his mad dash across the lawn to stand over the downed captive. "As for you, Thomas, a mere court-martial for defrauding the army isn't enough punishment for you and your stepbrother."

Thomas jerked up his head, his eyes wide in surprise.

Harold nodded and smiled triumphantly. "That's right. We know who you are. Coop discovered the family connection and also identified you as the messenger who relayed confidential information from here to Questa Springs," Harold said, taking grand satisfaction in informing him. "Now tell us where Webster is hiding out or you might bleed to death before your court-martial."

Thomas stuck out his chin and glared belligerently at Harold.

"Harold, take a walk, will you?" Coop requested. "I think Thomas prefers to pass along that information in private."

"Like hell—ouch!" Thomas yelped when Coop applied persuasive pressure to his injured hand.

Clearly Harold wanted to be present for the interrogation, but he finally turned around and walked off to the spacious mansion on the hill. Hell of a castle, Coop mused as he appraised Alexa's home again. If the visit to her house to confer with Harold earlier wasn't enough to convince Coop that he and Alexa lived in different worlds and hailed from vastly different backgrounds nothing would. He wasn't far off the mark when he teasingly referred to her as princess. She was as close to royalty as Coop would likely ever get.

When Harold was out of earshot, Coop turned his attention to Thomas. He resorted to several tried-and-true tactics that prompted criminals to volunteer crucial information. It wasn't long before his prisoner broke the silence.

"He's waiting for me at Rose's Pleasure Parlor," Thomas gritted out grudgingly.

"Ah yes, Lily's infamous sister," Coop said, making certain Thomas knew that he was aware of the information network that had been set up in the territory. "One last question. Who has been providing the information that you pass along to your stepbrother?"

"Go to hell," Thomas snarled hatefully.

"Been there a time or two. The devil sends his regards. He's counting your days until you take up permanent residence with him," Coop retorted as he applied more pressure.

"Ambrose Shelton," he squawked in pain then gasped for breath. "The arrogant bastard didn't even realize Rose pumped him for information when he paid his weekly visits. Then she double-checked what she'd heard with another of her clients, Ben Porter, who had a loose tongue himself. Then Rose, damn her fickle hide, decided to take on another client against my wishes and I—"

When Thomas stopped talking abruptly and clamped his mouth shut, Coop dug his knee a little deeper into Thomas's spine. "Go on. I'm listening."

"It has nothing to do with the information network," he ground out.

"Perhaps not but you've piqued my curiosity." Coop applied another degree of persuasive pressure and said, "You might as well know that I won't let you up until you spill it."

Thomas groaned in pain, cursed Coop foully then said, "Rose betrayed me with another man."

Coop frowned and wondered how a prostitute could be loyal, given her chosen profession.

"She started playing favorites with him and I went after him with a shotgun one afternoon. She swore I was the one she really cared about. But she was looking for better connections that I could provide."

Coop thought Thomas should have selected a higher class of woman, but considering that he was a liar, swindler and a thief, he supposed Thomas had gotten exactly what he deserved.

Satisfied with the information that would lead to several convictions, Coop came to his feet to haul Thomas up beside him. The future-*former* quartermaster of the territorial commissary was on his way to jail.

Coop gave a shout to summon the two police officers who were waiting at the house. After they marched Thomas away, Coop strode back to the stables to fetch Bandit.

Harold was waiting for him. After Coop gave the boiled down version of his conversation with Thomas, Harold shook his head in dismay. "And to think I was there—" He shut his mouth, muttered under his breath then added, "The flower sisters need to be shut down immediately."

"On my way through Albuquerque I informed the marshal about the information network at Daisy's Pleasure Haven. He's shutting it down today," Coop reported. "I'll have the police arrest Rose after I locate Webster and Lily." Coop's gaze narrowed sternly. "I refuse to let Webster sneak off again. He caused Kate and Alexa too much pain and anguish. I want to make damn certain he's behind bars."

"So do I." Smiling gratefully, Harold extended his hand to Coop. "I am indebted to you and so is Alexa."

Coop lifted his shoulder in a nonchalant shrug. "As I explained to you earlier, Alexa was directly responsible for uncovering crucial information and tying it together to give us the leads we needed to solve the case."

"Don't remind me," Harold said, grimacing. "She took a more active role in the investigation than I wanted. I'll never be able to restrain that headstrong daughter of mine now that she's had a taste of adventure and excitement."

"No, probably not, so I suggest you don't try. She's meant for greater challenges," Coop said before he strode off to grab Bandit's reins. "After I tie up the loose ends at Rose's Pleasure Parlor, I'll circle back here before I head south to my headquarters."

"My thanks, Coop," Harold called after him.

"You should be more grateful than you even realize," Coop said under his breath.

Harold was unaware of how much effort it required for Coop to walk away from the only woman who truly mattered to him. Which was exactly why Coop had made a solemn pact with himself to have no future contact with Alexa—for her sake as well as his own. She needed and deserved a man who traveled in the same social circle. Someone dignified and respectable, who carried Harold's stamp of approval. Not a rough-edged gunfighter whose secretive past had to remain dead and buried because it would reflect badly on Alexa and Harold.

Two more arrests and you can ride away for good, Coop told himself as he trotted into town to enter Rose's Pleasure Parlor.

A quarter of an hour later Coop greeted the unsuspecting Elliot Webster with two loaded pistols and the terse command to raise his hands above his head—and keep them there.

"What are you doing here?" Webster asked in stunned surprise. "And what happened to your limp?"

"The limp was Alexa's idea to throw you off track," Coop informed him. "She's the one who figured out how you were passing privileged information and selling military supplies."

"Alexa?" Webster hooted, his hands still over his head, as Coop demanded.

"Yes, my partner in investigation. We worked this case together. You should know that she never had the slightest intention of marrying you," Coop took great pleasure in telling him.

Webster sniffed disrespectfully. "For damn sure she won't want a commoner like you so don't think you'll have more luck getting hold of her family's money than I did."

"I wasn't planning to ask her to marry me," Coop replied as he grabbed one of Webster's wrists, and secured him to the carved bedposts.

Hell, he'd been the *first* to realize that he was the *last* man Alexa needed.

"By the way, Gil Henson sent a telegram stating that Alexa sent him out to retrieve the incriminating ledger as evidence of your shady business dealings."

Webster scowled at the news.

"In addition, the hired guns you sent to start the fire at your competition's store have agreed to testify against you." Coop grinned wickedly. "Good luck with your upcoming court case and your stepbrother's court-martial. I'm sure justice will prevail."

Webster muttered and swore profusely.

Coop summoned several law officers to transport Webster to jail, along with Lily and Rose Brantley. All three of them glared mutinously at Coop, but he didn't pay the slightest attention. He simply mounted Bandit and rode away.

A rueful smile pursed his lips as his thoughts drifted back to the bittersweet memories that were never far from mind. Damn, he was going to miss Alexa like crazy. Her touch, her indomitable spirit, her quick wit. The feel of her luscious body moving intimately against his in the heat of passion…

Coop squelched the erotic thought. For one reckless, whimsical moment, he glanced in the direction of Questa Springs, the town that was nestled in a plush green valley between the hazy mountains to the southeast. Then he convinced himself that he could never go back because he wasn't strong enough to leave her twice.

Alexa would make a full recovery. Caring, reliable friends surrounded her. She didn't need him anymore and he needed to accept another assignment that would occupy his time and his mind.

On that sensible thought, Coop trotted off to deliver his final report to Harold before riding back to his headquarters.

Alexa felt considerably better by the time the city-wide celebration began. The two local bands were stationed at opposite corners of the town square, playing lively tunes. There was enough food placed on the makeshift tables to feed an army. Countless citizens stopped by to thank her for her contribution of exposing Elliot Webster for the conniving shyster he was.

"Can't thank you enough," Percy Hampton said as he halted in front of her. "Now that my partners and I have moved into the vacant mercantile store, business is booming again."

"You should hire Miguel to run the shop," Alexa suggested. "My father and I can offer sterling recommendations. He is honest, trustworthy and responsible."

"Do you think he might be interested?" Percy asked before he sipped his wine. "After I received the telegram from your father, notifying Barrett and me that we both will be providing beef and trained saddle horses for the forts and reservations, I realized we won't have much time left to run the store."

That's the way Alexa had it figured, too. "Indeed. And why allow Kate's fine education to go to waste?" Alexa purposely massaged her mending arm, silently reminding Percy that she had taken Kate's place as hostage and that his daughter might have died if Webster hadn't decided to put excessive pressure on her father to extort money and favors.

"Together with Kate's head for numbers and Miguel's organizational skills they will make a grand team." Alexa planted the seed and smiled enthusiastically. "Besides, they get along splendidly and they have known each other forever. In addition, they have great respect and affection for one another."

"Grand idea, Alexa. Kate has become increasingly restless of late." He stroked his chin thoughtfully. "I don't think my daughter is going to be satisfied with allowing me to arrange her marriage and see her settled into the position of running a household quite yet. After nearly losing Kate during that fiasco with Webster, I must admit that I've become a bit more lenient and open-minded toward my daughter."

Open-minded enough to allow Kate to marry a man you probably consider beneath her so-called social class? Alexa wondered.

Well, she wasn't going to bring up that touchy issue tonight. She had paved the way by encouraging Percy to make Miguel and Kate business associates. They would have to take the next step, if that's what they really wanted. Time would tell if they were willing to stand up to Percy in order to be together.

When Percy wandered off, several citizens dropped by to praise her on organizing the fine party. Alexa sipped her wine—and nearly choked on it when she saw her father step down from a carriage full of unexpected arrivals.

"Dear God!" she squealed as she took off in an unladylike dash across the town square. "Bethany? Is it really you?"

To her amazement and delight, Alexa watched her younger sister alight from the carriage, looking positively enchanting in her gold satin gown. "How...when...why...?"

Bethany chortled as she hugged Alexa close, ever mindful of her mending shoulder. "You sound exactly like Papa when I showed up unexpectedly at his office door. The only difference is that he blacked out when he saw me and we had to use smelling salts to revive him."

"I was also reeling from the shock of discovering that Kate Hampton, and then Alexa, had been abducted and held for ransom," Harold defended himself before he dropped a kiss on Alexa's cheek. He stared disconcertedly at her. "We will discuss, at great length, your firsthand involvement in that investigation later, young lady."

"It was quite exciting," she said, undaunted, and then gave her father a one-armed hug. "I must confess that I loved every moment it of it. Except for the hostage ordeal, of course."

"I was afraid that would be the case," he mumbled.

Alexa turned to face her sister directly. Bethany had become the striking image of their mother. Statuesque and aristocratic. Curly chestnut-brown hair surrounded her bewitching face. Exotic brown eyes that tilted at the corners mesmerized and beguiled. Her full, cupid's bow lips and her dazzling smile were destined to break men's hearts—if they hadn't already. Alexa noted that several men in attendance had stopped to stare at her. Indeed, Bethany reminded her of a fairy goddess in the form-fitting gown that glistened in the lantern light.

"I'm surprised Mother permitted your visit to a place she always referred to as the uncivilized outpost of society," Alexa said as she clutched her sister's hand and held on tightly. "How did you talk her into letting you visit?"

"Permit?" Bethany sniffed. "She practically ousted me from Grandmama's home because she said that no matter how hard she tried she couldn't groom the Quinn out of me. She claims I turned out more like you and Papa than she thought possible." She smiled dryly. "Besides, she didn't want me underfoot any longer. She flitted off to Europe with her latest admirer, who is as much of a lush as she is."

Bethany surveyed the town square that glowed with makeshift lanterns then she studied the partygoers milling on the lawn. "This is a quaint town. I like it. I believe I'm going to enjoy making my home in this rugged territory," she said then added, "I'll enjoy it even more because you and Papa are here and I won't be dragged to all those snobbish soirees in Boston that Mama constantly forced me to attend."

"I hate to burst your bubble, little sister, but Papa's political functions can be stuffy," Alexa warned her.

"I'll manage," Bethany replied, with all the naive confidence of an eighteen-year-old who was destined to be wooed and courted because of the potential benefits of her father's social and political status.

Alexa had learned her lesson five years earlier when she became infatuated with a smooth-talking adventurer who plied her with flattery and seemingly devoted attention—then spent his evenings tumbling around in another woman's arms, just as Elliot had done. Alexa had been humiliated and hurt deeply back then. However, her deep abiding feelings for Coop taught her that she hadn't been in love with the suave adventurer. She'd simply been swept off her feet by her idealistic and romantic expectations.

"Alexa, I am so terribly sorry about your ordeal."

She pivoted to see Ambrose Shelton staring miserably at her as he stepped down from the carriage. The persnickety gentleman she remembered had become humble and apologetic.

"I'm recovering nicely, Ambrose," she assured him. "No need to fret on my account."

"I have been fretting nonetheless." He gestured to Ben Porter, who moved up beside him and looked every bit as contrite and remorseful. "We had no idea that Rose Brantley was discreetly pumping us for information about Webster's government contract renewal. Not to mention other matters of state that she passed along for a price. We were both fools to think that she was merely an interested citizen who liked to keep updated on politics and territorial improvement projects."

"I feel awful about this!" Ben burst out as he clutched her hand and pressed a kiss to her wrist. "Can you ever forgive us?"

"Please forgive them and be quick about it," Harold inserted as he shot both men a withering glance. "They have apologized to me so many times this week that we barely have had time to tend to important business."

Harold's countenance changed as he drew Alexa aside. "As for you, young lady, Mr. Cooper explained your extensive and active participation in the investigation. Although he praised your effective techniques and tireless effort—"

"He did?" she cut in.

"Yes, he did. He is very thorough and no-nonsense. I like him." He paused a moment then wagged his finger in her face. "You took your involvement much further than you initially indicated. You made a nervous wreck of me, Lexi."

"I'm sorry if I stretched the truth and worried you, but I discovered my true calling," she insisted. "I seem to have a natural aptitude for investigation and I intend to pursue it."

"I was afraid you were going to say that," Harold groaned. "Do I have to suffer through another ransom demand in the future? If so, I strongly oppose your chosen profession. It is going to take some getting used to."

Alexa smiled in satisfaction. "Although you aren't necessarily pleased, I thank you for acknowledging my right to make my own choices."

"Something Mother refused to do," Bethany inserted sourly.

"I'll use another name so no one will extort money from you because of our family connection," Alexa promised her father.

Harold hugged her gently. "I said I wouldn't object to your lifestyle, Lexi, but that doesn't mean I won't worry about the dangers you might encounter."

He turned to his younger daughter. "And don't think I'll allow you to go into business with your sister. At least not immediately. Someone has to become my social planner and hostess until I get the hang of it."

Alexa noticed her sister's pleased smile. She obviously yearned to accept responsibility. She was eager to do something, *anything* besides live with Mother's unreasonable expectations. As for Alexa, she was thrilled to pass on her obligations as her father's hostess.

Of course, now she was jobless and that was unacceptable. She would drive herself crazy if she didn't have a purpose.

"Introduce me around town, Lexi," Harold requested as he linked his elbows around his daughters' arms. "I've been encouraged to run for public office so I might as well get to know more voters."

Beaming with pride and contentment, Alexa introduced her family to her new acquaintances. The celebration turned out splendidly, though she hadn't expected to enjoy herself quite so much. Later, however, when the lanterns on the town square were extinguished and everyone retired for the night, loneliness greeted her at her hotel room door.

Alexa stared at the bed, wishing desperately that Coop were here with her. A wave of emptiness swamped her when she laid her head on the pillow. Where was Coop? she wondered as tears flooded her eyes. Did he think of her at all? Did he miss her, even a little?

Odd, she mused as she swiped at the tears. Now that she had her freedom and her father's blessing to make a life for herself it seemed a Pyrrhic victory. She needed Coop back in her life, wanted him in her bed. Maybe she should resort to Webster's tactics of taking Coop hostage and forcing him to agree to her terms.

The deliciously wicked thought made her smile. She fell asleep, not the least bit surprised that Coop had the starring role in her wild, erotic fantasies.

Chapter Nineteen

Coop strode into his office in Albuquerque then scooped up the pile of mail that had been slipped under the door. More than a week had passed since he'd wrapped up the Webster/ Thomas case. He'd eagerly taken another assignment that had him riding the rails to the Santa Rita Copper Mines and Silver City to catch a trio of thieves who had been preying on prospectors.

Unfortunately he'd resolved the situation more quickly than he would have preferred. Now forbidden thoughts and whimsical dreams of Alexa tormented him. Damnation, where were the time-consuming, complicated cases when he needed them? Now he was back in his office that fronted his modest two-room apartment, with nothing but time on his hands and an unforgettable woman on his mind.

Life just didn't get much worse than this.

A wary frown furrowed his brow when he heard a rustling noise coming from his sleeping quarters. Drawing his six-shooter, he shouldered his way through the door. His jaw practically dropped off its hinges when he saw Alexa, dressed in a silver gown, standing before him like an illusive dream shimmering just beyond his reach—the same way she'd been the whole cursed week.

He cocked a brow when she draped herself seductively on his bed. He noted the sling on her arm and the provocative smile playing on her lush lips. Desire and longing hit him like a runaway freight train. He had to brace against the doorjamb for support. Bumfuzzled, he glanced around his room. For a trained observer it certainly had taken him long enough to realize Alexa had placed vases of colorful flowers on the round table, washstand and end tables on each side of his bed.

He glanced speculatively at the door, then at the window. "How'd you get in here?"

"I told you before that I'm not without my resources."

"What are you doing here?"

"Delivering flowers."

"I can see that. Is this your new occupation and you're practicing on me?" he teased.

She smiled in tolerant amusement. "No, I brought them to butter you up."

He eyed her suspiciously, but he became hopelessly sidetracked when his hungry gaze roamed over the full swells of her breasts then descended to the trim indentation of her waist—and drifted up again. "Why do you need to butter me up?" he questioned, completely preoccupied. "Did you accept an assignment for me without consulting me first?"

Her grin grew wider and her blue eyes twinkled mischievously. "In a manner of speaking, yes. You're very good at these guessing games."

"I pride myself in being a good detective, princess. I'm used to putting two and two together."

"A very good detective indeed," she purred as she crooked her finger at him. She patted the empty space beside her on the bed. "Let's see if you can solve this puzzle."

Like a dutiful puppy, he sat on the very spot she indicated. Then, to his astonishment, she grabbed two sets of cuffs from inside her arm sling and secured his wrists to the bedposts. He was still staring incredulously at her, wondering why he'd fallen for that fake-injury-trick when she'd made him use it in Questa Springs recently.

"Damn but you're sneaky," he said as he watched her discard the sling.

She beamed in delight. "Thank you for the compliment. I'm trying to polish my skills of subterfuge and ingenuity in my investigative work."

"I've seen you in action already. I'm impressed. Now let me go."

"Thank you…and no."

He glanced around curiously. "Where's Miguel? Surely he didn't allow you to come alone."

"He's too busy managing the mercantile store in Questa Springs to bother with me."

Coop arched a surprised brow.

"I caught Percy at a weak moment and got him to agree to hire Kate and Miguel to run the store."

"Nice going," he complimented.

Her smile faded and all playfulness vanished as she stared intently at him. "I want a job."

"No one is stopping you from getting one," he replied. "In fact, I raved to your father about your skills and techniques so he wouldn't put up any resistance when you declared your independence and resigned from hosting his stuffy parties."

"So he told me. And thank you for that."

"You're welcome. I also met your sister. Extremely attractive, by the way. But then so are you. Bethany is a lot like you in temperament, too, I noticed. I hear your mother kicked her out. Later rather than sooner, as in your case."

Alexa nodded. "As it turned out, Mother didn't care much for either of us. It took Bethany a little longer to realize she was every bit a Quinn, because she was without Papa's daily influence in her life. But her true colors came shining through and now she is Papa's social director and party hostess."

She stared determinedly at him. "Now, about my new job."

"What job is that?" he asked as he lay abed, his wrists secured to the bedposts.

"I'm prepared to buy into your detective business," she negotiated.

"No," he flatly refused. "Besides, you couldn't afford my price. Not even with all of your daddy's money."

Alexa stood up and circled to the foot of the bed. She crossed her arms over her chest and stared him down. "It's because I said I loved you. That's why you headed for the hills before I regained consciousness, isn't it? That's why you are denying me employment now, isn't it?"

He shifted awkwardly and glanced away, refusing to meet her unblinking stare. "I knew you were riding an emotional seesaw after your ordeal. I didn't hold you to what you said."

"Why? Because you didn't share my feelings and that was the easy way out?" she fired at him.

"We both know you didn't mean it," he retorted. "You said yourself that you tried hard not to care about me. I know why you don't want to."

Alexa cocked her head and arched a delicate brow. "Really? I can't wait to hear this. Why do you think I didn't want to fall in love with you?"

"Because we lead different lives. We come from different backgrounds, *princess*," he said emphatically. "My tumbleweed lifestyle takes me all over creation while you attend high society's most envied functions." He inclined his head toward the modest furnishings in his compact home. "Your family owns a sprawling palace and I reside in this cramped space."

She flicked her wrist dismissively. "That is neither here nor there. I am applying for a job as your coinvestigator."

"I'm not hiring you," he said unequivocally.

"No?"

"No, it won't—"

His voice dried up when she stepped onto the foot of the bed then sank between his legs. "I'm not finished negotiating," she informed him. "You don't have to pay me. I'll work for nothing if I can use your body for pleasure…at my whim."

Her hand settled on his thigh then moved steadily upward. When he groaned in sweet torment, she grinned gleefully.

"You're considering it, aren't you? Admit it, Coop."

"I cannot believe you would stoop to these underhanded tactics, just to get a job," he said, his voice thick with undeniable desire.

Her fingertips glided boldly over the fabric covering his arousal. "I want what I want," she told him, unabashed. "If it's information for a case, I will be persistent. If I want *you* then I will be relentless. I'm not settling for less than the best."

She straddled his hips then bent to brush her mouth over his sensuous lips. She was starving to death for a taste of him. She was putting her pride on the line, just to be with him on any terms. But she wasn't taking no for an answer. If nothing else, she would be his secretary, his janitor, whatever she needed to be, as long as she could be a part of his life.

"I'm not riding an emotional high at the moment, Coop. I still love you," she admitted softly. "You don't even have to love me back. Just let me into your life."

Then she kissed him for all she was worth, aching to convince him to hire her, to become her lover. Whatever he could spare. She was that determined to be a part of his life because anything less was a meaningless existence.

"Let me go, Alexa," he commanded hoarsely.

"I don't think I can. I tried but life just wasn't any fun without you."

He smiled. "I meant unlock the cuffs."

She shook her head, sending the curly blond tendrils into a frothy cascade over her shoulders. "Nothing doing. I intend to be extremely persuasive and persistent."

She unbuttoned his shirt to brush her fingers lightly over his muscular chest. She skimmed her lips over his nipples and felt him arch instinctively toward her. She trailed her hand over the band of his breeches then slipped her fingers beneath the fabric.

She glanced into his vivid evergreen eyes and saw hungry need flickering in his gaze. If nothing else, she knew that she still had the power to excite him. It was a start, she encouraged herself. In time, he might even come to love her—a little.

"Say it, Coop," she whispered as she stroked him intimately. "Say you'll hire me."

"I can't. I love you too much, damn it," he said, and then groaned in pleasure.

Alexa's hand stalled and she glanced at him, startled. "You love me?"

"I just said so, didn't I?" he muttered grudgingly. "And thank you so much for dragging that out of me."

She smiled, extremely pleased—yet confused. "You love me but you won't hire me?"

He nodded his tousled raven head. "I can't bear to see you hurt. It nearly killed me when you were kidnapped. I sweated blood when I heard Denton shoot at you that night in the canyon. The thought of losing you nearly drove me crazy. It also brought back too many terrifying memories from my youth. I couldn't live with the torment if I couldn't protect you from harm while we're working together."

She cupped his face in her hands and kissed him thoroughly, adoringly. "If I'm with you, learning to be as reliant and skilled as you are, I'll be fine," she assured him confidently. "Just give me a chance, Coop. I delight in working with you."

He shook his head again. "Not without a marriage license to go along with it," he insisted. "Your father probably won't approve of me, but I want the whole forbidden fantasy or nothing at all."

Pleasure sizzled through her and she smiled impishly. "I suppose you want Daddy's money, like my previous suitors."

"No. Fact is, princess, I might not live like royalty but I do have a tidy nest egg of bounties and salaries I haven't taken time to spend. It's you I want."

"Good, because I purchased Elliot's ranch and hired Selma Mae Fredericks to handle the household duties while we take our cases. Since that set me back a bit, I was hoping I could sign an IOU to buy into your business."

Coop strained against the cuffs to kiss her hard and hungrily. "You drive one hell of a hard bargain. But okay, you win. Partners. We'll headquarter at your new ranch. Now let me go."

"Permanent partners?" she prodded as she spread a row of featherlight kisses over his neck and cheek.

"Absolutely." He moved suggestively beneath her hips. "Turn me loose so we can seal this deal."

She discarded her gown then unlocked the cuffs. Coop lay there admiring her shapely body and the irrepressible spirit reflected in her smile. He marveled at his inability to tell her no after spending a week telling himself he could live without her if he really tried. But he had only *existed,* going through the paces, finding not one ounce of enjoyment without her.

When she leaned down, the peaks of her breasts caressing his chest, Coop couldn't think of one single reason why he shouldn't give into her on any issue.

"I'm crazy about you," he murmured as he glided his hands over the curve of her hips then took his sweet time touching every glorious inch of her body. "I realized I was in serious trouble the night I discovered you had cleverly duped me with that Mr. Chester disguise."

"That was also the night I realized my feelings for you had become entirely too personal," she whispered back. "I'm crazy about you, too, Coop. Love me for the rest of my life."

He rolled her to her back and braced himself on his forearms to stare adoringly at her. "I'll love you for the rest of mine and forever after, princess," he vowed faithfully before he offered all that he was to the woman who held his heart…

* * * * *

THOROUGHBRED LEGACY
*The stakes are high when it comes to love,
horse racing, family secrets
and broken promises.*

*A new exciting Harlequin
continuity series coming soon!
Led by* New York Times *bestselling author
Elizabeth Bevarly*
FLIRTING WITH TROUBLE

Here's a preview!

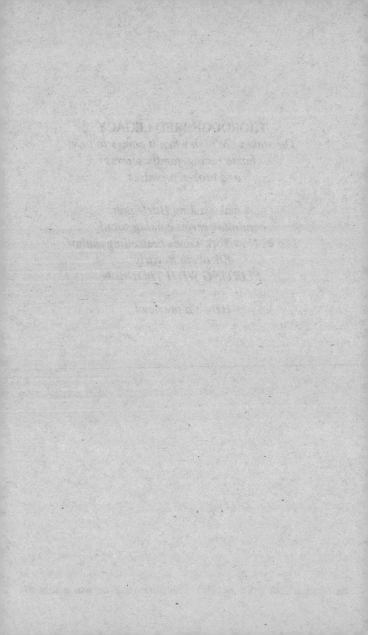

THE DOOR CLOSED behind them, throwing them into darkness and leaving them utterly alone. And the next thing Daniel knew, he heard himself saying, "Marnie, I'm sorry about the way things turned out in Del Mar."

She said nothing at first, only strode across the room and stared out the window beside him. Although he couldn't see her well in the darkness—he still hadn't switched on a light…but then, neither had she—he imagined her expression was a little preoccupied, a little anxious, a little confused.

Finally, very softly, she said, "Are you?"

He nodded, then, worried she wouldn't be able to see the gesture, added, "Yeah. I am. I should have said goodbye to you."

"Yes, you should have."

Actually, he thought, there were a lot of things he should have done in Del Mar. He'd had *a lot* riding on the Pacific Classic, and even more on his entry, Little Joe, but after meeting Marnie, the Pacific Classic had been the last thing on Daniel's mind. His loss at Del Mar had pretty much ended his career before it had even begun, and he'd had to start all over again, rebuilding from nothing.

He simply had not then and did not now have room in his life for a woman as potent as Marnie Roberts. He was a horseman first and foremost. From the time he was a schoolboy, he'd known what he wanted to do with his life—be the best possible trainer he could be.

He had to make sure Marnie understood—and he understood, too—why things had ended the way they had eight years ago. He just wished he could find the words to do that. Hell, he wished he could find the *thoughts* to do that.

"You made me forget things, Marnie, things that I really needed to remember. And that scared the hell out of me. Little Joe should have won the Classic. He was by far the best horse entered in that race. But I didn't give him the attention he needed and deserved that week, because all I could think about was you. Hell, when I woke up that morning all I wanted to do was lie there and look at you, and then wake you up and make love to you again. If I hadn't left when I did— the way I did—I might still be lying there in that bed with you, thinking about nothing else."

"And would that be so terrible?" she asked.

"Of course not," he told her. "But that wasn't why I was in Del Mar," he repeated. "I was in Del Mar to win a race. That was my job. And my work was the most important thing to me."

She said nothing for a moment, only studied his face in the darkness as if looking for the answer to a very important question. Finally she asked, "And what's the most important thing to you now, Daniel?"

Wasn't the answer to that obvious? "My work," he answered automatically.

She nodded slowly. "Of course," she said softly. "That is, after all, what you do best."

Her comment, too, puzzled him. She made it sound as if being good at what he did was a bad thing.

She bit her lip thoughtfully, her eyes fixed on his, glimmering in the scant moonlight that was filtering through the window. And damned if Daniel didn't find himself wanting to pull her into his arms and kiss her. But as much as it might have felt as if no time had passed since Del Mar, there were eight years between now and then. And eight years was a long time in the best of circumstances. For Daniel and Marnie, it was virtually a lifetime.

So Daniel turned and started for the door, then halted. He couldn't just walk away and leave things as they were, unsettled. He'd done that eight years ago and regretted it.

"It *was* good to see you again, Marnie," he said softly. And since he was being honest, he added, "I hope we see each other again."

She didn't say anything in response, only stood silhouetted against the window with her arms wrapped around her in a way that made him wonder whether she was doing it because she was cold, or if she just needed something—someone—to hold on to. In either case, Daniel understood. There was an emptiness clinging to him that he suspected would be there for a long time.

* * * * *

THOROUGHBRED LEGACY
coming soon wherever books are sold!

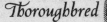

Thoroughbred *Legacy*

Launching in June 2008

A dramatic new 12-book continuity that embodies the American Dream.

Meet the Prestons, owners of Quest Stables, a successful
horse-racing and breeding empire. But the lives, loves
and reputations of this hardworking family are put at risk
when a breeding scandal unfolds.

Flirting with Trouble

by *New York Times* bestselling author

ELIZABETH BEVARLY

Eight years ago, publicist Marnie Roberts spent seven days
of bliss with Australian horse trainer Daniel Whittleson.
But just as quickly, he disappeared. Now Marnie is
heading to Australia to finally confront the man
she's never been able to forget.

*The stakes are high when it comes to love, horse racing,
family secrets and broken promises.*

A new exciting Harlequin continuity series coming soon!

REQUEST YOUR FREE BOOKS!

 Harlequin® Historical
Historical Romantic Adventure!

2 FREE NOVELS PLUS 2 FREE GIFTS!

YES! Please send me 2 FREE Harlequin® Historical novels and my 2 FREE gifts (gifts are worth about $10). After receiving them, if I don't wish to receive any more books, I can return the shipping statement marked "cancel". If I don't cancel, I will receive 6 brand-new novels every month and be billed just $4.94 per book in the U.S. or $5.49 per book in Canada, plus 25¢ shipping and handling per book and applicable taxes, if any*. That's a savings of 20% off the cover price! I understand that accepting the 2 free books and gifts places me under no obligation to buy anything. I can always return a shipment and cancel at any time. Even if I never buy another book, the two free books and gifts are mine to keep forever.

246 HDN ERUM 349 HDN ERUA

Name	(PLEASE PRINT)

Address	Apt. #

City	State/Prov.	Zip/Postal Code

Signature (if under 18, a parent or guardian must sign)

Mail to the **Harlequin Reader Service:**
IN U.S.A.: P.O. Box 1867, Buffalo, NY 14240-1867
IN CANADA: P.O. Box 609, Fort Erie, Ontario L2A 5X3

Not valid to current subscribers of Harlequin Historical books.

Want to try two free books from another line?
Call 1-800-873-8635 or visit www.morefreebooks.com.

* Terms and prices subject to change without notice. N.Y. residents add applicable sales tax. Canadian residents will be charged applicable provincial taxes and GST. This offer is limited to one order per household. All orders subject to approval. Credit or debit balances in a customer's account(s) may be offset by any other outstanding balance owed by or to the customer. Please allow 4 to 6 weeks for delivery. Offer available while quantities last.

Your Privacy: Harlequin Books is committed to protecting your privacy. Our Privacy Policy is available online at www.eHarlequin.com or upon request from the Reader Service. From time to time we make our lists of customers available to reputable third parties who may have a product or service of interest to you. If you would prefer we not share your name and address, please check here. ☐

HH08

Royal Seductions

Michelle Celmer delivers a powerful miniseries in
Royal Seductions; where two brothers fight for the
crown and discover love. In *The King's Convenient Bride*,
the king discovers his marriage of convenience to the
woman he's been promised to wed is turning all too
real. The playboy prince proposes a mock engagement
to defuse rumors circulating about him and restore
order to the kingdom…until his pretend fiancée
becomes pregnant in *The Illegitimate Prince's Baby*.

Look for

THE KING'S CONVENIENT BRIDE
&
THE ILLEGITIMATE PRINCE'S BABY

BY MICHELLE CELMER

Available in June 2008 wherever you buy books.

Always Powerful, Passionate and Provocative.

COMING NEXT MONTH FROM

HARLEQUIN®
HISTORICAL

- **THE LAST RAKE IN LONDON**
  by **Nicola Cornick**
  (Edwardian)
  Dangerous Jack Kestrel was the most sinfully sensual rogue she'd ever met, and the wicked glint in his eyes promised he'd take care of satisfying Sally's every need....
  Watch as the last rake in London meets his match!

- **AN IMPETUOUS ABDUCTION**
  by **Patricia Frances Rowell**
  (Regency)
  Persephone had stumbled into danger, and the only way to protect her was to abduct her! But what would Leo's beautiful prisoner do when he revealed his true identity?
  Don't miss Patricia Frances Rowell's unique blend of passion spiced with danger!

- **KIDNAPPED BY THE COWBOY**
  by **Pam Crooks**
  (Western)
  TJ Grier was determined to clear his name, even if his actions might cost him the woman he loved!
  Fall in love with Pam Crooks's honorable cowboy!

- **INNOCENCE UNVEILED**
  by **Blythe Gifford**
  (Medieval)
  With her flaming red hair, Katrine knew no man would be tempted by her. But Renard, a man of secrets, intended to break through her defenses....
  Innocence and passion are an intoxicating mix in this emotional medieval tale.